A
DANGEROUS
GOODBYE

D0836235

BOOKS BY FLISS CHESTER

THE FRENCH ESCAPES ROMANCE SERIES

Love in the Snow
Summer at the Vineyard
Meet Me on the Riviera

A
DANGEROUS
GOODBYE

FLISS CHESTER

Bookouture

Published by Bookouture in 2020

An imprint of Storyfire Ltd.
Carmelite House
50 Victoria Embankment
London EC4Y 0DZ

www.bookouture.com

Copyright © Fliss Chester, 2020

Fliss Chester has asserted their right to be identified
as the author of this work.

All rights reserved. No part of this publication may be reproduced,
stored in any retrieval system, or transmitted, in any form or by
any means, electronic, mechanical, photocopying, recording or
otherwise, without the prior written permission of the publishers.

ISBN: 978-1-83888-644-8
eBook ISBN: 978-1-83888-643-1

This book is a work of fiction. Names, characters, businesses,
organizations, places and events other than those clearly in the
public domain, are either the product of the author's imagination
or are used fictitiously. Any resemblance to actual persons, living or
dead, events or locales is entirely coincidental.

For my ever-adventurous great-aunt,
Glenys Barker 1918–2011

CHAPTER ONE

France, August 1944

My darling Fen,

I fear this may be my last letter to you. If you are reading this, then in all likelihood I am dead. I'm sorry to let you down like this, I think we would have had a jolly old time together in the years to come.

One last puzzle for you, honeypot… Where I have been posted, I cannot tell you. I muddled up Agen Cathedral for the hotel at first. You may wonder, lastly, why, with airmen of note around, I got so disorientated, but there you go. A glass of Burgundy soon saw me right, though, and the other fellows here are second to none.

I want you to know that I shall have died with your face in my mind, your name on my lips. Believe this, my darling, I loved you from the first moment I set eyes on you – and if we cannot be together after this ghastly skirmish is over, then I want you to find happiness elsewhere, and enjoy a life of fiendish puzzles and heavenly love for always.

Ever yours,
Arthur

The letter had arrived in the afternoon and Fen had found it waiting for her on the well-scrubbed kitchen table in the farmhouse. A few minutes beforehand, the postman, cycling along the lane that bordered the field, had called out to the group of land girls, all volunteers in the Women's Land Army, as they checked the twine on the bales; August's heat had brought the harvest forward by a week or two and now it was September the West Sussex fields were brown with stubble but peppered with bales of golden straw and the finer, greener hay.

Her friend Kitty Harris had waved back at him with an acknowledgement, then rested her hand on Fen's shoulder. The cry of 'Letter for you, Miss Churche' shouldn't have caused a sensible girl like Fen to drop her bale cutter and shake slightly, but she knew – *she just knew* – that this wasn't a rushed note from her mother or a gossip-laden stream of consciousness from an old school friend. She knew it would be news of Arthur and she'd run straight back to the farmhouse to read it.

The words, his words, puzzled her. *Didn't they always*, she thought as she remembered how she and Arthur had written little clues for each other in their letters.

'More crossword lovers than star-crossed lovers,' he'd joked that June day back in 1943 when they'd taken a modest picnic into the parkland beyond the farmhouse where Fen was billeted. They hadn't had more than a few slices of home-baked bread and a small amount of cheese, but that didn't matter as they had busied themselves working on their own puzzle, hoping to send it to *The Daily Telegraph*. 'That's what we should call ourselves,' he'd said in between mouthfuls, 'our setter name…'

'Rationed Cheese?' Fen had known that wasn't what he meant and had laughed and ducked as he had playfully thrown a chewed-on piece of crust at her head.

'No Fen, *Star-crossed*. It's got a nice ring to it.'

And it had, and they had finished off setting their cryptic puzzle as the sun dipped behind the horse chestnut trees. Moments later, Arthur had leapt up and cried, 'Dash it all!' before hastily collecting the picnic together. He had almost missed his ride back to his quarters outside Guildford; a straw-haired fellow in a Land Rover was waiting for him at Fen's digs when they'd got back, tapping his watch and looking every bit the part of put-upon patient friend. Still, it had been a rare day off for them both and its puffy white clouds and light breezes had lulled them into a sense of never-ending afternoon. He'd kissed her briefly before he climbed into the military vehicle and she'd known then that he was the one for her.

Fen closed her eyes at the memory, and before long others nudged their way into her mind. His spectacles with their round, dark rims and his dark brown eyes behind them. The way his neck always smelt of Palmolive soap, no matter what time of day she embraced him. His insistence on always carrying a penknife, a handkerchief and a small ball of string 'just in case'.

And, of course, the dance when they'd met in the spring of 1943. She remembered the smell of wet wool – all those scratchy uniforms caught out in a summer shower just before the dancing had started – mingled with tobacco and the boiled beef being served in the dining room. Fen, Kitty, Dilys and Edith had all decided to walk down from their farmhouse billet, on the outskirts of Midhurst. They had arrived at the Spread Eagle, a medieval coaching inn at the bottom of the high street, just in time for the Lindy hop – a dance so chaotic that Fen had decided she better wait for something a bit less fast-paced for fear a twisted ankle could render her useless for the rest of the war.

She and Dilys, a quiet but pretty Welsh girl, who, like Fen, had joined the Women's Land Army back in 1940, had hung back by the steaming tea urn and watched as several Wrens – the nickname given to those in the Women's Royal Naval Service – poured something from a hip flask into their teacups. Fen's memory was hazy as to where Edith had got to, though she remembered some talk later on of a tall Canadian chap. Kitty, dear Kitty, who by her own admission was a bit of a jive bomber, had made a beeline straight onto the dance floor, finding herself a partner in no time at all.

Fen wished she could simply join in like Kitty could, but then Kitty had such an open disposition, despite her hard upbringing, and would do almost anything to be loved, to be laughed with, to be part of something. Fen on the other hand had always been an outsider; it came with the territory of being brought up in a country that wasn't your own. Lily L'Étranger – or Lily the Foreigner – was what her French classmates had called her in Paris back in the 1920s. Trust her father, Professor John Churche, to move them to the most artistic and creative arrondissement of Paris when she was a child, only to bring them back to sedate Oxford when she was eighteen, just when Paris was getting fun. Still, her teenage sorties to the Revlon and Max Factor counters at Galeries Lafayette, that gilded world of fashion and opulence, had opened a few doors for her when it came to kindling friendships and talking make-up with the other girls back in boring old *Angleterre*.

'Are you dancing?' A voice in her ear had switched her attention away from the giggling Wrens and towards a rather handsome and open, friendly face.

'Not yet. Unlike them, I haven't the means to get the old confidence up.' Fen had nodded towards the other girls and their almost flagrant use of the hip flask and the man – Arthur as she would later discover – had smiled, his nose crinkling under the bridge of his glasses.

'Well, I can't help with the contraband, but I can do a *fine* foxtrot or *wonderful* waltz.'

Fen remembered how fun that night had been, from that point onwards at any rate. The dark-haired, chestnut-eyed captain had made her feel instantly at ease. He'd been there with a few other young men, and an Italian-looking girl, who threw her head back and laughed whenever Arthur's friend said something.

That was the thing about the war, you found your friends quickly and stuck with them. Fen had been lucky with her placement as a land girl – after finishing her agricultural training at the college in Plumpton, she'd been posted to West Sussex and met Kitty, Edith and Dilys and, of course, old Mrs B, who was the widow of the tenant farmer who had rented the farm from the grand estate down the road. Together they looked after the place, carrying out the work that local young men would have done if they hadn't gone off to war.

A friendship, Fen always thought to herself, is a *real* friendship once you've been out in the fields together, rain or shine, either planting out crops or ploughing the rough clay soil, your wellington boots getting stuck in every rut, or sitting up late at night on fire-watching duty with not much more to keep you warm save a blanket and a flask of hot tea, counting the seconds between blasts during the worst nights of the bombing raids that covered southern England.

Fen had spent many days and nights with these three and knew they were her real friends, despite their differences and backgrounds. Kitty was young, still not yet twenty, and relatively local. Fen suspected she came from a rather rough household and joining the Woman's Land Army was as much a means to get out from under her father's feet – and fists – as any dutiful calling.

Dilys was the daughter of a Welsh Chapel preacher and had grown up in a farm-like manse house in the Welsh valleys. She'd joined up as she reckoned she knew a thing or two about farming, and it turned out she wasn't wrong. She was Mrs B's favourite, and just about everyone else's too, due to her calm manner and general kindliness.

And then there was Edith from the East End of London, tall and awkward and with a fondness for anything fanciful. She would be a fairy or a princess if she could, but God had decided, in his great wisdom, that instead she should be five foot nine of clumsiness, and for this she found it hard to forgive him.

The four of them had made fast and firm friends, however, and dances such as the one at the Spread Eagle were what made their eyes gleam for days afterwards and kept them up at night, whispering remembrances and gossip about who was dancing with whom and if so-and-so's dress hem had been an inch too high to be proper or an inch too low to be fashionable.

The tea urn, the heat of the dancing bodies and the warm paving stones outside, doused in summer rain, had all seemed to be steaming, or was it Fen's memory that gave a hazy feel to that first night she'd met Arthur?

Arthur had indeed finally encouraged her out in front of the band, and she had jived and swung with him, laughing all the time at his terrible jokes and the funny faces he had pulled as he flung her around the dance floor. Flushed with dancing and the excitement of the night, Fen had barely noticed the hour hand of the large wooden-framed clock creep towards eleven – and as khaki-clad soldiers led blushing local girls out to their cars or to more private places, Fen had felt Arthur's hand on her arm, and she'd turned to face him.

'I don't even know your name. I'm Melville-Hare. Captain. Arthur!' he had laughed. 'Smooth as always. Let's start again. I'm Arthur.'

'How do you do, Arthur,' Fen stuck her hand out to him while trying not to smile too much at his charming ineptitude. 'Churche. Fenella Churche.'

'Fen Churche, like the…'

'… Station, yes.'

They'd both burst out laughing and for once she hadn't minded her name being quite so similar to one of London's more famous termini.

'Well, Miss Churche, if I may, can I write to you?'

Fen opened her eyes and blinked away the tears. Arthur *had* written to her. Two or three times a week, and they'd met up too. He could never say exactly where he was based, but he would borrow a Land Rover or hitch a ride from the other chaps who were stationed at his digs. Sometimes his letters came with thick black redaction lines across the text, and when that was the case, Fen had to work extra hard to decipher the clues he would lay out for her. They were easy, by and large, and especially so when you knew the context. When he wrote *meet me in your Revlon don't you think?* she knew he wasn't asking her to tart up but was suggesting a trip to London, it being a classic 'hidden' type of clue, the answer being sandwiched between *RevLON* and *DON't*. And, of course, there was one letter full of clues… like *For you, unravelled, an emerging gent I am…* that had led to her accepting his proposal of marriage.

She looked down at the letter in her hands. Was this full of hidden messages too? She had to admit that as far as farewell letters went it was rather an odd one, mentioning airmen and Agen Cathedral.

Oh.

Ohhh.

Fen smoothed out the letter and read it again. The bit about the cathedral and the airmen, it really didn't make any sense. Who would mix up a hotel – and no doubt his quarters wouldn't have been the *Georges V* exactly – with a cathedral? *A crossword setter, that's who.*

'Muddled up…' she muttered to herself. 'So it's an anagram. Of Agen Cathedral.'

Fen turned the letter over and with a pencil she wrote all the letters of AGEN CATHEDRAL in a circle. Her eyes sketched across the letters, willing them to fall into place, but they just wouldn't. She scrubbed it all out in frustration and wrote the letters out again, in a different order and jiggled up within the circle. Suddenly ANGEL sprang to her from the jumbled letters.

Fen bit her bottom lip. She was onto something all right. Arthur – her puzzle-loving Arthur – had sent her a message from… Her eyes filled with tears as she silently completed her own thought… *Beyond the grave.*

She laid her pencil down and cradled her head in her hands as she imagined what bombed-out dugout he might be lying in. Would she ever find him? She didn't even know whereabouts in France he was; he had been mobilised so quickly that they'd not even had a chance to have an engagement party or, to Fen's shame and regret, meet each other's parents. So what was this then, this letter? *In all likelihood I am dead.* German forces were in retreat, it was true, more than likely wreaking havoc in their wake, but he might still be alive, despite his fears…

'I have to do this, I can do this.' If there was any chance of finding out what had happened to Arthur, Fen knew the clues to where he had last been were in that letter. In a life that had been dominated by duty and secrecy, he was letting her know, in his own way, where he had been stationed, and if there was any chance of finding where his journey had ended, she needed to know where it had begun.

Taking up her pencil, she concentrated once more on the wordplay.

'… For the hotel at first…' She chewed the end of the pencil as she worked out the clue. 'The hotel at first… the first letter of hotel is H. So if I…' her words turned into scribbles and she added an extra 'H' into the anagram of AGEN CATHEDRAL.

Angle… angel… cat… death…

'Oh! Archangel Death. Gosh.'

Fen sat up straight and felt the bones in her back click into position. Long days in the fields were excellent for general health, but not so kind on a back, especially one that before the war had been more used to hunching over a desk, either studying or, once she had graduated with her degree in Modern Languages, working as a translator for a firm of copywriters in London.

'So the next one. The airmen…' Fen found the clue and read it out loud, for no one's benefit but herself, but she found sounding out the clues sometimes gave away more than reading alone could. '*You may wonder, lastly, why, with airmen of note around, I got so disorientated…* I may wonder, Arthur, yes!'

She poised her pencil and started to jot down some letters. AIRMENOFNOTE. As before, the letters formed a circle.

'*Around*, you see,' she muttered to herself, once more trying to find new words in the mess of random letters. She knew this wasn't the whole clue and read it through one more time.

'Aha!' She added a Y – it being the last letter of *why* – to the circle of letters and hunched over the page, staring at them as she held her face between her hands.

Nothing. She could find nothing in the bunch of random letters. Tone… foot… font… toon… fountain…

'No U. Oh balderdash!' Fen flung the pencil down, but not too far, and her determination to solve Arthur's puzzle made her square up to the letter again.

A glass of Burgundy saw me right though…

'Burgundy… France. Aha… of course not fountain, but,' she checked the letters, 'Fontaine.'

She worked through the letters that were left, 'OERMY or YOMER?' She tried a few more possibilities out as Kitty walked in.

'Still at it, Fen? It's gone ten.' Kitty laid a hand on Fen's shoulder and peered at her work. If she'd had an opinion about Fen writing all over the last letter her fiancé would ever send her, she didn't show it and just squeezed Fen's shoulder. 'Cup of cocoa?'

'If there's some going, then yes please. And, Kitty?'

'Yes?'

'Do you know if Mrs B has anything like an atlas here? Or a map of France at least?'

Kitty put the old kettle on the stove and exhaled, blowing air out through pursed lips. 'An atlas you're more likely find in the town library, I suppose, or up at the big house. You could ask Mary if you could look.' She was referring to one of the other land girls, Mary, an aristocratic young lady from the north of England who had managed to get a room in the big house itself. 'Though I'm not sure she's taking visitors after Lord Bigwig found her in the hay barn with Johnny Borthwick the other day. Still, poor love needs some excitement before she's married off to some other toff, I've no doubt. Anyway, I'm sure Mrs B's got a map of France though, wait here.' Kitty moved the kettle off the hotplate onto the warming side of the stove and disappeared through the low door of the kitchen into the dark passageway beyond.

Fen, despite the cheering diversion of some gossip, really was starting to feel rather exhausted. It had been quite the day, from all the physical work before the afternoon post, then the reeling horror of realising that Arthur was most likely dead. But it hadn't been a black-edged telegram, or were they only sent to *real* family? Perhaps fiancées didn't count and weeks, even months ago, Arthur's parents had known what she only feared; that he wasn't coming home.

Kitty reappeared with a battered old map in her hands. 'Thought I'd seen it somewhere. I think it's Mr B's from the Great War, but I doubt, bar the odd crater, that France has changed all that much.'

'Thanks, Kitty, you are the very best, you know.' Fen shook out the old map and found the right area for Burgundy. *Now to find a Fontaine somewhere...*

Four eyes and two cups of cocoa worked their magic and Kitty triumphantly pointed out a large village called Morey-Fontaine, close to the famous Château du Clos de Vougeot.

'That must be it!'

'Oh Kitty, you're wonderful, you know that?'

Kitty, who had never been called wonderful in her whole nineteen years, smiled a little and nodded.

'I wonder how the Archangel Death fits in with a charming little Burgundian village?' Fen pondered.

'I think Herr Hitler saw to it that *he* visited most places.'

'Yes. I don't suppose there's many villages in France that haven't had him fly over them these last few years.' Fen reached out and held Kitty's hand in hers as they thought for a moment about all the lives – and loves – lost in France since the war began.

'Maybe Morey-Fontaine has some sort of connection with him? The Archangel.' Kitty put the idea forward and it made Fen wonder who the Archangel of Death was, and why, indeed, he had some special connection to the village Arthur was so desperate to tell her about?

CHAPTER TWO

Luckily for both Fen's mission to find out more about archangels, and for her aching back, the next day was a Sunday, which meant church and an enforced rest from the fields. Mrs B was keener than mustard that if she must have so many young ladies in her house she would ensure their spiritual sustenance as much as their physical one, and the best way to stop her sudden influx of girls being compared to a bawdy house (for some billets did indeed get that reputation) was to frogmarch them all, willingly or not, to church every Sunday.

'I don't know what I should be thanking 'im for.' Edith spoke out rather loudly between verses of 'Now Thank We All Our God'.

'Shush, Edie,' Kitty glanced over to where one of her cousins was sitting, several pews behind and on the other side of the nave. Fen knew Kitty worried constantly that her father would kick up a stink and demand she come home, to take on the work he and her mother couldn't manage now the boys were gone, especially if word ever got back to him that she was on some sort of free ticket and enjoying herself a little bit too much.

Fen raised her eyebrows at her in solidarity; Edith was good fun at times but also a bit of an attention-seeker. She'd flapped her hands around wildly earlier as a bee had buzzed around their hats during the welcome, and now, since no one had paid her much attention, she seemed at it again.

'*Ai-eee!*'

'*Shhhh!*'

'*Whatever is the fuss?*'

The group of young women were shushed by those in the pews around them and Edith in particular was told to 'just be quiet' by Mrs B.

'What is it?' Dilys whispered to her, once the next hymn had started.

'Got bloody stung, didn't I?'

'There, there,' Dilys whispered, the words sounding even more comforting due to her soft Welsh accent. 'Suck the sting out, else it'll swell if you're unlucky.' Dilys was always the one who knew about countryside lore and how to fix almost anything like that.

'Tch, it's too late, look at my bleedin' arm!'

The girls all looked at Edith's swelling wrist and each had their own reaction. Fen frowned at the commotion, Dilys patted the poor girl on the shoulder and muttered another 'there, there', and Kitty looked sheepishly over at the ever more irritable Mrs B.

The service came to an end, not before Mrs B had insisted they all take Holy Communion, and they filed out according to their pew into the aisle and from there out to the September sunshine.

Fen found the vicar, a Reverend Smallpiece, and shook his hand.

'Thank you, Vicar,' she started the pleasantries. 'Such an interesting sermon.'

'Thank you, dear girl.' Smallpiece took his hand back and used both of them to flatten his stole against his surplice. 'I find the preaching of Romans 12 particularly poignant this year: "… offer your bodies as a living sacrifice".' He raised his hands up as if he was back in the pulpit.

Fen swallowed quickly, not wanting to think too much about the sacrifices made in France, by Arthur in particular perhaps, recently.

'Can I ask you a question, Reverend?' She felt bad interrupting him, but out of the corner of her eye, she could see her friends waiting not-so-patiently by the lychgate, milling around like chicks next to Mrs B, their mother hen, obviously stalling so Fen could catch up and walk back to the farmhouse with them.

'Of course, my child, what is it?'

'The archangel of death, do we have a name for him?'

'He is never mentioned in the Bible, my dear, but I think we know him from other scriptures as Azrael.'

'Azrael.' Fen repeated the ancient name and then thanked the vicar and headed over to her friends.

'Thanking the vicar?' Mrs B looked approvingly at Fen. 'The only excuse worth having for keeping my roast waiting.'

'Sorry Mrs B, I just had… well I wanted to—'

'No matter, let's hurry and we'll be home soon.'

The other girls dropped into line behind her, the talk still mostly of Edith and her now bandaged, thanks to Dilys's headscarf, arm – but Fen was deep in thought. *The archangel of death was Azrael.* It felt an odd sort of connection to Arthur and didn't quite sit right. Although, in crossword terms, they were both six-letter words starting with A, and even darling Arthur wouldn't have gone so far as to describe himself as an angel…

She reached into her pocket as they walked along the footpath through the fields that led back to the old farmhouse and felt the softened paper of Arthur's letter. Its presence gave her some comfort and, to herself as much as to anybody, she whispered, 'What are you trying to tell me, my darling?'

She sighed, pulled her hands out of her pockets, adjusted her Sunday-best hat and ran a little to keep up with Kitty, who was regaling Edith and Dilys about the latest flick she'd heard about starring her heart-throb, Cary Grant.

'Tell me, duckie, something's bothering you, isn't it?' Mrs B was knitting in front of the fire late on Sunday evening. The long scarf was an odd mix of navy-blue wool and some grey left over from the three balaclavas she'd already knitted for '*those poor fellas in them boats*'. Fen was helping her by sewing some knitted squares of more brightly coloured wool together for '*them poor tots in London with no roofs over their blessed little heads*'.

'I think Arthur is… missing.'

'Had one of them telegraphs, have you?'

'Telegram,' Fen couldn't help but correct the older woman. 'No. But I got a letter from him and I think he was trying to tell me something about his death.'

'Oh deary, I am sorry.' Mrs B's knitting needles fell unusually quiet. 'Spit it out then, what makes you think he's a goner?'

'Well, he's given me a clue or two—'

'Oh he's a right one for always doing that, isn't he?' Mrs B interrupted, starting up her knitting again.

'One of them I'm pretty sure leads to a small village in Burgundy called Morey-Fontaine.'

'Sounds fancy.'

'And the other spells out *archangel death*.' Fen looked up from her needlework to see if her words had had any effect on Mrs B. As a keen churchgoer, Fen knew she was on rocky ground blasphemy-wise if she went around dropping the names of the choirs eternal.

'That's what you were chatting to the vicar about earlier, was it?'

'Yes.'

'Well, Smallpiece is an educated man and there's not much he don't know about scripture and the like, but if you need to find out more, you can look in Mr B's old country almanac. Has some odd things in it, I can tell you. Birdsong and harvest times, yes, but also Catholic saints and whatnot.' She put her knitting down and pushed herself up out of the chair with a small grunt. 'I'll find it for you.'

'Thank you, Mrs B. Really.'

Fen concentrated on her sewing until the older woman came back into the room.

'I'd have never put purple and orange together, but it's a jolly little blankie you got going on there.' Mrs B took the baby blanket out of Fen's hands and replaced it with the almanac. 'Must be that French bit of you.' It wasn't said unkindly, but Fen wondered if she should apologise for the slightly clashing *avant-garde* feel to the charity blanket. Instead, she nodded some thanks to Mrs B and tucked her feet in under her as she leant back in the armchair and started flicking through Mr B's old book of country lore.

'Gosh,' Fen exclaimed to the room, which was now home to both Kitty and Dilys, as well as Mrs B. With Fen absorbed in flicking past mowing competition results and flags of the world, Mrs B had had to rope in more volunteers for her blanket stitching. Edith was upstairs setting her hair with some concoction she'd read about in *Home Chat* magazine, but Kitty and Dilys were both sitting on the floor, needles in hand, vying for room in front of the fire.

'Found something useful, duckie?' Mrs B asked.

'Rather. And you were right, Mrs B,' Fen laid the large, and still slightly dusty, book down on her lap. 'There's a whole list of Catholic Angels of God here.'

'Does it include us?' Kitty chirped up, risking a clip round the ear. Instead she got a stern look from the old woman, which didn't stop her from continuing. 'Miss Pettifer always said that we English were angels, hence why the Romans called good old England that. Angel-Land. Perhaps I'm an "angel Saxon"?' She clasped her hands into the prayer position and pouted piously, then giggled as Dilys, being Welsh, jabbed her playfully in the ribs.

'Shush, you silly girl,' Mrs B chastised her. 'Fen dear, what have you found?'

'Well, Kitty isn't right in this case, though there are a few angels listed that I had no idea were patrons of various things. According to the Franciscans, Michael, Gabriel and Raphael are all angels of death.'

'Makes you shiver, don't you think?' Dilys said, but stared into the fire as she did so.

'But also patron saints of the blind, in Raphael's case, and Germany of all places for all three of them!'

'Well, I think that's quite enough of all that now.' Mrs B made to move around a bit in her armchair. 'Dilys, be a dear and switch on the wireless. I think we could all do with a nice change. Put it on the Light Programme side and let's see if that funny RAF show is on, what's it called again, Kitty?'

'*Much-Binding-in-the-Marsh*. Oh let's, those chaps are such cards.'

Fen closed the almanac and smiled, pleased too of a change of subject. But the names of all the archangels stayed with her: Azrael, and now Michael, Gabriel and Raphael. They sounded more like Renaissance painters than archangels, but she kept the knowledge tucked away as she laughed out loud with the other women over the Sunday-night comedy broadcasting.

CHAPTER THREE

One Year Later – Late September 1945

Fen stared out of the train window at the empty green and brown fields of France as they streamed past her. Just over a year had gone by since she had received the letter from Arthur. A year in which she'd continued to work on the farm, tending the crops while Britain's farmer-soldiers had liberated towns across France. There had been little in the way of highlights, save the odd dance or visit home, and everything she'd done had been tainted by his loss.

As much as they could, her parents had kept her informed of her brother Andrew's progress in North Africa – he was fighting on that front against Rommel. Oxford, they told her, was a shadow of its former self, with some colleges requisitioned by the military and others struggling to fill places as so many young men had been called to the front. At least its glorious architecture had been saved; rumour had it that Herr Hitler himself had ordered it preserved as he wanted to make it his new capital, though more practical minds pointed out that the German bombers would have had to have flown unscathed past London and its barrage balloons and anti-aircraft placements to get to it. Fen had offered to come home to help her mother in her tireless work for the famine relief fund, but as she'd anticipated, they shared her belief that her work in the fields should take priority. On those short visits home, though, Fen had reassured herself that her parents were surviving the war in as genteel and comfortable way as possible.

Kitty had been a real friend, more like a little sister really, and let Fen talk about her plans to go to France to find out what had happened to Arthur. They'd spent the cold nights of 1944's winter planning her train journeys and saving coupons for appropriate clothes and travel garments. Timetables had been hard to come by, but luckily the stationmaster at nearby Haslemere had done his best to find out what trains were still running from the docks in northern France. They'd also joined Mrs B in bidding farewell to Edith, who'd decided that having a baby on her own wasn't what she wanted and that the baby's father's family in Canada could share the load, even if he had never reappeared.

'Left me his visiting card, didn't he?' Edith had moaned as she'd stroked her massive belly. 'Even if the poor bugger never made it home.'

They'd made a special trip to Southampton to see her off, and Fen had shed a small tear as they'd waved the large ocean liner away from the dock.

Mrs B had caught pneumonia in March, it had been such a cold and damp one, and the three of them that were left had taken time out from their field duties to nurse her back to health. She'd been laid up until almost VE Day itself, and the girls were mighty glad she was well again and able to join in the town's celebrations. They'd downed tools and helped to hang criss-cross bunting along the high street and, between them, they'd saved up ration tokens for sugar and flour. The farm's cherished chickens meant they had never been short of eggs, so they made a dozen cakes for the town's children to enjoy at a celebratory tea party. The war was finally over; it didn't seem real.

And every single day she had thought about Arthur and the Burgundian village that he had coded to her in that last letter. She'd tried contacting the War Office, but she'd come up against a wall of silence; their staff were either overstretched or unable to help her, and one letter she received even denied Arthur's existence at all, or claimed he was safely at work in London in some unheard-of branch of the Air Ministry. This obfuscation and hurtful bafflement only made Fen all the more committed to getting herself to France, to find out, using his own clues, what had happened to him and if, hope beyond hope, he was still alive, recuperating perhaps in some field hospital or friendly farmhouse.

'*Docked newspaper man got confused going to America – how dull.* Seven letters.' She was stumped. 'You're no help.' She spoke down to the little terrier that was tied via a string to a valise, which in turn was attached by a thin rope to the belt of the gently snoring gentleman in the seat across the carriage from her.

The dog cocked its head on one side and growled slightly.

'*Je m'excuse, monsieur,*' Fen blinked an apology at the dog and then turned back to the window briefly before staring down at her crossword. 'Come on, old girl, what would Arthur do?'

'I don't know who Arthur is, but can I help?' The snoring had stopped, as had the growling, luckily, and the old man who had the valise tied to him was now sitting more upright. 'You'll find I have better manners than my friend here…' he indicated the small dog, 'but sometimes I think he might be the brains of the operation.'

Fen smiled at him, and repeated the clue. A few minutes passed in silence, apart from the noises of the train as it clattered on its rails over the farmland beyond the window. The old man closed his eyes again and Fen wasn't sure if he was deep in thought or if the snoring would start up once more. She felt a bit awkward staring at him and so creased the folded edge of the newspaper slightly firmer and sketched a quick doodle with her pencil.

At last he spoke. 'No, sorry, not a clue. I've never got those cryptic ones.'

Fen nodded at him and was about to carry on staring at the fiendish clue when a thought niggled at her. This man was obviously British too, and yet here he was on a train to Dijon as well. Her curiosity got the better of her and she asked, 'Are you travelling for work or…'

'No.' The old man gave her another smile, and then continued, 'I think my boy was lost along the Maginot Line, he's half-French, you see, and was called up early in the war. We all thought it was phoney for so long, didn't we? And he was married here, with a child on the way. Then the real war started and we heard nothing. My wife and I…' he started to cough a bit and Fen knew it was to disguise a lump that had formed in his throat, so she started talking instead.

'I'm going to try and find my fiancé. I thought we were so lucky as he was stationed back in England for so long. I asked him, of course, what his role was, but he never gave me a proper answer and then he was suddenly under starter's orders and off right after we'd got engaged.' Fen paused and looked down at her fingernails, clean at least, but in desperate need of a manicure after the years spent in the fields.

She flexed her fingers and realised it must look odd to this fellow passenger that she wasn't wearing any sort of ring. 'Never even got the chance to get one, you see. We thought it would be incredibly fancy to try and go to London and perhaps even take tea at the Ritz as a very special celebration, but he never came home,' she said, still staring at her hands. The letter he'd proposed with, that clue about unravelling gents… it was the only *engagement ring* she'd been given. 'It all seems so unfair,' Fen continued, 'because my Arthur is – was, I suppose – such a gentle soul and so much more at home with his pipe and slippers and one of these,' she pointed to the newspaper in her lap, 'and I can't imagine him here *fighting*. He always said he was meaner than he looked, but really I think old Growler down there has a sterner countenance.

'And look at these villages that we keep passing. Some don't look like they've been touched at all, as if it was all someone else's problem, someone else's fight.' She looked out of the window and then started up again, more to herself than to her companion. 'It's not that he wasn't young and fit and eminently capable, it just seems a waste to have not had him in Whitehall or somewhere…'

Fen looked back towards the old man and realised that the reason he hadn't interjected was that he was sound asleep, his gentle snore adding another rhythmic sound to that of the train itself. Fen held in a snort of laughter and shook her head. She picked up the crossword and, with eyes afresh, suddenly saw the answer to her five down…

'Of course,' she picked up her pen and wrote in the seven letters. 'A newspaper man is probably EDITOR, but docked so no R. Mix that up and add US and hey presto. TEDIOUS. A bit like me, eh Growler?'

Unsurprisingly, she got no response from Growler, or his owner. All the same, a somnolent companion was better than many, and Fen pondered over what he'd said before she'd bored him to sleep. The so-called Maginot Line was meant to have been France's wall of defence, except the Germans had both ripped through it and skirted around it when no one was really watching, leaving thousands dead, hundreds of thousands wounded and almost half a million taken prisoner and that was the end of the 'phoney' war, as they'd called it. And Burgundy was so close to where both the Maginot Line and the demarcation zone had been. It must have been a battlefield of sorts, literally and strategically, and Fen wondered, what with Arthur's working knowledge of French and brains the size of Big Ben if perhaps, *just perhaps*, he wasn't a normal infantryman at all?

A few more hours passed and Fen decided that the rocking of the train wasn't so bad that she couldn't put pen to paper and write a letter back to Mrs B and her friends. She'd promised to keep them up to date with her mission. Mrs B, who had quite a kind heart once you got past her sometimes gruff exterior, had sent her off with a special bar of Fry's chocolate she'd been saving. She had made Fen promise to write, if only to give her something jolly to read out to the girls of an evening now the wireless was on the blink. Kitty and Dilys were still lodging with Mrs B, not so much for war work now as to help the older lady out while they decided how best to carry on with their lives.

Somewhere near Dijon, France, September 1945

Dear Mrs B, Kitty and Dilly,

I promised I'd keep you informed, so here it is, my adventure so far.

Mrs B, thanks for the sandwiches, they went down a treat on the crossing from Dover to Calais. And luckily didn't come up again even though the Channel got quite choppy halfway across!

The boats are loaded with soldiers, however, and I was lucky to squeeze onto one that the Red Cross had requisitioned to ship in supplies to the wounded who can't yet leave France. It's all frightfully sobering and covering this distance in a relatively short time (27 hours and counting from Haslemere!) makes one realise how close we all were to it, even in the fields of West Sussex.

I boarded the evening train to Paris along with a dishevelled bunch of travellers, and I must say I was glad to see the City of Lights appear out the window, not only because I adore the place, but because it meant I could nudge the snoring salesman off my shoulder, who hadn't paused for a silent breath since Lille.

I arrived terribly late at Madame Coillard's (good idea, Dil, to look up my old art teacher!) and then left early the next day. No time to take in the sights or seek out my old haunts – maybe next visit – as I had to dash from her apartment to the Gare de Lyon to catch the train to Dijon. I have to tell you a bit of what I saw, not because I want to shock or upset you, but I feel I've seen history in front of my very eyes and perhaps at its darkest point.

In Paris, at the stations, there are soldiers just lying there on stretchers on the platforms, covered in dirty sheets with rust-red stains on them. I can't bear to think of those poor men who made it off the battlefield, only to be left on a station platform… And the walking wounded fare no better really. They look so gaunt, so pale, except for stained bandages smeared with the blood and mud of the battlefield.

I'm sure this isn't the cheery adventure you wanted to hear about, so instead I'll tell you of the latest fashions I saw… Yes, fashions! Can you believe that the women here still have the most exquisite clothes, I think they might have magicked them up, or at the very least be much more deft than me with a needle! And get those hair rollers heating up – fashions here are for big curls on top and longer hair at the back – très chic!

I wonder how Edith is doing in Canada and if Duke's parents have warmed to her? Will write again soonest.

With fondness, Fen

PS Kitty, you asked me to teach you how to solve crosswords… well, I'll do what I can from afar! Let's start with a simple anagram, shall we? Remember how the answer is always one word from the clue – and one word will tell you it's an

anagram, something like 'twitches' or 'confused', look for that
marker! So, here we go... 'The City of Lights in mixed-up
pairs (5)' – it's an easy one!

Writing the letter and coming up with even a simple clue for
Kitty occupied Fen until she disembarked at the nearest station
to Morey-Fontaine. She hadn't wanted to burden her friends with
some of the other sights she'd seen as she'd crossed Paris, such as
the young woman, who had looked a lot like Kitty, being mobbed
by men and women alike, her shaven head daubed with a large
black swastika. The woman next to Fen on the bus had spat out
the word '*tondue*' – meaning shaven one – as they'd driven on and
Fen had gleaned from her that there were lingering recriminations
for those deemed to have collaborated with the Germans. French
women accused of selling Nazis their bodies or exchanging a private
few hours with them for basic essentials such as food and clean
clothing were shaved and dragged through the streets.

The thought of that shaven-headed woman had stayed with her
as she'd arrived at the Gare de Lyon and boarded the train to Dijon.
The train journey itself had been long: the constant delays as they
were held at sidings while engines pulling carriages of exhausted
troops, refugees or supplies took priority on the tracks. But, finally, she
disembarked at the somewhat isolated station and though she allowed
herself a small shudder at the loneliness of the place, she at least felt
a little bit closer to finding out what had happened to her Arthur.

Like many small, rural stations this one was not much more
than a house next to a platform and there was nothing in the way
of maps, information or notices – all things that must have been
taken away a few years ago to impede the occupation. Still, the
familiar yellow of the *boîte aux lettres* gave Fen some hope and she
happily slipped the letter she'd finished writing on the train into
it, hoping it might get back to England before she did.

Fen was pleased to have a copy of Mr B's old map of France with her. She and Kitty had painstakingly traced the roads and landmarks from the original, aware that something as precious as Mr B's regulation map shouldn't leave the farmhouse and Mrs B's protective care.

Fen now flattened out the tracing against the white wall of the station house. She wasn't surprised that there was no stationmaster about to help her, she doubted it had been a job with much longevity during the war, what with the railways being used for everything from troop transport to black-market smuggling, from what she'd heard. So, she took her bearings and found what she decided must be the road that would lead to Morey-Fontaine.

As she started walking, knowing that her destination was now only a few miles away, she felt more optimistic than she had for long a while, or at least since Arthur's letter had arrived. Perhaps it was the fact that the sky was blue and the road, though dusty and potholed, was flat and quiet, or maybe it was something to do with being back in France. After all, Fen had lived in Paris from when she was a small girl until she was eighteen and sometimes felt more French than English. Perhaps that was why she had planned this hare-brained mission to find Arthur – it wasn't just *him* calling her over the channel, but France itself.

Haaaarrrrruuuuuuuaahhhhh. The horn belted out its klaxon-like sound, but too late to warn Fen of the truck's approach.

'Blimey!' she cried as she fell over into the ditch beside the dusty road. She felt like shouting out some of the slightly riper words that she'd picked up from the returning squaddies at Dover, but almost as soon as the truck had forced her from the road, it was gone and out of sight, and certainly out of earshot. A large dust cloud and the settling silence of the empty road was all that was left of the accident.

'How rude!' Fen climbed back out of the ditch and found her suitcase where it had been flung out of her hand, a glancing blow from the truck striking it several feet in front of her. Luckily, the sturdy leather and decent catches hadn't been damaged and her undergarments weren't shredded all over the road, but still, this wasn't the welcome to rural France she'd been hoping for.

She dusted herself off and patted down her hair, feeling completely out of sorts, not to mention a bit battered and bruised.

'Oh dear,' she said to no one but the birds scavenging in the dust, as she saw how dirty her hand was now. 'Only one thing for it.' She squatted down by her suitcase, unclipped the catches and found inside a clean handkerchief and a brightly coloured scarf. Fen cleaned her face as best as she could with the hanky and wrapped the scarf around her head, as she always had done when she was at work in the fields, using it to tame her chestnut curls that escaped from her victory rolls.

Feeling a bit more herself – she did like to look her best where possible, even if it was only a slick of lipstick and a pinch to the cheeks instead of rouge – she clicked her suitcase shut and carried on along the road. She had, in the panic of the moment, kept her wits about her and made a mental note of the colour and make of the vehicle. Needless to say, she spent the rest of the walk into Morey-Fontaine going over in her head exactly what she'd say to the owner if she ever saw that big dirty grey Citroën again.

Finally, as she reached the outskirts of Morey-Fontaine, the vast stone tower of the church came into view. The village was larger than she had anticipated though, and it took her a full twenty minutes or so to navigate the narrow, and occasionally winding, streets until she found herself in what looked like the main square.

'Place de l'Église…' she read out loud to herself, seeing the stone plaque with the square's name high up on the wall of one of the shuttered buildings.

The church, built of greyish-beige stone, did indeed dominate one side of the square, which itself was looking rather down at heel, unsurprising given the fact that the local community had probably been too distracted by the war to get round to tending the marigolds. Large plane trees created welcome shade within the square and Fen walked underneath them to find herself at the grand Romanesque doorway at the front of the church. She looked up at it and studied the solid, reassuring permanence of the ancient stone arches. Her childhood had included many trips out to villages and small towns like this one, and she remembered how her father would read from his Baedeker's guide, his voice fading out of earshot as Fen would walk away from him, her mother and brother, her fingers trailing over the sun-warmed walls of whichever church they were visiting until she met an obstacle – a buttress, a door, a broken paving stone. She much preferred to soak in the buildings this way; feel them, touch them, notice them, rather than rely on mere facts and dates to tell her about them.

The caw of a raven broke her nostalgic train of thought and she shook her head clear of old remembrances and walked towards the church, her arm stretching out as she got closer, ready to touch the stone, the expectation of its warmth and the familiar grainy surface bringing back her memories. She had barely touched it when her eye was drawn to the parish noticeboard, the legs of the slim, wooden cabinet planted in a stone trough that spilled over with weeds and long grasses. The notices were out of date and sun-faded, but it wasn't them that caught her eye. It was the name of the church: SS Raphael et Gabriel. *The Archangels of Death.*

Fen caught her breath. She had been right. Arthur's clues had led her to the correct village. The anagrams of Morey-Fontaine and Archangel Death made utter sense now – he'd given her the village and, if that was ambiguous, the name of the church in it. She was definitely in the right place. Her pride in her clue-solving capabilities was marred, of course, by the heartache that accompanied it; the reason *why* he had left her the clues. *So that she could find out what had happened to him.*

With her resolve all the stronger, she looked around the town square and tried to work out what to do next. Having grown up in France, she knew as much about its culture as its language (and she could speak the lingo as well as the most earthy of Burgundian farmers), so she knew that the place to head would be the town hall. There, the *maire*, or local mayor, would know exactly what had gone on in this small town during the war, both officially and unofficially.

Fen cast her eyes around the square, looking for a signpost or some hint as to where the mayor's office might be. She wandered over to the centre of the square and placed her sturdy old suitcase down. Stretching out her hand and swinging her arm around to get some blood flowing back into her fingertips, she paced the square until a noticeboard under one of the trees caught her eye. Feeling like it would be quite safe to leave her suitcase unattended, and pleased not to be lugging it with her at every step, she hotfooted it over to the noticeboard to take a look. It was a large wooden cabinet-style structure, with the notices roughly nailed onto a board behind two glass wooden-framed doors. The cabinet stood on slightly shaky-looking legs that were dug deep into a large stone planter, itself overspilling with unkempt weeds and wild flowers.

Fen scanned the notices, but there was nothing pinned to the board about the local *maire* or the hours he kept. She caught sight instead of her reflection and noticed that her headscarf was a bit skew-whiff. She adjusted it and patted down her hair, making sure her hairpins were doing what they were meant to do.

As she was checking her appearance, she happened to glance at a faded advertisement: 'Workers Needed', it declared. She read on: 'Domaine Morey-Fontaine seeks labourers for winery and vineyard work. Board and lodging included.' The small print pointed her in the direction of the local château, so local in fact that it was just the other side of the church.

With the sun starting to fall behind the rooftops of the buildings and a rather unsubtle rumble patrolling through her stomach, Fen walked back to her battered suitcase and picked it up, hoping that the advertisement was still in date and that the château of Morey-Fontaine might be willing to hire her – and, more importantly right now, feed her too.

CHAPTER FOUR

Château Morey-Fontaine was named after the small town, or perhaps it was the other way around and the town had sprung up, back in the mire of medieval Burgundy, because of the presence and protection of the solid stone house and the sanctity of its church.

Either way, it was impossible to miss the ancient building. All Fen had to do was follow the monumental, sand-coloured stone walls around from the front portico to the east end of the church to find herself in a pleasant little grove of fruit trees. From here, she could see the château itself and in between them she could make out what must have once been formal gardens.

The ground was dusty underfoot as she covered the short distance between the orchard and the house, but Fen could tell that once, maybe only a few years ago, these would have been well-kept lawns. Lichen-covered, dry, stone bowls were all that were left of the ornamental fountains, the cherubs no longer spouting water, their mouths cast in pouts, whistling in the wind.

Unkempt bushes lined the path, and Fen tried to make out the original shapes of the topiary cut they once must have had. The bushes looked sparse and their outer branches were yellowed by the dry summer. The borders, no doubt once ornately planted, had been given over to a vegetable patch and Fen recognised the brownish skins of onions poking up through the soil and a few green beans hanging off a limp plant. A prickly-leaved artichoke sat majestically in the middle of the bed, its heavily laden head, regal purple in flower, nodded at Fen as she walked past and then up the broken stone steps to the château's main terrace.

'Hello, monsieur,' Fen spoke not to the owner of the château, but to a plump fluffy black and white cat, which had appeared on the terrace as she reached the top of the steps. His gleaming coat seemed to mock the scratched-up earth and dry, dusty terrace around them. *If fresh vegetables had been in short supply during the occupation*, Fen thought to herself, *then mice certainly hadn't.*

Fen gave the cat a quick tickle between its ears and then looked up at the building itself. From where she stood, she could see warm stone covered in vibrant red Virginia creeper, its straggling feelers climbing up between elongated stone-mullioned windows towards the roof, which was a dark terracotta with a decorative diamond pattern set into it. It reminded Fen of the highly decorated buildings she'd seen in Dijon when she'd stretched her legs between trains.

She put her suitcase down and walked along the terrace to the right of the building, where a fairy-tale tower, of which Rapunzel would be proud, connected the old, medieval wing to another, larger and slightly more recent three-storey section, making the whole building a solid L-shape in design. Looking up at the tower that loomed above her, Fen saw that at each corner there was a small turret. They clung to the tower like limpets and it was only the reassurance that they obviously hadn't crumbled for the last few hundred years that gave Fen hope that her adventure wouldn't be prematurely ended by falling masonry.

All in all, the château, though monumental in parts, was a modest one. More of a *grand maison*, as her mother would imp-ishly say.

A thin wisp of smoke rising from the chimney hinted at life within the house and, picking up her suitcase, Fen walked back along the terrace in front of the older part of the building until she found a small gate in an evergreen hedge. She pushed it open, cringing at the loud creak it gave as she slipped through, and found herself in the central courtyard of the château.

'Bonjour! Madame?' Fen called to the woman in the courtyard who was hanging sheets on the line. She was bent over the washing basket and Fen wondered if her voice had been lost on the breeze that had suddenly whipped through the buildings.

'Madame? Bonjour!' She tried again and this time the woman turned to face her – a much younger woman than Fen had assumed from the unfashionable clothes that she wore.

'Je m'excuse… mademoiselle,' Fen apologised, although the disgruntled young woman didn't relax a muscle in her face, which was a picture of pure irritation. She was dark-haired and slim, her face pinched and sallow, as if she had spent the war drinking vinegar rather than fighting off Germans. She was young though, and it struck Fen as odd that she still wore a skirt and pinny instead of overalls. Fen felt sorry for her in her old worsted, calf-length, shapeless piece, which somehow made even the workaday overalls Fen had spent most of the war in look like high fashion.

There's no colour to her, Fen thought, subconsciously reaching up to check that her own brightly coloured headscarf was still in place, keeping her curls at bay.

Before she could apologise for her *faux pas*, the woman started talking in a stream of rushed French.

'Who are you, coming here, surprising me like that, with your madame this and madame that? *Bof!* You could have given me a heart attack!' The woman looked Fen up and down. 'Dressed like a duchess but dirty like a tramp!'

Fen, who was unsure whether it was her smart skirt – she'd worn one of her best to travel in – and rather natty headscarf or her travel-weary and dirty face that had offended the woman, waited until the flow of objections stopped before replying, her French rusty, but falling back into place as she spoke. '*Mademoiselle*, I am sorry to cause you any offence. I am here looking for work and lodging as advertised on the town noticeboard.'

'*Parisienne?*' The maid indicated that she thought Fen was from Paris, the use of the feminine lending its own connotations to the word and Fen understood what she meant. The women of Paris, as she'd seen for herself, with their fashions and more cosmopolitan culture, were often regarded cautiously by more rural folk, who perhaps saw higher hemlines as heresy rather than *haute couture*.

'No, I'm from England, but I have lived in France before. My name is Fenella Churche.'

'*Eh bien,*' the woman looked a little mollified and placed her hands on her lower back to arch it out before she returned the introduction. 'I am Estelle Suchet. I am the housekeeper and nursery maid. The mistress is in the kitchen, I'll take you through.'

Fen thanked her and followed her across the courtyard, listening to the mutterings of the maid as they went. 'Who does she think she is? Like she'll last more than a minute in the fields with that silk scarf. Ha. She'll be gone soon enough, I'm sure. Though her accent is good, I'll give her that, though it's far too *Paris* for my liking.'

Fen smiled to herself, not mocking the young housekeeper, but glad that although the war may have ravaged the country around them, the women of France were still as opinionated as they ever had been.

Estelle led her out of the sunshine of the courtyard into the cool of a small hallway and from there into the large vaulted-ceilinged kitchen of the château, where she left her and returned to her laundry. The overwhelming feeling was of stone – massive pale blocks of it created the walls and the deep fireplace, which once would have housed an old-fashioned spit, such as you would have roasted a whole pig on with a kitchen boy slowly turning it for hours and hours. Now there was a large black stove set into the soot-darkened recess, with copper pans hanging above it from cast-iron hooks.

Fen's eyes moved up the chimney breast, thickset with stone and a carved family crest. It had likely once been coloured in heraldic blues and reds, perhaps a flash of gold, but those hues had long since faded and been tarnished by the black smoke of countless cooking fires. She could make out three fleurs-de-lis, the gold of their original colouring smutted with soot, and the azure blue behind them now mostly grey and blackened, too. There had obviously been an accident at some point, perhaps a copper pan wielded too energetically, but one of the smaller stones of the fire surround was freshly mortared into the chimney breast and it stood out starkly, clean against the soot. In the centre of the kitchen was a long, well-scrubbed wooden table. Near to where Fen stood, by the door to the hallway, the table was laid with dishes and cutlery, ready for dinner. Fen subconsciously touched her rumbling stomach and hoped she would be sitting there soon enough. The table was exceptionally long, however, and whoever would be dining there later would only take up about a third of it. At the far end, a woman was pounding bread dough into submission, her dark hair swept up into a chignon but tendrils around her face swinging rhythmically with her kneading.

'Bonjour, madame,' Fen hoped she was on safer ground, and that this was indeed the lady of the house, although she was only wearing a simple cotton dress, nothing fancy.

'*Yes?*' The woman looked up from her dough and spoke.

Fen introduced herself, and once again she was met with an inquisitive 'Parisienne?'

'No, madame, I am from England and I…' Fen stopped talking, not because her French wasn't up to it, but she hadn't really thought terribly far ahead as to how she was going to explain her sudden appearance in Burgundy. She and Kitty, in all their planning over timetables and rationing coupons, had never thought of the need for a cover story. Perhaps it was the less-than-friendly greeting from both women, or the fact that the kitchen's high stone walls seemed to suddenly bear down on her, but she stopped in mid-sentence and decided that it might be best not to explain about Arthur and her search for his whereabouts to this stranger.

As the lady stared at her, though, her impatient eyes demanding an explanation, Fen grasped around inside her mind for inspiration.

'… I am travelling in order to write about the, er,' Fen stalled before plucking an idea out of the air, 'the, er, churches of the Côte d'Or region.'

'That is a very niche subject matter, mademoiselle.'

'Yes, it's a passion of mine. Churches.'

'And what is your name?'

'Fenella. Fenella Churche.' Fen realised how silly this all sounded now. A Miss Churche writing about churches…

She held her breath as madame pounded the dough. Finally, she stopped and spoke to Fen as she peeled the sticky dough from her fingers.

'*Bon*. We need help in the vineyard and the house. I assume you can work?'

'Yes, of course. I was in the Women's Land Army, I worked the fields and—'

'*Bon*.' Madame cut her off. 'You will sleep with Estelle. *Estelle!*' The call brought the housekeeper running back in from the courtyard. 'Show Mademoiselle Churche to your room, you will share.'

The look of disgust on the maid's face was hard for Fen to miss, but she bravely smiled at the pair of French women and picked up her suitcase.

'But, *madame*…' the maid whined.

'Shush, Estelle, you used to travel the countryside in a caravan, you can share a room in a château!'

Estelle scowled but beckoned for Fen to follow her out of the kitchen and into the dark passageway that led to the bedrooms.

Before they left the warmth of the kitchen, Fen asked madame one more thing.

'Madame, if you don't mind, may I have your name?'

'Of course, my name is Madame Bernard. Sophie Bernard. My husband is Pierre. I will introduce you to the household at dinner. Six o'clock. Don't be late.'

Fen thanked her hostess – or rather employer – and caught up with the disgruntled housekeeper. *A stranger is just a friend you haven't met yet*, Fen repeated the mantra to herself as she followed Estelle from the kitchen through a door that led into the grand tower that Fen had looked up at from the terrace.

The tower itself served the purpose of linking the vaulted kitchen wing to the three-storey living quarters and was home to the most monumental staircase. Climbing it was like clambering through a fossilised ammonite, the smell of the stone musty and chalky, the air damp and cool.

'Sharing a room! It is not right! I am not a child!' Estelle chuntered away to herself as she led Fen up the spiral staircase. Fen was careful to follow in Estelle's footsteps and keep to the widest part of each stair tread, as the steps narrowed to nothing at the cylindrical centre of the tower. Even so, her suitcase still accidentally bashed against the stone every now and again as she lugged it up with her, causing Estelle to tut under her breath. Needless to say, Fen wasn't too keen on the pairing either, but the house suddenly seemed a large and potentially unfriendly place, so she wasn't about to complain about having the company, however sour.

Soon enough, they arrived at the first floor, where an elegant painted blue door looked incongruous next to the solid stone surrounding it. As soon as the pair walked through it, Fen noticed that the architecture of this wing was different from the kitchen and tower, and she imagined that it must have been added to the medieval building later on.

The door opened onto a corridor, and Fen thought that the decoration, though not in its first flush of youth, was more elegant than the older part of the château. Light flowed in from large, unshuttered windows on the left-hand side and, as they walked along, Fen caught sight of the courtyard she'd been in a few moments earlier.

On their right were the bedrooms, and each door was painted in the same pale blue as the rest of the woodwork. One, two… Estelle stopped in front of the third door along and laid her hand on the door handle. She turned to look at Fen and gave her what felt like a final accusatory glance, a once-over up and down as if vetting her for the room, and then turned the large brass knob to open the door.

'Wait here,' the housekeeper demanded of Fen.

As she stood, Fen cast her eyes around the corridor, noticing the cobwebs high up in the cornicing and the dust on the skirting board. Mrs B would have had a field day in here, her duster and mop at the ready. Fen was busy fantasising about how her former landlady would react, and what choice words she'd use to describe the slatternly state of the cleaning, when Estelle reappeared and finally allowed her to enter their bedroom.

Fen picked up her case and walked in. The room wasn't beautiful, but it had the potential to be so, with the proportions that you'd expect from a fine eighteenth-century building. Wide, dark wood floorboards were covered with a couple of threadbare rugs, and between Fen and the two large almost-floor-to-ceiling windows there stood two small single beds. But oh, the view from the windows… Even at this distance, Fen could see gently rolling slopes covered in vines, with a copse here and there in the distance. It was stunning countryside, different to the more wooded Weald of West Sussex, but a lovely sight all the same.

Fen was just edging past the beds to get a better look when she heard a 'Tsk, non, non, non,' from Estelle.

'Sorry, am I in the way?'

'Of course, but it is not that, that is your bed there.' Estelle pointed towards the one nearest the door.

Fen placed her suitcase down on the floor next to it, glad to let go of the heavy weight and stretch out her fingers.

Estelle sighed heavily, as if every action Fen took was specifically designed to annoy her, and then did a cursory show round of the room. She opened the doors of a large grey armoire and pointed out the hanging space. *She's barely got a thing in there*, Fen thought and in that moment went from being slightly overwhelmed by the whole situation to pitying the housekeeper, whose dresses only took up a few inches of hanging space.

'When you've finished gawking,' Estelle closed the armoire's doors and indicated the chest of drawers, which was also painted grey, and positioned between the two windows.

Once, Fen thought to herself, *this grand house must have had someone living here with an eye for detail and the money to commission such matching furniture*. Now, it was merely a room for a housekeeper – *and one with barely a stitch to her name either*, Fen realised as Estelle indicated that only two of the drawers in the chest were hers.

'Don't you dare go through it though. Or go poking your nose around any other part of this room.' Estelle waggled her finger at Fen, who was already nodding her head. 'And under the bed is the pisspot and where you can store your case. Just don't confuse the two in the middle of the night!' This last, crass, *bon mot* sent Estelle into paroxysms of cackling laughter.

'I will try,' Fen assured her, glancing around as the maid still chuckled to herself. In between the beds was a small table, on which stood a framed photograph of a man and an oil lamp. A lack of electric supply was understandable in a rural, obviously run-down château. But a *potty*? Plus, she'd noticed that there was a large pitcher and bowl on top of the chest of drawers – put there no doubt for the ladies' daily wash. Fen wondered if enquiring about the plumbing would irk her new housemate even more, and she decided to leave it and hoped she might find something resembling a bathroom when she was alone and able to explore.

Estelle suddenly snatched the framed photograph away from Fen's eyeline. 'There is work to do, I'm sure *madame* would like you to make yourself useful before dinner.' She slipped the frame into one of the capacious pockets of her apron. 'Don't linger over the unpacking, unless you are actually *Parisienne* and have trunks and trunks of silk stockings and fine wools that I am missing?' Estelle did a bad impression of a detective looking for clues with a magnifying glass and then laughed. '*Bof*, well, I am busy. Until dinner, *à bientôt*.'

Estelle bustled past Fen and left the bedroom, closing the door behind her. Fen counted to three, and then let out a long sigh. She sat down on the bed and winced as the metal springs gave their best impression of the string section warming up before a concert. She gave the bed a cursory bounce and the noise worsened so she stopped and sat in the still, silent room. She stared at the dust motes that danced around in the sunlight that streamed in through the large windows.

'What a funny old place, with some funny old people,' Fen said to herself under her breath. And then she let herself, just for a moment, wonder how diverting Arthur would have found it all.

CHAPTER FIVE

Fen unpacked her suitcase, laying out her clothes on the single bed before deciding whether they should be hung up in the wardrobe or folded into a drawer. She hoped she'd brought the right things, and thought of what Kitty had said before she left about 'baking in the French sunshine'. Fen smiled as she remembered their giggles…

'It's Burgundy, Kitty, not exactly the Riviera!'

'Yes, but it's still more thrilling than a wet weekend in West Sussex…'

'To be fair, most things are more thrilling than that!'

'And you get to have a proper adventure. Like Joan Fontaine in *Frenchman's Creek*!'

'As long as I'm not paddling the wrong way up the *creek* in Morey-*Fontaine*, we'll be fine…'

And who knew where this adventure would lead her?

She settled on folding her dungarees and jumpers into one of the empty drawers and hanging her other Sunday-best skirt and blouse in the armoire. Other than what she was wearing, she had one more stout pair of shoes with her, some pumps and, of course, her short wellington boots, all of which she lined up in the bottom of the large wardrobe.

'That's odd,' Fen whispered to herself as she noticed that a thin layer of dust covered most of the bottom shelf, except for a rectangular patch where a box or case might have recently been stored. Someone had obviously recently had cause to move whatever it was before any more dust could gather.

She shrugged and moved back to the bed where she'd left the handkerchief that she had used to wrap around a silver frame that contained a photograph of Arthur. She carefully unfolded it and placed the frame on the rickety bedside table so that she could see it from her pillow. She remembered the day they'd been to the photographic studio and had the portraits taken. Then, a few days before Arthur was sent abroad, they'd given each other these little love tokens. Fen wondered where the matching silver frame that contained the picture of her was? Lost, no doubt, to some roadside tinker now, sold on for cash or perhaps dirty and corroding in a ditch.

Fen dabbed her eye with the hanky and decided to stop herself from getting too maudlin by exploring the rest of the corridor.

Most of the doors were locked, which seemed odd to Fen in a family home, but then she had to admit that nosy parkers like her could be exactly the reason why they were. She could only imagine that each room was like her and Estelle's – high-ceilinged and rather stark, but all with that glorious view over acres of green vines. After trying a few locked doors, she had, much to her relief, found a bathroom.

Why Estelle had made such a fuss about the potty was beyond her when the château was home to one of the most impressive thunderboxes Fen had ever seen. The contraption – a flushing lavatory, the seat of which was solid wood and throne-like in its size – was in a bathroom that also contained a wide, old metal bath with a geyser hung unsteadily above it. *So baths could be had, but your life might be in danger with every drip of steaming water*, Fen thought. She noted the large, but cracked, basin too and wondered if any money had been spent on the château before the war.

She chided herself for comparing the place to her accommodation back in West Sussex – the farmhouse there had been updated by the landlord shortly before the war and the bathroom had had every convenience, from hot running water to a detachable rubber hose for washing your hair.

Fen nipped back to her bedroom and picked up the large porcelain pitcher from the chest of drawers. She tested the geyser and stood back as it spluttered and spat into action, dispensing steaming water into the jug. She topped it up with cold water from the basin and walked with it back to her bedroom.

Fen closed the door behind her and then washed her face and fixed her hair, her chestnut-brown unruly curls never quite sitting perfectly no matter how carefully she pinned them. She looked at her reflection and saw her hazel green eyes with their dark lashes stare back at her. They looked weary, though, and Fen wished she'd been able to bring some of the make-up that Edith had left at the farmhouse. A dab or two of that concealing cream would do nicely right now! She still lived by her mother's maxim of 'it's nice to look nice' and she wondered if there was a touch of *Parisienne* about her after all?

Content enough with her little fix – a dash of lipstick finished off her tidy-up – she sorted out the last few bits and pieces from her suitcase and remembered what Estelle had said about where to store it.

'Off you go,' she said to the sturdy old case as she knelt down and pushed it right to the middle of the space under her bed. Then 'Ouch!' as a splinter from one of the floorboards caught her finger. Sucking at it hard, Fen began to get up, but something caught her eye. Under Estelle's bed, she noticed not just a suitcase, much like her own, but a metal strongbox, a cardboard archiving box and a whole heap of newspapers. 'Aha,' Fen took her finger out of her mouth and looked at the splinter.

A hoarder after all, she thought as she prised the slither of wood out from under her skin, *and I bet one of those boxes would exactly fit that dust-free space in the wardrobe…*

Fen's sense of duty to her new employer and to the privacy of her new room-mate had curbed her natural curiosity about whether the boxes under Estelle's bed had recently been moved, and she retraced her way back down the spiral tower staircase to the kitchen. Sophie Bernard was nowhere to be seen, but Fen noticed that one more place had been set at the dining end of the long farmhouse table. This simple act of welcome cheered her heart, and almost brought another tear to her eye. She was so far from home, in a place where she knew no one, on the hunt for her fiancé, who was, she had to face up to it, more than likely dead. *But perhaps, just perhaps he isn't…* She'd almost expected him to be in the kitchen when she came down the stairs, so convinced was she that she'd cracked his code. Everything pointed towards this being the village…

Fen let that tear slide down her cheek as she leant against the long table. The Archangels of Death had more than likely been here and taken her Arthur with them. A shiver went down her spine and she had no sooner wiped the tear from her eye than Sophie Bernard appeared from a doorway near the stairs.

'Are you all right, Mademoiselle Churche?'

Fen felt embarrassed, but far from stiffening her resolve, this act of kindness seemed to weaken it, and it was all Fen could do to nod her head and press her lips together in a vain attempt to stop the tears from coming.

'There is not much time to set you a proper task before dinner.' Sophie's tone was soft and motherly and Fen was grateful that she hadn't pushed her to explain herself more. 'But go and get your bearings. You know the way to the church, yes?'

Fen nodded, if she spoke, she worried the words would get caught up in sobs.

'*D'accord*, well if you leave by the gatehouse or go around the terrace away from the church, you'll find the vineyard. Maybe you saw it from your bedroom? There is a winery too. I will serve dinner at six o'clock. It's early, but it suits the hungry men and the children.'

Fen nodded again and as she took her leave of Madame Bernard, her emotions got the better of her. The heat from the stove and the smell of cooking onions had made her feel quite nauseous, and she was barely out into the fresh air and late-afternoon sunshine by the time the real tears came and she couldn't help but have a little cry.

'Come on, old thing,' Fen gave herself a talking-to as she walked across the courtyard of the château, dabbing her eyes with her handkerchief. What would Kitty have told her? Or her brother for that matter? 'Don't be a fathead, silly.' The sound of her own voice uttering such a childish phrase in these grand surroundings caused Fen to giggle; absurdity always made her laugh. But at least she had managed to cheer herself up a bit and she kept up the good work by whistling a jolly tune as she crossed the courtyard, dodging under the washing still hanging on the line.

She looked up at the windows of what she thought of as 'the bedroom wing', though, of course, it was the landing windows that looked over this courtyard. The bedrooms had a view of the vines on the other side of the building. And it couldn't all be bedrooms, surely? Not the whole wing?

Fen decided to have a peak and stood on tiptoes to look inside the elevated ground-floor windows. As she strained to see in through the dusty glass, her fingers grappling with the creeper that hung tantalisingly over the windowsill, she heard footsteps behind her. Losing her balance, she quickly let go of the wide stone sill and stepped back to solid ground before turning around. But there was no one there, only a jackdaw pecking at the dried grass.

Fen looked up at the building once more and noticed the late-afternoon sun glint especially brightly in the window of one of the tower's four precarious corner turrets. She stared at the turret a while longer, wondering if she'd see the bright reflection again, but there was nothing to see up there apart from a few birds circling overhead, probably finding their roost for the night.

Fen shrugged and turned. She tried whistling and found herself holding the old familiar tune to 'Pack Up Your Troubles'. She'd remembered her grandfather singing it as he bounced her on his knee; it had been popular just before she was born, during the Great War, the war to end all wars, until this one came along that was. Fen kept whistling, determined to jolly herself up before she met her new workmates. It was over now, the Allied Forces had won, the Nazis had retreated and Herr Hitler was dead. Fen made a promise to herself – when she'd found out what had happened to Arthur, she'd give herself a new start. 'No more looking back, only forward.'

'Talking to yourself is a sign of madness.' The gruff but educated English voice startled Fen, who hadn't realised that she'd been vocalising her thoughts.

'And interrupting a lady while she's talking is a sign of terrible manners.'

'Even when she's only talking to herself?'

'Especially then.' Fen paused and looked at her companion. He was tall and fair, and if his voice hadn't sounded like it was from the classrooms of Eton, she'd have described him as looking like a grubby tinker or a labourer. There was ingrained dirt in the creases of his once-white linen shirt and his dust-covered, greenish-grey woollen trousers were wrapped tightly around his calves with dark green puttees.

Before Fen could introduce herself or ask for his name in return, the Englishman was gone, striding off towards a small door at the base of the tower.

'How rude!' Fen muttered to herself. She was shocked by his bluntness but was pleased to see him; surely it was a stroke of luck to come across a fellow Brit about the same age as her, and, judging by his clothes, demobbed from the army. When he had the grace to hold a proper conversation with her, she'd be sure to ask him about Arthur.

Fen carried on walking around the walls of the old house, trailing her fingers along the brick and stone and keeping her thoughts to herself, along with any jaunty tunes going round her head. *Had Arthur been here?* She thought back to his letter. He'd told her about this village, identified it by its name and church and then… '*A glass of Burgundy soon saw me right, though, and the other fellows here are second to none.*'

She took a deep breath in as she realised that Arthur had actually pointed her towards this very château. What had Sophie Bernard said? There was a vineyard and a winery right here. *A glass of Burgundy…* This was the place, if anywhere, in Morey-Fontaine that you would find one! As for the other fellows being *second to none*, she wasn't quite sure, but that Englishman sure as hell was her best lead to finding Arthur so far.

Fen soon found herself at the base of another tower, this one a gatehouse with a wide archway running through it. She slipped out of the late-afternoon sunshine and into the cool of the stone-chilled shade.

'Halloo,' she called into the vaulted ceiling, but the only reply was the soft cooing of a dove, sitting high up in one of the corners.

'Coo to you too,' she said to the dove, before checking her watch. Time enough to keep exploring.

She walked across a small lawn and through some trees to a track, which followed along the side of a vineyard towards a winery building. If the house and its courtyard had been a quiet and contemplative sort of place, the opposite could be said about the hum of activity happening in the vines. Along with the late-afternoon bird calls, Fen could hear the buzzing of the bees in the nearby hives, the crunch of the dirt track beneath her feet and the sound of men and women singing, the voices far apart but joined in unison in the jaunty little tune.

As Fen looked between the rows of vines, she saw the workers with heavy-looking wicker hods on their backs, each person cutting bunches of grapes and tossing them gently into them. Fen didn't want to be caught staring, so hurried along the path towards what she thought must be the winery. It was a modern, single-storey, cinder-block affair with a few small windows up near the roofline. Its large concrete slabs were a poor relation to the stone used for the château and the town.

As she got closer, she heard men's voices raised, not in anger, but shouting directions and generally barking orders. 'Lift, lift, wait… All right, yes, now!'

She was about to mosey on in and introduce herself when out of the corner of her eye she spotted something that made her catch her breath. 'Hell's teeth!' she swore. There, parked in front of the winery was the grey Citroën truck that had run her off the road only an hour or so ago. It was identical, down to the canvas cover she'd seen flapping around as it drove off at speed and the tow hitch that was, for whatever reason, painted red. 'You little blighter.'

Fen stood with her arms crossed for a while, working out what to do. She was about to charge into the winery and find out who owned the vehicle, when she heard the deadened clank of the church bell chime the quarter-hour. Taking a deep breath in, and exhaling slowly, she decided not to storm into the winery and find the culprit of her brief stint in a ditch there and then and instead turned back towards the house.

'Fools rush in…' she counselled herself, fully aware that this whole escapade could be classed as some fool's errand of sorts. She took another couple of deep breaths and then whispered to herself, '… Where perhaps archangels have feared to tread.'

CHAPTER SIX

Estelle was nowhere to be seen when Fen got back to their shared bedroom. She still had a few minutes to spare before dinner and thought she should at least change out of her dusty travelling clothes.

Compared to the activity in the vineyards and the commotion in the winery, the house was quiet, and the bedroom even more so. The silence was almost overwhelming and Fen suddenly felt very isolated, very alone and as if her mission, which had once been so clear-cut in her mind, now seemed such a risky folly. She had never been homesick in her life before, and she wondered if this feeling of being unsettled and a bit unsure of herself was that, or just plain old loneliness.

She sat on her bed and bounced up and down a few times to make the springs squeak and the sound of it, though not at all pleasant, was at least some sort of noise in the emptiness of the room. She reminded herself that she had to be careful with the family and other workers she might meet over the dinner table in a few moments. If Arthur had been posted to this town, well, then there would be a reason why he wasn't here now. A rather fatal reason.

Fen shuddered, then shook herself free of the icy sensation that had run down her back. She mustn't be late to the communal dining table and she had to get herself together. Yes, she was alone in this vast old château, there was no sign of Arthur and she may well have walked into the vipers' nest.

Better make the best of it, old thing, she thought to herself as she rose from the bed, giving the springs one more chance to speak their mind, and then opened the armoire.

She changed her blouse for a less grubby one and took her headscarf off and pulled a comb through the curls that fell down the back of her neck, loosened from her hairgrips. She walked over to the mirror and pouted her lips ready for a top-up of the red lipstick that she decided no girl should be without, be it in the fields of Burgundy or on the Champs-Élysées. As a finishing touch, she pinned a small cameo brooch, made of ivory and edged in gold, to her cardigan. It had been her grandmother's and her mother had given it to her when she left to start working in London before the outbreak of the war. She wasn't sure if it was quite her thing, it being Victorian and not entirely *à la mode*, but it meant a lot to her as a connection with home, with her parents and with a happier time.

Walking down towards the kitchen, Fen heard the church bell chime the hour. It was six o'clock on the nose and she braced herself for meeting more of the château's occupants.

Someone here must know what happened to Arthur, she thought and then set herself the mental task of merely observing tonight and not start asking awkward questions before she'd taken the lie of the land. It would be like having a good read-through of all the clues in a crossword, sitting on your hands so you weren't tempted to jot things down, before starting the actual clue-solving. And not to mention excellent fodder for another letter to Mrs B and the girls.

Fen entered the kitchen and smiled at an elderly man who was sitting at the head of the long, well-scrubbed wooden table.

'Good evening,' she greeted the old man in her perfect French and was relieved when he looked up at her and smiled. His skin was deeply tanned and even more deeply wrinkled and his white hair floated like a halo above his head, the bald patch in the middle making him look like a medieval monk. *How apt, for the setting of this vast medieval kitchen*, Fen thought.

Before he could say much more than a quick greeting back, Sophie Bernard strode into the room, shouting at the man behind her, who held a young boy in his arms while another was being dragged along by his mucky hand. Both were dirty with soil and dust and Fen caught the end of the conversation and realised that the man was being told off for letting the young boys play out in the vines so late in the day.

'Now there is no time to wash their dirty faces, Pierre. And today we have another English…' Sophie had paused as she noticed Fen standing near the table. 'Well, good, here we have you and on time. Pierre, for goodness' sake, get those children to the table.'

Fen stood aside and let the children past. The youngest one peered up at her, frowned, and said, 'Who dis, mama?' at least that's what Fen thought he said; her ability to understand French was one thing, but toddler-speak was quite another. Fen looked down at the blond-haired child and winked, while, luckily, Sophie Bernard took the cue and introduced Fen to the family.

'Miss Churche, this is my youngest, but perhaps loudest, son, Benoit.' She walked over to him and ruffled his blond mop, then patted him on the bottom and encouraged him into the old man's waiting arms. 'And Jean-Jacques is there hiding behind my husband, Pierre.' At this point, Pierre lifted up the larger boy, still by Fen's estimate only about six years old, into his arms.

Fen waved at him but got nothing but the back of his head in reply as he buried his face into his father's shoulder. She smiled as she noticed Pierre absent-mindedly play with the little curl of brown hair that sat at the nape of his son's neck, before he gently set him down on one of the chairs around the table.

'I wouldn't worry about him,' Sophie reassured Fen. 'Ever since he was a baby, he's been in my skirts and hiding behind chair legs. Our little coward, eh, poppet?'

Fen wasn't sure if she should nod and agree with Sophie's comment about her son, and judging by the expression on her husband's face, he wasn't sure he liked the idea of his eldest son being introduced to a stranger in such a way. He looked like he was about to speak up for the child when Sophie continued.

'And this is Clément, Pierre's father. Papa to us and the boys, head of our household here.'

Fen turned to the old man and reached out a hand to him in formal greeting. He extracted one of his own hands from under his wriggling grandson and returned the handshake.

'Good evening, mademoiselle, it is a pleasure to have you here.'

Estelle appeared at the kitchen door and, without saying much to anyone, sat herself at one of the places furthest away from the old man at the head of the table. Before she knew it, though, young Benoit was off his grandfather's lap and onto hers and she shrieked as his grubby hands grabbed at her skirts and dirtied her pinafore.

'*Ooh la la!*' she exclaimed, but Fen could see that she was smiling behind her admonitions. There was something so charming about the whole scene and Fen felt all her fears about being surrounded by strangers diminish as she took her cue from the housekeeper-cum-nursery-maid and sat down opposite her at the table.

Once Sophie and Pierre, plus the shy Jean-Jacques were seated, Fen noticed that there were two more place settings left to fill. One might be for that English chap she'd met in the courtyard earlier and one for… She didn't dare hope that there might be another Englishman yet to come out of the woodwork – *her* Englishman.

Fen wasn't sure what the protocol was next. This was far removed from her parents' rather erratic suppers that would come as and when her mother or father could get their nose out of a book, or the jovial if well-mannered evening meal served up at Mrs B's farmhouse. Her heart ached, thinking that right now Kitty and Dilys would probably be sitting down to whatever Mrs B had cobbled together from their rations and the glut of vegetables, thanks to a summer of constant care in the veg patch. They'd be giggling over some local gossip, no doubt, flushed cheeks made pinker from the warmth of the stove. At least she would be able to take great pleasure in describing this place to them, so different it was to the cosiness of Mrs B's kitchen, though a family home too nonetheless.

The thought of writing them another letter raised her spirits further and she looked around the table for inspiration. She could imagine her next letter now…

They're a funny bunch all right, very rustique *if that's the word. Mrs B, you'd be in awe of the stove, set as it is in such a deep and magnificent fireplace, but absolutely spotless and garlanded, if you will, with the most wonderful display of glistening copper pans hung above it. The light from the new electric bulbs (this part of the house at least seems to be connected to the electric supply) glistens off them in the most beautiful way.*

I've met the family now, I think, and they're all very pleasant. Dark-haired and Gallic, to be sure, except for the grandfather, who has skin as brown as a nut but hair like a dandelion clock, and the youngest child, who is as blond as one of those cherubs Rev Smallpiece paints on his Christmas cards.

No need for jealousy on the fashion front either, Kitty, as the ladies of this house seem to favour simple cotton and very outdated skirts, though I must admit to only being here a few hours so far, so we'll see. I mustn't judge too harshly, though, as there has been a war on and they really can't have had much in the way of choice or interest, I suppose, while trying to fend off the Nazis…

Fen was happily musing over what else she'd write when a noise from the doorway announced the arrival of the tall Englishman whom Fen had met earlier.

'I'm sorry, I'm sorry,' he apologised to the waiting diners and sat himself down in the chair next to Fen. 'Hubert and I were in the far field, checking the Pinot grapes,' he spoke in fluent French, and Fen was impressed at his perfect accent and mannerisms. She was sure he was English, wasn't she?

'And where is Hubert?' Sophie asked, drumming her fingers on the table.

'Still at the winery, he sends his apologies.'

'Apologies… men are always sorry for something. *Eh la.*' She shrugged and then pressed her hands together into the prayer position and Clément mumbled a grace.

After that, Sophie and Estelle got up from their chairs and brought the cassoulet and freshly baked bread to the table. They served the men first, starting with Clément, then Pierre, the young boys, then the Englishman and finally Sophie, Estelle and Fen.

'Hello again,' Fen had waited until the family and Estelle were engrossed in their own conversation about local politics before she introduced herself to the man she thought was a fellow countryman. 'We didn't introduce ourselves earlier, I'm Fenella Churche.' She would have stuck her hand out for a formal shake, but it was a little awkward in that he was sitting right next to her at the table.

She waited for a reciprocal greeting and snuck a glance sideways at the sun-beaten face, rough stubble and straw-like hair of her neighbour. If there was a man who suited his environment more, she couldn't think of one. Instead of speaking straight away, he raised his ice-blue eyes up from the cassoulet and turned to meet hers, the intensity of his stare making her feel distinctly uncomfortable.

'I say,' Fen flustered, 'I do think you could at least let me know your name.'

'Lancaster.' The way he said it, she felt like it was about to be followed by rank and number, as if she were the captor and he the reticent prisoner. But a moment later he continued. 'Fenella Churche. Fen Churche. Ha, like the station?'

'Yes,' Fen sighed and looked heavenwards but was pleased that her bizarre birthright had at least broken the conversational ice.

'And you're Lancaster. Like the bomber?' She wondered if he was a man who couldn't take teasing. But there was something in his demeanour that seemed familiar to her and reassured her that he wouldn't take offence. Somehow, he reminded her of Arthur, even though he was much stockier, blonder and far more dishevelled than she'd ever seen Arthur look, especially at a mealtime.

'James Lancaster actually. Captain.'

'It's a pleasure to meet you, Captain Lancaster.' Fen felt less at sea now she knew his name.

'And you, Miss Churche.'

'Oh please, call me Fenella. Or Fen. I really don't mind.'

He nodded. 'So what brings you here? I take it you're not with the War Office or on some official business?'

Fen wanted to tell him there and then about her mission to find Arthur, or at least find out more about what happened to him, but she reminded herself that as friendly as this man was currently being, he was a stranger and had not proved himself trustworthy – yet.

Sit on your hands, Fen, she reminded herself, *this is only the read-through...*

'No, nothing like that. I'm an enthusiast on churches.'

'Nominative determinism as its very best.'

'Excuse me?'

'Never mind. Churches though. Are you expecting to find anything of interest in this one?'

'Oh, I see,' Fen caught up with the captain's joke about her name and then kept going as he stayed quiet, spooning cassoulet into his mouth. 'Well, I'm here to write about them for our local rag. I've heard there are some excellent panels dedicated to the archangels.'

'Not that I know of,' he barely looked at her as he spoke, seemingly more interested in his food. Eventually he put his spoon down and turned to her. 'What are you really doing here?'

His question in all its stark bluntness took Fen completely by surprise and she had to admit she was relieved when, at that very moment, Sophie leant across and caught her attention, asking her to pass the bread back up to the family end of the table.

'You are joining us at an excellent time, mademoiselle,' Clément Bernard had the sort of natural *bonhomie* that one would expect from a rural winemaker. 'We are mid-harvest, and, God willing, it will be a good one. The war is over and the grapes are ripe – we have suffered much over these last years, but finally He smiles upon us.'

'Amen,' his son, Pierre, spoke up.

'You know it will be like 1918 all over again. The end of war always brings a good vintage.' The old man looked to his son for affirmation and received a nod in reply.

'Were your vines terribly affected by the occupation?' Fen asked, genuinely curious.

'No,' it was Pierre that chipped in, 'the army left them pretty much alone, but our weather seemed to hate the Germans as much as we did. Plus, it's been hard getting the manpower as so many of our local men left the countryside to fight.'

But one or two came to fight for you, Fen thought to herself.

'I think the town was more ravaged than the vineyards,' Pierre continued. 'Nightly raids on properties, the sight of rows of soldiers goose-stepping their way around the square. The local hotel was overrun with them, like vermin.'

'It must have been…' Fen couldn't think of what to say, everything she could think of seemed inadequate.

'Then the random shootings started and the patrols became more frequent. We feared for our lives, all of us.'

'That's enough now, Pierre,' the soft voice of Sophie urged him to stop. 'You'll give our new guest nightmares.'

'It has been a nightmare for us.' Pierre punctuated the end of his sentence with a mouthful of cassoulet.

'I'm sorry, Miss Churche,' Sophie apologised for her husband, who merely shrugged.

Fen was just protesting that Pierre had every right to describe the last few years as nightmarish when Clément interrupted.

'Right, no more talk of the past. Let us talk only of our tomorrows – here's to a brighter future for us all in the long term,' he raised his glass, 'and in the short term, literally tomorrow, we will be celebrating the holy day of our church's saints, Raphael and Gabriel.'

'Oh how marvellous!' Fen was truly cheered by the thought of a party, not to mention the opportunity to meet some of the townsfolk and find out more about these saints. 'What will the celebrations be like?'

'Oh,' Sophie chipped in, 'do you not celebrate like this, a fête, in England?'

'Well, to us a fête is sometimes associated with a church, but not a saint, although Mother always joked that most of the ladies who ran it were absolute saints.' Even in her near-faultless French, her sentiments obviously confused the French around the table.

Captain Lancaster, who Fen felt was eyeing her up extremely oddly, helped her out, 'Fenella means that fêtes in England are a little different than they are to the ones here. More cake, less carousing. More sedate, you could say.'

'But jolly fun all the same.' Fen felt like the captain wasn't sticking up for the home team as much as he could do.

'Well, here, mademoiselle,' old Clément took over the conversation, 'you will see that at our fête we eat and dance late into the night. It will be a double celebration this year, as although the filthy Nazis stole our relic,' he thumped his fist down on the table in the first sign Fen had seen since she arrived of some sort of retaliation against the recent occupation, 'not to mention a lot of our wine, it is thanks to the bravery of our Resistance fighters and our Allied friends that we are now free of the Germans.' He spat down onto the floor as soon as he mentioned that nation.

Sophie tutted and Estelle stared at Clément.

'I suppose it is I who will be clearing that up?'

'I'm sorry, dear Estelle.' Clément reached across the table and clumsily tried to take her hand. He settled for patting it and then sat back in his chair. 'I'm so heartbroken for my sons, my church, our pillaged wine and for *belle France* herself.'

Fen knew all about these Gallic mood swings; she'd seen enough of the *pastis* drinkers in the local bars near their apartment in Paris to recognise an old man slightly in his cups.

She noted the plural of the word sons, but decided to let it pass. Instead, she asked Sophie more about plans for the next day's celebrations. 'Shall we need to prepare anything for the fête? I can bake something for you if you'd like?'

'That's a very nice thought, Miss Churche,' Sophie answered, 'but I think you will be needed in the vineyard all day, isn't that right, Pierre?'

'True, true, I'm afraid we can't afford you to be here as merely our resident cake baker! Full board,' he swept his hand over the table, indicating the meal they'd all shared, 'and lodging just for a cake?'

Fen nodded while the French family laughed and she sat back as the conversation turned back to the harvest, feeling more than a little chastised. She hadn't meant to cause any offence and told herself off for not taking her employment with them more seriously. This was a vineyard in the middle of harvest after all.

Lancaster glanced sideways at her, that intensity back in his eyes.

'They've been through a lot.'

It was all he said. Comforting women was perhaps not his strong suit, and before long he too had chipped in about the harvest and his voice was lost in the cacophony of the dinner table.

CHAPTER SEVEN

By the time the church bell thudded out ten clanking rings the next day, Fen had been hard at work for more than two hours. She was pleased that she'd packed her kit of sturdy overalls and rubber boots, as although the sun was shielded by a light covering of cloud, the work among the vines was tough. The discussion around the dinner table last night had mostly been about the harvest, and the mysterious Hubert had joined the table half an hour after they'd started eating.

Fen had known, really, that the spare place couldn't have been laid for Arthur, but still, seeing the Gauloises-smoking Frenchman walk in had made her a little sad. Hubert Ponsardine, who looked as weather-beaten as Clément but with none of his joviality, had tucked into what was left of the cassoulet and talked solely about the current state of the harvest. Clément had argued that they had started too early and the rest of Burgundy wouldn't start until October, but Pierre and Hubert together insisted the grapes they had left, having survived an early frost and a bizarre summer cyclone, as well as the strafing of bullets from retreating Luftwaffe, were ripe and ready, and the juice already coming from the first pressings was of excellent quality.

'We won't be alone in trying to make the best out of this harvest,' the winemaker had said, pulling a piece of bread in two, one bite of it clamped between his yellowing teeth. 'Already they're saying this will be a better year even than the best of the 1930s vintages.'

'That is welcome news indeed,' the old man had sat back in his chair and lit his own thin cigarette. 'If it's so, you might even be able to fix that terrible truck of yours, Hubert!'

Fen blushed. She hadn't seen more than one at the winery earlier and it didn't take a genius to work out that the one that had almost killed her must obviously belong to this Hubert chap. Luckily, Sophie had indicated to her that she might like to help clear away the plates at that moment, which rather stopped Fen from denouncing Hubert and his appalling driving there and then.

'You have come at a very convenient time,' Sophie had said to her, as she had helped her wash the dishes after the meal. 'Although when I first saw you I had hoped to have you here with me to help in the house, I see now that I will lose you totally to the vines. You don't mind field work, do you?'

'Not at all.' Fen had then been at pains to express how she was used to outdoor work; she needed more time to find out about Arthur and becoming indispensable would help with that. Being able to give Hubert a piece of her mind too would be an added bonus.

'It's very important to this château, you see, this harvest. Without a good wine this year, we will be... well, I shouldn't talk of the occupation,' she had glanced back towards the table where the men were still sitting and then whispered, 'but whatever happens we need a good harvest...' her voice faded to nothing as she scrubbed the plates clean.

'Don't worry, madame, I am here to help.'

And so Fen had turned up bright and early the next day to the winery to meet Hubert and receive instructions. Gauloises cigarette firmly wedged between his teeth, he'd done not much more than issue her with a large wicker hod – just like the ones she'd seen the workers labouring with the day before – and a pair of secateurs, and this less-than-warm welcome into the world of grape picking gave Fen the confidence to pull him up on his driving yesterday.

'Monsieur Ponsardine,' Fen thought the formality of using his surname would help her cause, 'I do feel like you might owe me an apology.'

Hubert, who had already turned his back on her and was heading into the winery, stopped and turned to face her. He slowly took his stubby cigarette end out of his mouth and held it between his finger and thumb. 'Excuse me?'

Fen wasn't sure if it was wise to continue, especially as Hubert then closed the gap between them with a few purposeful steps, combined with quite a threatening look.

'For, well, for yesterday. With the...' Fen stammered slightly but managed to raise her hand, still holding her newly acquired secateurs, towards the grey Citroën van.

Hubert stared at her, then rolled his tongue around his teeth and spat on the floor. Fen wanted to fill the silence with more explanation of the accident, but there was a menacing aspect to the winery manager's countenance that made her open and close her mouth a couple of times before clamming up.

'Hubert!' the call came from behind the vehicle and broke the stand-off.

Fen released the breath, which she hadn't been aware that she'd been holding, and was more than slightly relieved when Hubert turned on his heel and followed the voice over towards the vines.

'How rude!' Fen managed to whisper to herself, hoping the less-than-pleasant winemaker was now out of earshot. She bent down and picked up her wicker hod, noticing the slight shake to her hand as she did. She hated confrontations.

You need to keep this job if you're going to find Arthur, she reminded herself as she stumbled over the roughly ploughed, summer-hardened soil between the vines until she got to her allotted post.

*

As the hours passed, the wicker hod on Fen's back grew gradually heavier as she neared the end of a row of vines. After it was full, the manoeuvre for unloading it into a large well-head-sized basket had to be performed and the trick was to do it without throwing out her shoulder or losing any grapes as she teetered over the edge of the massive container.

She realised that not only had her arrival in the village been exceptionally well-timed for someone wanting work, but that there were technically a lot more people involved with this vineyard than had dined at the Bernards' table last night.

As her body worked in an almost mechanical fashion; identifying, selecting, cutting, placing, walking, tipping… her mind slipped back to supper the night before. Her excellent French had allowed her to eavesdrop on the family's conversation and among the small talk about the harvest she'd heard a few more names, including those of two men – Jacques and Thierry. From the way that Monsieur Bernard's face had sunk when they were mentioned, Fen inferred that perhaps they were the sons he had alluded to. *Seems like this poor family took a real pasting*, she'd thought to herself as she'd strained to keep listening, hoping to glean anything that might relate to Arthur.

On that front, sadly, she had been left wanting, although she did now know an awful lot more about how the mayor's daughter's poodle was the prime suspect in a sausage theft, how the German-created potholes would be a disaster for next year's Tour de France race and how it was only now coming to light that the neighbouring vineyard had hidden their wine from the thieving Nazis by pulling a kitchen dresser over the door to the cellar, concealing it for the duration of the occupation. Hubert had bristled at the thought of wine being stolen by the occupiers and had made his feelings very clear on the matter with a few well-chosen expletives.

'That Weinführer, Spatz, was a bastard.' Clément had spat at the floor in disgust. There had been a murmur from the men in agreement, while Clément had continued, 'At least we—'

'*Shh*, Papa,' Pierre had stopped his father from saying any more and Fen had wondered if it was on her account.

She stretched her back and looked up over the vines. She saw the heads of the other workers bobbing up and down, methodically selecting the bunches of grapes, cutting their stems and placing them in their hods. She picked up a few words here and there, mostly curses as knives slipped or perfect bunches of grapes fell to the hard, dry ground. Otherwise, the fields were quiet, save for the whinnying and solid plods of the horses that carted the massive baskets of grapes back to the winery.

Fen, never one to shirk from her duty, went back to harvesting, and in her head she pretended Arthur was next to her, prompting her to 'give him a clue'. *Perhaps a riddle would be more apt*, she thought to herself as she recounted the chain of events that had brought her to this vineyard, deep in another country, so far from home. *Who am I? My first is in graft, but never in grapes; my second makes eyes from a possible yes; but my third will say no...*

'Oh Fen!' she scolded herself out loud and then berated herself more quietly. 'Stop pretending Arthur is here now. And stop making up silly games when you should be working out what's happened to him!'

Muttering to herself, she finished her row of vines and carried the heavy hod to the collecting basket. Once she'd heaved the grapes into it, she paused to adjust her headscarf. Years of working in the fields had made her relatively strong for her size, and it had also given her the ability to know exactly how to tie her scarf and smooth her hair without needing a mirror. Though she did miss having Kitty next to her to tell her if her scarf was completely skew-whiff, or Dilys to lick a hanky and rub dirt smuts from their faces. War work had been hard, but it was bearable – and sometimes even the slightest bit jolly – with best friends.

Fen sighed and had no sooner finished adjusting her rather snazzy, or at least she thought so, scarf when the gruff voice of Captain Lancaster behind her made her start.

'This isn't Saint Germain, you know. I don't think it matters to the grapes what you look like.'

'It matters to me,' Fen turned around to see him staring at her, his silhouette looming large against the recently reappeared sun, swollen by the fact that he was carrying two hods, not just the one like she was.

'I don't think the Bernards pay you to look pretty.' He dumped the contents of his hods into the cart, then turned and walked back towards the far end of the vineyard from whence he had come.

'How rude! Again!' Fen rested her hands on her hips and, for no one's benefit except her own, said out loud, 'You'd think the only other English person out here would be a bit more sporting than that!' But as Lancaster disappeared down another row of vines something occurred to her. She was sure that at no point had she told him, or anyone here in Morey-Fontaine, that ten years ago, or so, her family had lived near the *École des Beaux-Arts* in that area of Paris beloved by artists and academics called Saint Germain.

Lunch was brought to the workers via a horse and cart – bread and cheese and, of course, wine, though Fen would have preferred to have slugged down a bucket or two of fresh water. Some of the workers, those near enough to home, had sloped off back to their own kitchens or shaded gardens, for a home-made meal and a comfier seat. But Fen didn't mind sitting on the ground, just resting her legs and stretching out her back was good enough for her, plus the bread and cheese were most welcome.

Lancaster appeared from one of the rows, another two hods on his back for the final dump into the grape cart.

'Here, come and eat.' He may have been rude to her earlier, but Fen wasn't about to lose the best lead she had when it came to finding out about Arthur.

'Water?' he asked.

She nodded a 'yes please' and he disappeared for a moment or two before coming back to where she sat, in the shade of the grape cart with an earthenware bottle.

'There's a pump at the end of the rows; you should drink as much as you can out here in this heat.'

'Thank you,' Fen was too grateful for the chance to slake her thirst to try and stand up for herself and mention that she knew full well the benefits of hydration, having worked in the fields for the last few years. 'I was worried it might be Chardonnay for lunch.'

Lancaster smiled and Fen wondered if the gruff exterior was merely that: a mechanism for coping with what he'd seen in the war. She was itching to ask him something, anything, about why he was here in France, when Sophie came past, carrying an apronful of apples.

'Here, windfalls from this morning. They're fresh.'

Fen and James took one each and bit into them.

'Thank you, Madame Bernard.'

'Please, Fenella, call me Sophie.'

Fen nodded and was about to strike up some more conversation, but Sophie walked on, handing out the fruit to the other workers.

'How did you know that I grew up in Saint Germain?' Fen decided to come out with it.

'Did you?' His reply was innocent enough.

'Yes. And I assumed you knew, as you commented…'

'Just a throwaway phrase. I didn't realise everything I said was so analysed.'

'It's not, I mean, I didn't think that much of it, you know, I…'
Fen was flustered and feeling more and more like an idiot, so she
changed the subject. 'This fête tonight should be a gas, don't you
think?'

'Perhaps not so much now they don't have a relic to parade
through the square.'

'What *was* the relic? I know it must have been quite special and
all that, I mean, I know how Catholics feel about these things. The
toe of Job, or the eyelid of the Virgin, or suchlike.'

The captain snorted. 'It was a piece of the True Cross actually.'

'Oh. Big-time stuff then. Christ's cross itself. Lumme.'

'And the Nazis took it away, but not without a fight.' He stopped
talking and his words hung in the air.

Fen opened her mouth to ask him what had happened, but he
had scrambled up to standing and strode away from her, without
a backwards glance.

'How rude…' Fen said, but this time she didn't feel affronted,
more like perplexed. James Lancaster knew a lot more about what
had happened around here, but he sure as anything wasn't going
to let her into any of his secrets that easily.

Lunch was short, but Fen was happy to get back to work; the
motion of the labour helped her mind relax somewhat and she
started to plan out how she was going to start looking for Arthur.
One thing was clear at least, he wasn't here now and she hadn't yet
done a great job yet of working out if he ever had been.

A frown set itself on her forehead and she puzzled on. She had
been so sure that she had the right village. All his clues had brought
her here and finding Captain Lancaster was an obvious connection.

'What's an Englishman like him doing here? I'll have to break
cover and quiz him later.' Fen told the vines her plan. 'And if he

knows nothing about Arthur, well, then I guess I'll have to go home.' The thought didn't sit easily with her, for what was there for her at home? And nowadays, where was home? And with whom? With her parents, of course, but she was a twenty-eight-year-old, well, spinster. She should live alone, or at least try and find her way in the world without hanging onto her mother's apron strings.

If only Arthur hadn't...

No, keep the faith, Fen, he might be alive... But then where are you, my darling?

Maybe Kitty, Dilys and she could share a flat... that would be something to look forward to perhaps. The thought cheered her a little, though it was scant compensation really, and she progressed through the rows of vines, selecting and cutting the ripe grape bunches, trying not to imagine what the rest of her life would be like back in England without her beloved fiancé.

By the time she'd finished for the day, her allotted vines picked of all their jewel-like fruit, she was adamant that the fête tonight would turn up something, *anything*, about Arthur. She hoped a quick nap and a freshen-up would set her up for some serious investigating.

CHAPTER EIGHT

'*Vite! Vite!*' Estelle was chivvying Fen along as she applied her lipstick. Even with her year of saving coupons, Fen had hardly anything with her in the way of party clothes, except her Sunday best, so decided it would have to do, along with a jazzy headscarf. Estelle had squeezed into a skirt and jacket that looked like they might have once both come from separate suits sometime in the early 1930s, and was now standing at the door of the bedroom, holding it open impatiently.

'I'm hurrying, I'm hurrying!' Fen said, then smacked her lips together and pouted into the mirror.

'*Ooh la la*, it's the village fête not the *Folies Bergère*!'

Lipstick applied and final accessories tweaked – Fen had chosen to wear her cameo brooch and Estelle had made a corsage from some lavender – the two women hurried downstairs and were in time to catch the Bernard family as they bustled around the kitchen getting ready. The weather was still warm and Clément and Pierre had chosen to stay in their shirtsleeves, but Fen noticed that, like Estelle, Sophie had gone to the trouble of finding a two-piece suit and had teemed it with smart white cotton gloves and a striking feather-laden hat.

'Jean-Jacques! You will not be allowed out late, you know?'

'But, Mama!' his whine joined that of his brother as they tried to wheedle the promise of an hour or two later.

Fen smiled to herself, remembering being about Jean-Jacques' age and demanding, along with her brother, the same sort of late pass. Her parents hadn't been the types to expect Nanny to bring in a nicely washed and fresh pyjamaed child to kiss goodnight at about cocktail time, but they had insisted on proper bedtimes. Fen wondered if these children even knew what a proper bedtime was, but then chastised herself for her uncharitable thought.

Once the boys had been wrestled into jackets they most certainly felt were unnecessary, the family, along with Estelle and Fen, were finally ready. Benoit and Jean-Jacques ran ahead, and Sophie called upstairs to hurry James and Hubert, both of whom, Fen had found out from Estelle as they'd been getting ready, had rooms on the floor above them. 'They're no more than eaves rooms really, the old servants' quarters,' she had said sniffily.

A clattering of boots on stone heralded the men's appearance and they too were then ushered out of the kitchen so that Pierre could lock the large old wooden door. Fen watched as Clément beckoned the men to join him, a nod of the head indicating that they may as well get walking.

Fen sighed. She'd missed her opportunity to prise any details from the captain, although she was fairly relieved not to have to walk with the horribly unfriendly Hubert, and instead she joined Sophie and Estelle as they tried to corral the overexcited young boys as they careered through the vegetable patches.

They walked through the old formal gardens and then into the orchard that offered the grand house a little protection from the rest of the town. Soon they reached the church and Fen had to restrain herself from trailing her fingers along its wall, and instead listened as Estelle reeled off a list of the local people she had some sort of grievance with. She'd only managed to slander the butcher, and grocer's boy and the second cousin of the nearby cheesemaker when they reached the heart of the small town, the Place de l'Église.

And what a heart to a town, however small, it was. Fen couldn't believe this was the same dusty, quiet backwater that she'd arrived at only a day before. The square was alive with people, with the general hubbub focusing on the grand front entrance to the church. Townsfolk were mingling and filling the Place de L'Église with a wonderful atmosphere of expectation and gaiety.

The Bernard family were well met by all sorts of friendly grinning faces and hands were gripped tight and shaken warmly. Other people even seemed to like Hubert, who Fen had to admit to herself she was keeping a beady eye on. Jean-Jacques and Benoit tore off with a pack of similarly scuff-kneed children and were soon lost to their parents and negligent nanny, who seemed none too bothered by it all. In fact, Fen had noticed how Estelle had moved away from the family group and was talking to a tall, heavily browed gentleman in a dark suit and homburg hat. 'So that's why you were in such a hurry earlier, Estelle,' Fen noted, and smiled to herself, remembering how Edith used to chivvy all the girls along when she too was desperate to get to a dance.

'Love's young dream,' Captain Lancaster's voice in her ear startled Fen.

I must stop talking out loud, she thought to herself.

'Who is he?' There was no point being embarrassed in front of the captain now, plus her natural curiosity was getting the better of her.

'That's Pascal Desmarais, he's the local pharmacist.'

'And they're…'

'Courting, I think is the polite word.'

Fen and James stood in silence together for a moment, watching, as if mesmerised by the joyful look on Estelle's face as she gazed up into the eyes of her lover. She was quite transformed without the sulking scowl Fen had mostly received from her, and her face now looked far younger, the smile on her lips plumping up her rouged cheeks.

'It's rather wonderful, isn't it, to…' Fen wished she hadn't started saying that. Suddenly she felt terribly alone – albeit with a vast crowd around her – and blinked a tear or two away, resorting to a fingertip dab when they became more persistent.

'She met him through Sophie,' whether Captain Lancaster had noticed Fen's tears and was trying to move the conversation on, or not, Fen was grateful for the distraction. He carried on. 'Sophie used to collect the script for the tank-cleaning chemicals, but what with the boys and taking over the chatelaine duties at the château, she's less involved with the actual winemaking now. So Estelle started heading down to Pascal's shop and, hey presto, the future Mr and Mrs Desmarais.'

'You seem to know a lot about it.'

'Sophie's winemaking background or Estelle's love life?'

'Both.' There was a brief pause as they continued to watch the French couple. 'So, Madame Bernard, Sophie I mean, was a winemaker too? Isn't that rather uncommon? Not that I disapprove, what a wonderful job.'

'She studied oenology or some sort of biological sciences. Or was it petrochemicals? I can't remember. She was at the Sorbonne, I think.'

'Gosh. I studied in Paris too. Speaking of which, Captain Lancaster, how did you become so proficient in French? You speak it like a native.'

'James.'

'I'm sorry?'

'You don't have to keep calling me Captain Lancaster, you can call me James.'

'Thank you.' Fen wondered if she was going to get an answer to her previous question when James suddenly gripped her shoulders and turned her away from watching Estelle and Pascal to where a rustic sort of dais had been set up outside the door of the church. The crowd were quietening down now, shushing each other and peering over heads and hats to catch a glimpse of what was happening.

'Look there.'

Fen followed James's gaze as the doors to the church opened and several robed altar boys exited, carrying with them large silver crosses held aloft. They processed down the stone steps of the church to the dais. Another pair soon came along behind them with candles, more followed with yet more crosses and finally the priest, who carried in front of him a small casket, resting on a deep-red velvet cushion. When the vast church doors had been closed and the priest was stationed on the dais, the casket now resting on a lectern in front of him, the crowd finally fell to a complete silence.

'Friends!' The priest's confident voice carried well across the assembled crowd of villagers.

Fen looked around and estimated that there must be several hundred people amassed there, in front of the church, waiting expectantly for the priest. And he didn't disappoint. His speech was so full of drama it could have come from the Bard himself. He described to the townsfolk the story of the True Cross – its place in Catholic lore and how their church had been blessed by the archangels Raphael and Gabriel themselves and tasked with keeping safe the piece they had. He had paused and the crowd had waited. You could have heard a pin drop as far afield as Dijon; no one was making a sound. Then he grabbed one of the candles from an attendant altar boy and threw it against the wall of the church behind him.

'They tried to extinguish our light!' His voice was so powerful that some of the children, hitherto not that interested in the goings-on, started to whimper. The crowd took a collective breath in as he snatched another candle from the second boy. 'They tried to break our spirit!' Once more, the candle was dashed against the old stone wall of the church. The priest surveyed the faces of the crowd now and said, in more hushed tones, 'They stole our True Cross.'

Fen looked around and saw that she was no longer the only person with a dampness to their eyes. This local priest had the oratory skill of Churchill, or Herr Hitler himself, and the crowd, with hands fluttering, tracing the sign of the cross, was putty in his hands.

He continued, 'But they could never steal what is most important to us as Frenchmen and women. They could not steal our faith!'

An eruption of 'Amen' and more fluttering came at once from the crowd, as much an exhalation of released tension as anything.

The priest raised his hands, bringing them all to silence, and continued. 'And, thanks to the ingenuity of our best men and the good townsfolk here in Morey-Fontaine, even with their despicable Weinführer, they did not steal our wine!'

The crowd burst into applause and cheers, and Fen noticed how the priest had gone from wearing a look appropriate to his fire-and-brimstone sermon to one of complete joviality.

He left the dais with the altar boys, who seemed not at all surprised that they no longer carried candles, and indicated to the crowd that they should disperse. 'The good ladies have been cooking and carrying, go feast, go feast!' he shouted into the mass of people, who cheered and started to move towards the back of the town square, where trestle tables held plates of pies, pâté and cheeses and flagons of what must have been wine and water.

'Well, that was quite a show, good old Marchand.' James was smirking, like a man who was in on a joke that no one else understood.

'You mean it was all choreographed? The candle flinging and whatnot?'

'Yes, got to keep the crowd happy.'

Fen looked up at James's face and saw what she thought was pride. Could he have been in cahoots with this priest during the war? He seemed pretty chuffed with the whole spectacle.

'James, tell me, what or who is a Weinführer?'

James looked down at Fen and thought for a second before replying. 'The chap the Germans put in charge of stealing all the local wine.'

'Stealing?'

'Spoils of war.'

'Gosh.' Fen was amazed that such a position had been properly created and titled.

'They had them in Champagne and Bordeaux too, I think. Possibly the Loire. A way of siphoning the best of France back to the German high command.'

'But that's terrible, it's just stealing.' Fen suddenly felt very protective of the local wine, having spent a day toiling in the vineyard.

'Our chap, Heinrich Spatz, wasn't as bad as some. He tried to requisition the château apparently, although the Bernards saw him off. Negotiated that he stay in Hubert's family place the other side of the town so they could keep the cellars hidden at the big house.'

'Like the people they spoke of last night who hid the entrance to their cellar behind a kitchen dresser?'

'Sort of, yes.'

Fen shook her head in disbelief. 'There's so much I had no idea was happening out here. How did the Bernards manage to defy the Weinführer?'

James paused before he spoke. 'From what I hear, once they'd convinced Hubert that he couldn't just throttle him, Sophie volunteered to do the liaising. Feminine wiles and all that. Then they did the usuals.'

'Such as?'

'Well, when I arrived it was all about rebottling the *vin de table*, disguised as Nuit St Georges just for him. And siphoning off the confiscated wine from the barrels at the station before they were shipped out.' James chuckled to himself at the memory. 'Nasty business though, nasty business.' And then the steel was back in his eyes and he left Fen's side and blended back into the crowd of locals, who were all pouring themselves drinks from the flagons and bottles on the tables.

'How… interesting,' Fen said to herself, noting that, apart from her failure to ask James anything about Arthur or if he knew him, he certainly was a mine of information and she congratulated herself for finally getting more than a few words out of him, even if they weren't on the topic she was so desperate to find out about.

'Come, sit down, sit down.' Clément Bernard beckoned Fen over to his spot on the bench seat alongside one of the trestles that seemed to be defying the post-war austerity around them and was groaning with food.

'It helps that the town's fête coincides with the harvest,' Sophie explained, as Fen obviously looked jaw-dropped at the spread. 'It's mostly peasant food, but there's enough to go round. Come and join us.'

'Thank you,' Fen hoped her thanks conveyed more than her gratitude for the meal; she was grateful too for being so included by the family. That dastardly Hubert obviously hadn't mentioned anything to them about their little showdown earlier.

'They tell me you came to write about our church?' Clément was engaging Fen in conversation and she felt obligated to answer him, albeit still with a lie.

'Yes, although I'm not a proper journalist, just a hobby writer. I heard you had some lovely brass inscriptions around here.' Fen didn't enjoy lying through her teeth, but needs must.

'Not in this church, I'm afraid,' the voice was a new one and Fen found that the charismatic orator of a priest himself was now sitting next to her on the bench.

Up close, Fen saw that he was older than she had first thought, the lines sitting lightly, but definitely, on his brow. He was less tanned than the other villagers, and his frame was more slight than most of the men who worked in the vineyards and fields. He had dark, almost black hair, noticeable now his biretta was removed.

Once introductions had been made, he continued, 'We are less known for our brasses and more for our bravery in these parts.'

'I'm sure everyone did their bit.' Fen wasn't about to doubt the priest, especially after his bravado on the dais a few moments ago.

'But, round here, we had many, many brave men – and women. Speaking of whom, where's James? He hasn't gone back to England yet, has he?'

Fen followed the conversation across the trestle as Clément shook his head, his mouth full of baguette and cheese.

'He and the other Englishmen, the Baker Street Irregulars, they were marvellous. Astonishing bravery!'

Fen's ears perked up at this latest revelation. *Who were the Baker Street Irregulars?* Her curiosity got the better of her.

'I'm sorry, Father, I don't mean to interrupt, but there were Londoners here? In the war?'

'Londoners, Dubliners, Scots, Northerners, Southerners…'

'But Baker Street…?'

Clément swallowed and washed it down with a sip of wine. 'You're confusing her, Father.' He turned to Fen. 'I don't know how much you know, but your countrymen, and women, were sent over here in secret. Dropped in the middle of the night to help our Resistance network. They worked with us, sabotaging ammunition stores, communications, derailing trains, that sort of thing. I'm surprised a fluent speaker like yourself was never asked to join them.'

Fen was speechless. Her brain was working overtime. 'So Captain Lancaster wasn't an infantryman then? Who decided to stay here after it was all over?'

'No.' Clément laughed and Father Marchand continued the story instead.

Fen listened as she looked over to where James was sitting with some men, a few faces she recognised from the vineyards today, and, to his credit, blending in like a true native.

'James was sent from Baker Street, the London headquarters, with a couple of others.'

'Who?' Fen interjected so quickly she sounded like an interrogator.

Luckily, Father Marchand carried on with an explanation. 'There was that marvellous Italian girl, wasn't there?'

'She wasn't Italian, you fool, she was English!'

'But her hair was so dark.'

'A man of the cloth taking notice of a lady's hair?'

Fen was a little taken aback at how forward Clément was with the priest – Mrs B certainly wouldn't have spoken to Reverend Smallpiece like that – but she let the two men bicker as she processed the information. If Clément was to be believed, and why shouldn't he be, a secret network of Allied operatives had been dropped into the area. *But was Arthur one of them?* Realisation flashed across Fen's mind. Of course he must have been a secret agent. He was fluent in French, like her, his German had been more than passable too, thanks to his time in Berlin in the 1920s, and he was so clever with puzzles, plus his training had struck her as somewhat odd.

The War Office requisitioning country houses for accommodation was one thing, but now she thought about it, he never spoke of a certain regiment or barracks, only 'the chaps back at the digs'. What had that secretary at the War Office said? He was listed as being part of the Air Ministry. *A ministry that might deal specifically with parachuting agents into enemy territory!*

'Was there another Englishman with them?' Fen blurted it out, not caring any more if her cover of being a mere church enthusiast was blown. These two old men looked like they were the sort to be able to keep a secret in any case.

'Yes, young lady, there was.' Father Marchand turned his attention to her properly now. 'Are you looking for someone?'

At that moment the band started playing 'La Marseillaise' and Clément ushered the others around the trestle to their feet, hands clasped to their chests, singing the national anthem with true Gallic passion. As soon as the closing bars were finished, the musicians started on a folk tune and the benches around them emptied as townsfolk took to the middle of the square and started dancing.

Father Marchand's question still hung in the air between them and all Fen could do was give a nod before she felt a hand at her elbow and James was beside her, encouraging her to dance with him.

'Thought I should save you from the old double act over there,' he said as he escorted her deep into the mass of dancers, who were waltzing, oddly enough, to a tune that Fen thought sounded more like a barn dance reel. James's offer of a dance had surprised her to say the least, and though this was no chaotic Lindy Hop she was slightly reluctant to join the throng. *This might be an opportune moment to quiz James on what he knows however*, she thought and let him lead her into the pack and set the pace of their moves.

'They were telling me about secret agents,' she said, and felt the muscles in his arms tense as she said it.

'Fanciful talk of old soldiers.' James tried to laugh it off, but Fen shook her head.

'I lost someone in the war.' She decided some truth was needed if she were to gain James's trust. 'A very special someone. And we were crossword fans, you see, so he always said to me, if you can't work out your ten across, then try and get your six and seven down. And I think I've just got my six down.'

James gave her that look again, then quietly said, 'I lost someone special too. We all did.'

'But we don't all track them down to the village they laid clues for in their last letter home.'

'Did he now? Setter was a bit of a rebel then.'

'Setter? You mean Arthur, you know him?'

James was silent for a long time and if Fen hadn't been so firmly held in his arms and in the middle of a crowd of dancers, she'd have shaken him for an answer. The suspense was killing her. Suddenly, James broke free from their coupling and disappeared through the dancers, leaving Fen to apologise to revellers as they waltzed into her. She dodged her way out of the melee but had lost sight of James completely.

'How bloody rude. Again!' Fen sighed and placed her hands on her hips. She had been tantalisingly close to finding out about Arthur. She knew James must have known him. *Setter.* As code names went, it wasn't a bad one for a crossword enthusiast. Though she thought he might have chosen *Star-crossed…*

Left on her own, Fen glanced around to try and find a friendly face to talk to. The Place de L'Église itself was alight with candles and buzzing electric bulbs, and the light bounced off the glistening red faces of the dancing townsfolk. Fen spied Estelle in the mix with Pascal, and Hubert was dancing with a short, fat woman in a polka-dot dress. Fen didn't fancy heading back into the fray without a partner so wandered off to one of the tables and sat on a bench, looking around her.

She caught sight of the priest, Father Marchand, still in his purple dress robes, as he exited the church, leaving the door slightly ajar. He didn't come straight back to the festivities but scurried along the edge of the square until he stopped outside a decent-looking house, where he unlocked the door and slipped inside. Fen's eye was then caught by a swish of fabric and she was a little surprised to see Sophie Bernard leave the church a few moments after Marchand. She was adjusting her collar and patting down the front of her dress, but unlike Marchand she headed straight back to the centre of the square and deep into the dancers. She had a smile for every local person she knew, a hand on their shoulder and a kiss hello to many.

Fen was intrigued watching Sophie do her 'lady of the manor' act. *Had she just had a tryst with the priest in the church?* The thought was scandalous, especially if she could turn her hand to greeting the townsfolk so quickly afterwards. Fen made a mental note to work out what she thought about it later, as right now her mind was still turning over as to why James had suddenly left her in the lurch. He hadn't reappeared yet, so Fen decided she may as well eat something. She sat back down at one of the trestles and had just helped herself to a chunk of bread and some very runny cheese – a real treat when such a thing hadn't been seen in England since before the war – when Estelle, flushed from dancing, plonked herself down next to her.

'Pascal is a demon!'

'Not sure you should say that at a saints' day festival!' Fen teased Estelle, who gave a shrill, excitable laugh.

'*Aiieee*, they are the angels of death and we have seen so much death, they do not scare me!' Estelle raised a clenched fist up at the church tower, then stopped laughing. She shook her head. 'Can you imagine what life has been like for us?'

Fen took note of her sudden change of tone and knew now wasn't the time to list her wartime hardships and losses too. She let Estelle continue.

'You feel like you are a prisoner, not just in your own home, but in your own mind.' She tapped her finger to her temple to illustrate, getting a few baguette crumbs in her hair as she did so. 'You cannot walk around without being questioned, "What are you doing? Who are you seeing? Where are you going?" Eventually you start to question your own thoughts! "What can I say? Who can I trust?" It was hell.'

'I'm so sorry, Estelle, I don't think any of us in England really—'

'*Bof*, why should you care? Would I care if the war wasn't on my patch? I don't know.' Estelle bit into her cheese-covered bread and paused for a moment before continuing. 'And for the Bernards, losing the sons was terrible, terrible. Clément is doing his best to hide it all, but it's not the same here now.'

'I've been hearing about the Weinführer.' Fen was still aghast that a genuine role had been created within the German army to steal wine. 'And that the Bernards were in danger of losing the château completely.'

'Ha! Spatz!' Estelle spat on the floor. 'Well, if necessity is the father of invention than Spatz is the father of our inventive ways of hiding our wine.' Estelle laughed and picked at her teeth for a while, seemingly deep in thought. Fen followed her gaze over to where the young children were playing under the candlelit plane trees. Estelle then turned back to look at Fen. 'All's fair in love and war, is that not your English Shakespeare?'

'Yes,' Fen thought for a moment. 'Speaking of love, how long have you and Pascal been courting?'

'Forever it seems.' Estelle huffed. 'We found, what you might call a "mutual interest" in each other during the occupation,' she smirked. 'He was injured in the last war, he's a great deal older than me, you know – he is over forty.' She paused to make the point. 'So he was unable to join the army, but that saved him, you know.'

'And he's the pharmacist here?'

'Yes, nosy parker.' There was a pause, then. '*Tch*, this is no good. I will have to talk to that dratted Marchand.'

'The priest?'

'Yes, yes, the priest. Fat lot of good he is, though, refusing to marry us. You know,' Estelle was getting into her stride, 'he said he didn't believe that Pascal and I were marrying for the right reasons, can you believe it? The cheek of it! How is a celibate man to know what my reasons are!'

Fen wondered to herself, *Not so celibate perhaps*, but said nothing, instead mustering some sort of feeling for the Frenchwoman. 'So you are to be married, congratulations, Estelle!'

'Save your congratulations,' she practically snorted back. 'Until I have the ring on my finger. If Marchand doesn't get round to it soon, I will have his guts for garters!'

Fen felt awkward. She'd liked the charismatic priest when she'd met him earlier in the evening and it struck her as odd that he should refuse to marry two perfectly legitimate people, especially after so much suffering had gone on during the war. It posed the obvious question, to Fen's mind at least, of what he knew about them as a couple that Estelle wasn't letting on?

'Come on, ladies, join us!' Fen's thoughts were interrupted by Sophie, who pulled them both into the dancing. It was more of a Russian-style affair now, with rings of dancers skipping in ever-decreasing circles, the central couple spinning about, the dancers around them seeming to pulsate in and out like the beat of a giant heart.

Sophie ducked and shimmied into the very middle of the ring, where she took the hands of the central couple and started spinning the circle around. In a moment, another couple had ducked under their arms and were now spinning away in the middle. The whole dance was chaotic and seemed arbitrarily made up by whoever had the most energy and enthusiasm. A tea dance at the Spread Eagle, it was not. But despite all the chaos around her and the thoughts buzzing through her head, Fen started to enjoy herself.

The music reached a crescendo and the dancers whirled faster and faster in their circles, skirts twirling, faces puffed, hair frizzled and loosened, the whole effect was one of joyous excitement until the band came to the final chords, the guitars strummed a final time and the drums stopped. The lights at that moment, strung up along the trees and from poles in the corners of the square, flickered and died. The dancers were plunged into silence and darkness and no one uttered a word until a shriek shattered the spell and the lights, luckily, flickered back on.

'What was that?' Fen wasn't the only one to ask the question of a neighbour, then suddenly there was a cry of 'Over here!' and 'Help her!'

To Fen's horror, as she rushed in the direction of the shouting to see if she could help in any way, she saw it was Sophie. She was lying there in the middle of the town square, silent and still, a crumpled heap on the floor.

CHAPTER NINE

'Sophie!'

Fen watched as Pierre ran over to his still and silent wife. The crowd collectively held their breath before there were murmurs of 'She's talking, look!' and 'Eh, a bad fall, she'll be hobbling for weeks…'

'Thank the Lord,' whispered Fen to no one in particular, realising Sophie was all right, but she pushed her way through some of the crowd to see if there was anything she could do to help. She'd taken part in a few training sessions with the Wrens in the local parish rooms back in West Sussex and Mrs B had taught her how to tie a bandage properly, having nursed poor old Mr B before his wounds from Ypres got the better of them both. 'Can I help?'

'Mama?' Benoit had found his mother collapsed on the floor, but she was at least now resting in her husband's lap.

'Shush shush, little one,' she was unhurt enough to comfort him and stroke his hair but looked relieved when Fen appeared. 'Fen, could you take him? And find Jean-Jacques. It's time for them to go home. Where is Estelle?'

'I don't know, Sophie, but yes, of course. I'll find him. Come along, Benoit.' Fen genuinely didn't know where Estelle had gone, but then Pascal was nowhere to be seen either, so she assumed they had made use of the chaos to slip out of sight for an assignation.

All's fair in love and war, Fen thought, then tried to not to think too badly of her room-mate for selfishly slipping away while her mistress was hurt.

*

Fen had found Jean-Jacques quite easily – he and his friends were all throwing squishy plums at each other from one of the fruit trees by the church. She'd told him of his mother's injury, which had made him stop larking around instantly and start to cry, so now she had both him and Benoit held by their grubby hands as she walked back towards the house, luckily only a few paces behind Pierre and the injured Sophie.

'Ah! Ooh! Pierre, be careful!' Sophie reprimanded her husband as he carried her in his arms towards the château.

'It's not like you to turn your ankle, Sophie,' he admonished her, although there was no real malice in his voice. 'You're usually so sure-footed.'

'If you compare me to a mountain goat, Pierre, I shall wallop you with my handbag.'

He chuckled at his feisty wife and shifted her weight in his arms. Fen wondered if she should offer to get James to help, but Pierre walked on, all of them in silence, listening to the festivities still carrying on in the village behind them. He navigated past the vast stone buttresses of the church's southern wall and carried Sophie through the little orchard, with her occasionally moaning and chastising him for clumsily knocking her against a straggling branch or unkempt topiary bush.

'It really is swelling, I can feel it. Oh hell!'

'Perhaps,' Pierre paused to think and shifted Sophie's weight in his arms, 'Mademoiselle Churche can be spared from the harvest and run the kitchen and you can then rest for a few days, *ma chérie*.'

Fen's ears picked up at the mention of her name and she listened, relieved that at least her new role didn't sound too onerous. She wouldn't mind learning to cook a cassoulet from an immobile Sophie.

'Rest! As if we women ever rest,' Sophie teased him. They bickered like this as the group moved towards the terrace, across the dried-out lawns that had once been so beautiful and up the broken and chipped stone steps. Changing the subject, Sophie commented, 'I'll work on these gardens next year, but it's not such a bad old place, eh?'

Pierre shifted her weight in his arms and agreed with her. 'The gardens are a mess to be sure, *chérie*, but at least we have the grapes this year. Wine we can *sell* and then we can buy vegetables. And now the occupier's boot is no longer at our throats, we can sell the wines we hid, too.'

'They were not all so bad— Ahhhhoowwww!' Pierre had dropped Sophie with little warning by the door of the château. 'You brute, what did you do that for?' The threatened wallop from the handbag came at last.

Fen had to chuckle. Sorry as she was for Sophie's injury, she was enjoying this music-hall-style sketch.

'I'm sorry,' Pierre had lost whatever passion had suddenly overwhelmed him at the mention of the Germans and held his arms up to parry his wife's blows. '*Ma petite chou-fleur*, I'm sorry. How can I say sorry enough?'

'Get me inside, you idiot, and I'll think!'

Dutifully, Pierre opened the kitchen door and scooped his wife up.

'Fenella, can you put the boys to bed? I cannot see myself moving!' Sophie called out to Fen over Pierre's shoulder.

'Of course, Sophie. Come on, chaps.' Fen took it as her cue to let the Bernards go up ahead of her as she found some milk in the kitchen and warmed it over the stove for the boys. She caught snippets of the rest of the conversation between the Bernards as they gradually walked up the spiral staircase.

'… I know how… sorry… favourite pastries… Monsieur Fracan will have one or two… breakfast, please?'

With them firmly upstairs and the boys now relatively calm drinking their milk, Fen sat down and tried to think about what had happened that night. Clément Bernard and Father Marchand's words kept coming back to her. *The Baker Street Irregulars?* They sounded more like a Conan Doyle plot. But whatever they were called, it was now certain that secret agents had operated in the area and, more likely than not, her Arthur was one of them, along with James.

Speak of the devil, she thought to herself as the big kitchen door swung open and James and Estelle appeared from the darkened hallway beyond.

'What ho,' she called over to them.

'Hallo, we thought we'd lost you in the dancing.' James stepped back into the hallway and took off his cap and started undoing his work boots.

'Didn't you notice the kerfuffle? No more dancing for Sophie, I'm afraid, and I was tasked at bringing these vagabonds home,' Fen smiled at the boys.

'What happened?' Estelle asked as she bustled over and took over looking after the boys, wiping off their milk moustaches and generally tidying them up.

'It looked quite dramatic, but Sophie took a tumble is all,' Fen replied.

'You all came back here?' James came into the room, stood by the stove and warmed his hands.

'Slowly, yes,' Fen answered as she was waved to the boys, who were being taken upstairs by their nanny. 'Goodnight, you two,' and then to Estelle, 'I won't be long.'

Estelle shrugged and ushered the boys up the stairs.

'Something's got her goat,' Fen whispered to James.

'Probably Pascal, he's a funny old thing. Nice enough, but when you deal in chemicals all day…' James twisted his finger against his temple to indicate looniness.

This made Fen snort a little with laughter and she was pleased when James left the stove and sat down next to her.

'I'm sorry I left you mid-dance, it was exceedingly ill-mannered of me, it's just…' James paused.

Fen wanted to ask him all about Arthur, but something held her back.

Before she could speak, James carried on. 'There's nothing left for me back in London now, you know. Perhaps I should be a French peasant, as I obviously have the manners of one.'

'Did you know—' Fen was about to ask the question she'd been dying to since she got to France when the kitchen door flew open and Clément and Hubert, who was fast becoming Fen's nemesis, burst in, full of song.

'*Allons enfants de la Patrie. Le jour de gloire est arrivé…*' The two men belted out the familiar tune of 'La Marseillaise' at full volume.

James got up and pulled out his chair for the older man and let him slump into it, while Fen quickly exited her seat for the inebriated Hubert. James shook his head slightly and ducked back into the hallway to close the large front door.

'Assuming you're bedding down here for the night, Hubert?' James called and Fen heard the large bolt being drawn across the door. She thought back to Little Miss Polka-Dot and reckoned she had escaped a fate – or a fête – worse than death.

'Yes, of course he is!' Clément then hummed more of the well-known tune. 'He still has the stench of the Germans in his house, he must stay here whenever he wants! Another glass of *pastis*, Hubert? And, James and Fenella, you will join us?'

Fen looked at James, who suddenly seemed so much more at home. This *bonhomie* must have been what kept them all going through the war and she watched as he pulled three small glasses out of the dresser. He looked over to her and raised his eyebrow in a question, but Fen shook her head. As much as she wanted more information from James, she knew now wasn't the time to do it.

Clément probably knew everything too, but Hubert remained an unknown to her, and she wasn't entirely sure if she wanted to share a drink with the man who ran her into a ditch. What stung, though, just a little, was James's nod of agreement at her refusal. Tonight, this was the boys' club.

Fen waved at the men from the tower door and tried not to be slightly put out that there were few protestations at her leaving. She let herself into her and Estelle's room, as quietly as possible in case the other woman was already asleep.

'Not a sausage,' she whispered to herself at the sight of two empty beds and she let herself sink down onto her own cacophonously creaky one. She unpinned the brooch and placed it on her nightstand, the familiarity of it cheering her up. 'Thanks, Ma.' She touched it and much happier memories of a time before the war came to her: her parents dancing in their apartment in Paris, the meals they'd shared, her brother's sense of humour and her mother's perfume. In that moment she wondered if she'd ever be happy again like that, and if she did, would it be a huge betrayal. 'I wish you'd met him,' she spoke to the brooch as if it was her mother. 'You would have loved him really, almost as much I do.'

It was testament to Fen's strength of character that she managed to resist lying down and falling asleep in the clothes she was wearing, but as she undressed and washed her face in the large porcelain bowl of cold water, tears started to fall and one word persisted in going round and round her mind... *did*.

CHAPTER TEN

Fen woke with a start. The noise of Estelle leaving the room, no doubt heading to the old thunderbox down the corridor, roused her from her dreams. She rubbed her eyes – crying before bed always made them puffy and she had bits of 'eye crumble', as her mother used to call them, trapped in her lashes. At least one thing was looking up – Captain Lancaster – James – was treating her more like a fellow human being now. What had he said? There was nothing left in London for him any more. The thought of not feeling wanted back home made Fen feel terribly sad for the lost soldier, although the fact that he was now a friendly face in this stark corner of rural France was something of which she was rather glad.

'Don't be a pill,' she said to herself, trying out one of those Americanisms that had so amused her when she'd heard the local GIs use it back in West Sussex.

She got out of bed and went over to the washbasin, assuming Estelle would still be occupying 'the best seat in the house', as her brother used to say. She must add him and her parents to her list of letters owed – though Lord knows if he was back from North Africa yet.

Once washed as well as she could be in the circumstances, she donned her workwear and headed down to the kitchen for breakfast.

The kitchen was empty and Fen had to double-check the large wooden clock that she hadn't accidentally woken and dressed before dawn, but no, it was 7.30 a.m. and the sun was already up in the autumn sky. Hearing a gush of water come down through the pipework reminded her that a trip to the bathroom might not be a bad idea either, so she took the opportunity while no one was around to explore the ground floor of the other wing of the house. It was decorated much like the floor above, the one that housed the bedrooms, and, to Fen's relief, it was home to a lavatory, as well as a smart morning room and a library.

From the look of the formal rooms, she deduced that they were rarely used; the library even had a dust sheet covering what looked like a large central table or desk, and a glass-fronted cabinet of trinkets was home to quite a few cobwebs, as well as what looked like a selection of dusty family heirlooms and Great War memorabilia. The morning room's oriental carpets were neatly rolled up and leant against the panelled wall. Both rooms smelt musty and unused, Fen even ventured to think *unwelcoming*, so once she'd made use of the WC, she headed back into the kitchen and from there to the small hallway, where she pulled on her work boots.

Outside, the air was cool, especially in the shade of the buildings, and dew lay heavily on the grass on the central courtyard. The day would be a fine one though, she thought, as she peered up past the roof of the château and its tower to see a perfectly blue sky, scudded here and there with fluffy white clouds. A perfect autumn day. There wasn't a soul about, however, and Fen wondered if it was due to last night's revelries and resulting sore heads. She remembered how greedily the men had all looked at the *pastis* bottle last night before she had turned in and she knew from her own experience that the aniseed-flavoured spirit could slip down all too easily and have its revenge the next morning.

'Serves them right,' she muttered to herself, a little upset at how quickly she'd been dismissed from the *bonhomie* in the kitchen, and then walked over to the far side of the courtyard, where the sun was now high enough in the sky to peer over the château's roof. She sat down on an old stone bench and turned her face to the sun, soaking up its already warm rays and enjoying the peace. A quick movement next to her jolted her out of her reverie.

'Oh, hello, monsieur.' The fluffy black and white cat had jumped up onto the bench next to her. He was a handsome beast, all fluff and whiskers, which made him look more like a Parisian house cat than some farm scally who was more likely to sleep under the stars than be treated like one. 'I think we've got the right notion.' She stroked the soft fur on top of his head and smiled at the resulting purr. Perhaps the day was looking up after all.

She closed her eyes and leant back against the cool stone. Soon enough she'd be back in amongst the vines, or, if Sophie commanded it, scrubbing the kitchen floor or peeling potatoes, but for now she sat and took stock of where she was and why she was there.

Gradually, her sense of duty outweighed quite how much she was enjoying the catnap in the sunbeam and she opened her eyes. A glint of light coming from one of the turrets at the top of the tower caught her eye and she moved her head from side to side trying to make out what it might be.

'Any thoughts?' she asked the cat, who replied by jumping off the bench in pursuit of a fly.

Fen sighed and pushed herself up and off the bench and headed back into the kitchen, where, to her surprise, there wasn't a sign of anyone else and she was quite alone.

'No time like the present then,' she told herself as she took a leaf of paper from a stack that was sitting on the dresser. *I hope they don't mind*, she thought as she quickly penned a missive to Kitty and co.

Kitchen table, Château Morey-Fontaine
September '45

Dear Mrs B, Kitty and Dilly,

Quite a lot has happened in the last couple of days, so I thought I'd fill you in. No sign of Arthur yet – well, that's not strictly true, but nothing concrete. I'm pretty sure he was here and operating as a secret agent under the code name 'Setter'. The trail has gone cold though for now, until I find the opportunity to quiz James (Captain Lancaster) – a former soldier who has stayed out here (I'm not sure why) – about what he knows. And yes, Kitty, I think you would find him rather handsome, but I fear he's a lost cause and terribly grumpy.

Last night was the fête of the local church, but it was quite unlike any we have at home – much more like a medieval banquet, with raucous dancing and folk music. I can't pretend it wasn't fun, but it wasn't exactly tea, cake and a nice coconut shy either!

Fen paused and absent-mindedly sucked the end of the pencil she was using to quickly scrawl her thoughts. Would it be good for their morale back in West Sussex to know more about what life had really been like out here, the things Estelle had been telling her last night, and the reality of the Weinführer, or best to keep it light-hearted and jolly? The decision, at that moment at least, was taken from her as she heard the clattering on the stone spiral staircase of little boys.

Estelle followed the boys downstairs and headed straight to the stove to riddle out the ash and fill it with coal, but not before noticing the letter Fen had been writing and raising one interested eyebrow. Fen surreptitiously folded it up and slid it into a pocket of her overalls, hoping she'd find a few minutes to come back to it later.

By 9 a.m. – terribly late by normal standards but apparently *de rigueur* in this house after a fête day – most of the family were finally seated around the table in the château's kitchen. Hubert was sitting there, nursing his head in his hands and Fen smiled to herself, *Ha! As I thought. Serves you right!*

She was pleasantly surprised when Father Marchand arrived. She'd enjoyed his company last night and surely she'd been reading far too much into the situation thinking that a man of the cloth could be having an affair with a parishioner! Plus, she wondered if, since he knew so much about the disappearance of the relic and the spy network of British and French fighters, he might know something about what happened to Arthur. He was looking distinctly wan this morning, though, and complained of a broken night's sleep.

Always generous, he put it down to nothing more serious than over-enjoyment of the night before and as Fen sipped her tea, she listened to more of his stories about the locals in the village and their customs. Monsieur Fracan, the baker, for example was beyond reproach in his eyes, with a first-class ticket to heaven, due to the divine nature of his strawberry fruit tarts. '*Un ange!*' he exclaimed, before deciding he'd overdone it and resting back in his seat.

Estelle rolled her eyes at the priest, obviously still unimpressed at his refusal to marry her and Pascal when they had wanted.

'I know how you feel, Father,' Hubert sympathised with the hung-over priest and passed him the jug of ersatz coffee. Father Marchand waved it away with his hand.

'At least I have a clear conscience though, young Hubert.'

'What do you mean, Father?'

Before Marchand could explain himself, Pierre returned from the village with a basket of Monsieur Fracan's almond croissants – and the baker's angelic status was confirmed. Their appearance was met with much 'oohing' and 'aahing' and Fen assumed correctly that they had been a rare commodity in recent years.

Their aroma, mixed with the smell of the chicory coffee, filled Fen with such happiness that for a moment she forgot why she was in the château at all. Even James looked more pleased than usual. The company all politely waited for Monsieur Bernard to tuck in first, followed by his invalid daughter-in-law, who had her swollen ankle propped up on a stool by her chair, and before long the whole party were pulling apart the delightful pastries.

The whole party that was, save Marchand, who, although he agreed that, like Monsieur Fracan's patisserie, his croissants were 'manna from heaven', as a priest and so close to a saint's day he should surely abstain. Plus, he suggested that he may have overdone it on the wine last night and he felt a little queasy. He sipped instead from his coffee and nibbled cautiously on the end of one of Fracan's 'equally as divine' fresh baguettes.

'It must be jolly hard, being a priest,' Fen said to James, as she pulled apart the buttery dough and relished the sweet almond smell of the croissant before popping a chunk her mouth. She hadn't tasted anything so sweet and luxurious in years.

'Indeed. And I must say, compared to usual, he doesn't look that well on it.'

'Come now, Marchand,' it was Hubert who was pushing the basket with the last croissant in it towards the priest. 'You can ask for forgiveness during Mass this afternoon. Go on!'

'You are a bad influence, Hubert Ponsardine. *D'accord*, I will try one as Fracan has a gift given by God himself, I think!'

Father Marchand took the last croissant and pulled a face at the two young boys, whose fingers had been edging closer to the basket in the hope of stealing the last one for themselves, but who now giggled at the affable priest. Their laughter was infectious and soon the whole table was chuckling away.

Fen wondered if now was a good time, while the rest of the table were occupied, to ask James some more about Arthur. She turned to him and was about to speak when she realised, at that moment, something was very wrong. She followed the line of

James's gaze to Father Marchand, and then, with almost everyone else around the table, she gasped in shock as the priest's head fell forward and smashed against his plate. As he tried to raise himself up, Fen could see that his face was reddening and his neck was straining as he choked.

'He's dying, help him!' Sophie shouted, scrambling to get up but falling down in pain herself as she put too much weight on her ankle.

James and Pierre rushed to the priest as his body shuddered. Hubert pushed back his chair so violently that it crashed into the stove and splintered. He joined the other two men who were trying to restrain the uncontrollably fitting priest. There was nothing they could do, however, and in a few moments Father Marchand gradually stopped convulsing and slipped down to the floor, dead.

'*Mon dieu!*' Estelle cried, running from the room.

Sophie, who had clawed her way back to her chair, looked across at the dead man on her kitchen floor and promptly fainted to the ground. Pierre left the body of the priest and went to his prone wife, fanning her face and gently lifting her head off the stone floor.

With Estelle gone, Fen's thought was of the two small boys, their cheeky little faces now rigid in terror, looking at where the jovial priest had been sitting, telling them stories, only moments ago. Before she could whip them away, their grandfather interceded and pulled them by the straps of their dungarees off their chairs, like kittens being lifted by the scruff of their necks, to get them away from the scene of the death.

Fen then looked up at James and noted how his face wasn't just set into a grimace of remorse for the dead man, but something much more terse.

'What is it?' she asked.

'This is all wrong.' James had interpreted her meaning. 'This is no natural death. He's been poisoned.'

'Poisoned?' The voice was that of Sophie, restored from her faint by the ministrations of her husband, who was now helping her upright into her chair, her ankle still causing her obvious pain. As decent and competent as Sophie seemed to be, Fen never held much esteem for those who fainted in important moments, although she begrudgingly admitted that Sophie Bernard's sense of the dramatic was second to none.

Hubert seemed not to hear the accusation and was picking pieces of chair out of the hearth, obsessively finding splinters where there probably were no more to be found.

'That's right,' James continued. 'And, by the smell of it, cyanide.'

'Cyanide!' Fen was shocked and automatically brought her fingers to her throat, remembering the delicious almond croissant that had only moments earlier slid down it.

'Why cyanide?' Pierre asked, his voice trembling slightly.

'The smell is unmistakable.' James sounded assured.

'But we were eating almond croissants,' Sophie pointed to the empty basket on the table. 'The smell could just as easily be from them? It is almonds, yes? The smell of cyanide?'

'Yes, but…' James looked less sure now, a torrent of thoughts crossing his mind as surely as they crossed his furrowed brow.

'So anyone of us round this table might have been killed?' Sophie gasped and started coughing, clearing her throat of imaginary poison.

'Or it could have been administered by anyone around this table,' Pierre whispered. 'Anyone.'

'Or God himself,' Hubert had found his voice and then crossed himself as the rest of the room fell silent.

'James,' Fen caught him by the sleeve as the family turned to go back into the house, having seen off the mortuary cart from the courtyard of the château. It had seemed the most respectful thing to do, with Monsieur Bernard, Pierre and Hubert clasping their flat caps to their chests and James and Fen bowing their heads. Sophie, who had been taken upstairs to rest after the horrible incident, couldn't make it down, recovering as she was from her faint and her poorly ankle.

'Yes, Fen?'

'How did you know?'

'About what?'

'The cyanide. How did you know so quickly what it was?'

'It's the smell. It's unmistakable, like I said.' He shuffled his foot in the dry dust and grit of the courtyard.

'But, as Sophie pointed out, the smell could have been the croissants?' Fen was still finding it hard to believe that Father Marchand had been murdered, let alone by a poisoner in their midst. 'And poor Father Marchand may have had a seizure?'

'Yes and no. Look, Fen, I can't explain it now. I've got to go and…' his voice trailed off and Fen followed his eyes as he looked up towards the wing of the house where the bedrooms were. 'Are you OK?' He looked back at her and briefly touched the top of her arm.

'Oh, yes. I mean, it's a shock and terribly sad, but yes.' She paused. 'Thank you.'

At that, James left her and strode back into the house. It wasn't much of a leap to work out where he was headed and Fen wondered why he was so keen to get back up to his attic bedroom.

The answer was made painfully clear to her an hour later when the clanging bells of the gendarmerie's solitary working van pulled up in a cloud of dust outside the château. The morning had, quite understandably, been a sombre one since the priest's body had been carted off and, at Sophie's request, Fen and Estelle were quietly polishing the copper pans in the kitchen, which seemed to Fen now to be even more cavernous than when she first arrived only a couple of days ago.

The noise of the bell, so similar to the ones she'd heard as fire engines tore through Midhurst on their way to fight the fires when Chichester was bombed, startled them both and, within moments, the kitchen seemed filled with men – their flushed faces and nervous jiggling at odds with the quietude the ladies had been working in.

'Monsieurs?' Estelle addressed them, taking ownership of the room, to Fen's relief.

'There has been a murder and we are here to arrest the murderer!' The Chief of Police spoke in rapid French, but Fen could understand every word.

Arrest the murderer? How could they already know who had done it?

Estelle blanched and grasped the top of one of the kitchen chairs. Fen thought back to her admission last night… *I'll have his guts for garters…* but Estelle steadied herself and answered back to the policeman. 'Who is it you are here to arrest, may I ask?'

'The Englishman, Captain James Lancaster.'

'James!' Fen blurted out his name, then quickly put her hand to her mouth, but not before she felt all the eyes in the room – the four burly gendarmes, their chief of police and Estelle – all turn to look at her. 'It's just… I, well, I don't see why…?' Fen quickly shushed herself and watched as the policemen swarmed through the narrow doorway to the tower staircase.

As soon as their backs were engulfed in the tower's darkness, Fen saw Pierre, carrying Sophie, emerge into the light of the kitchen.

'Madame, Monsieur…' Estelle began to explain, but Fen noticed how Sophie and Pierre seemed to be ahead of them, no shock or panic registering on their faces. Pierre, especially, looked incredibly downcast, like he'd been struck in the solar plexus and left reeling.

'You knew, didn't you?' Fen's question hung in the air as the gendarmes re-emerged, bundling a cuffed James into the centre of the room. Fen could already see one of his eyes puffing up from what must have been a blow to his head and she reeled in horror suddenly at the realisation of how a person suspected of killing a Catholic priest would be treated in this God-fearing nation. 'James, they've hurt you!'

'It wasn't me.' One of his eyes was split at the brow, but both bored into her.

'He is the murderer.' Sophie reached up from her chair and handed over a paper bag to the Chief of Police. '*Monsieur Inspecteur*, here is the brass case and capsule of which I spoke. It is a cyanide capsule belonging to Captain Lancaster. It is broken and the poison used to kill our dear Father Marchand.' Sophie broke down into weeping snuffles as the bag was taken from her grip.

'Where did you find it?' Fen asked on behalf of everyone who was thinking the same thing. Although the other obvious question – *And why does he have one?* – was left unsaid.

Sophie, who was wiping away her tears with her handkerchief, merely waved Fen's question away and Fen got the feeling that Sophie might be too overwhelmed by the whole affair to answer. Or perhaps Fen hadn't been reading into what she had thought of as a tryst too much at all… and Sophie might have lost more than her local parish priest?

'It wasn't me… Pierre… Hubert…' This time, James's voice, and his entreaties to his fellow men, trailed across the kitchen as the gendarmes took him outside and opened the doors of the black police van.

Fen followed them, unsure of how to feel about everything. It was all so terribly and utterly confusing and horribly sad, but, still, something felt *wrong*. Something felt out of place. Like the answer to a cryptic clue that comes far too easily.

'James, I—'

'Listen, Fen,' he cut her off and shouted over the heads of the men bundling him into the van. 'Look to the church. You know what I mean. About Setter... about everything, just look to the church, Fen!'

CHAPTER ELEVEN

It just didn't make sense. Why would the priest be murdered by James Lancaster of all people? Why would an officer, albeit an ex-officer who was perhaps a bit rough around the edges, but an officer all the same, want the local priest dead? Also, James had seemed so fond of him… He had said something so odd too, when he was carted off by the gendarmes – 'Look to the church, Fen.' The words stuck in her mind. *Look to the church*. Well, the priest *was* dead, and *his* link to the church was obvious. But James had been talking about Setter, who she was sure was Arthur, not the priest.

Could this murder have something – *anything* – to do with what happened to Arthur? Fen didn't know, but she did know this; that James knew more about Arthur – her Arthur – than she'd had a chance to get out of him and she wouldn't get a peep more while he was at the Republic's pleasure in the local police station. She had to prove him innocent, if indeed he was, to get him free so that they could resume that conversation – or at the very least she had to present some sort of evidence to the desk sergeant that was powerful enough to grant her a cell-bound audience.

But where to start? There was the suspicion of cyanide, that was made clear by James, though admitting it so forthrightly had rather landed him in the soup. Sophie had apparently found a poison capsule – used and discarded by him – and alerted the police, even though she was the one suggesting that Fracan's croissants could be the root of the distinct almond smell.

'Right, let's look at this like a crossword,' Fen spoke to herself as she sat back down on the old stone bench she'd found earlier that morning. Hubert and his draconian ways in the vineyards could go hang for a bit, for, in Fen's mind, there was more important work to be done than picking some grapes. 'Let's say I'm stuck on my ten across. What do I need? Something solid and definite in my six and seven down, that's what. And in this case that has to be that we know for sure that Father Marchand was murdered – I suppose the cyanide capsule that Sophie found – we still don't know where – was proof of that. And the overwhelming smell of almonds, although that could have come from those delicious croissants.'

The château's resident mouser sought her out again and Fen found herself absent-mindedly stroking him as she pondered her clues. He settled down next to her and she carried on talking to him as if he were Watson to her Holmes.

'So, the croissants, they're another definite too. They were so rich with sugared almond paste, Lord knows where Monsieur Fracan found the ingredients… so it's little wonder that no one spotted any cyanide in them. But that's another thing, when did anyone break the capsule? Not while we were all there, surely?' she pointedly asked the cat.

With no audible reply, she kept her musings to herself. Forgetting for one minute who the capsule belonged to, or where it was found, the only person who could have tampered with the croissants was Pierre.

'And so we have it,' she couldn't help but inform the cat of her breakthrough, 'a place to start for our ten across. Six letters beginning with P – Pierre.'

The château seemed awfully quiet that afternoon, only to be expected, Fen assumed, after the death of the local priest, but, much to her frustration, Pierre was nowhere to be found. What she did find, however, was a very irate Estelle in the kitchen, with young Jean-Jacques and Benoit running around, in and out of her skirts. Typical of children not to notice the heavy cloud of suspicion and fear in the air – it was just like in the war, when small boys made aeroplanes out of sticks and leaves and made play at strafing each other, running down the country lanes at full pelt, shirt tails flapping in the air, seemingly unaware of the lives lost to the real thing.

Fen knelt down and spoke to little Benoit, urging him to show his elder brother quite how fast he could run around the vegetable patches – she would be timing them, *vite vite!*

A visibly relieved Estelle didn't go as far to as actually thank Fen, but in her own way she showed her gratitude by pulling out a chair for her and pouring a coffee for them both. Fen noticed the German branding on the paper package that contained the grains… *Ersatzkaffee. A gift from the occupiers, perhaps?*

Fen sat down with Estelle at the long refectory table and waited for the other woman to speak. It didn't take long.

'In all my days, I never thought I would see a priest killed here in this house! We are cursed!'

'Oh Estelle, I don't think it can be that.'

'What would you know? You are English – you are one of them, like *him*,' she thumbed her chin in the direction of the staircase, Fen assumed to indicate where James had last laid his head. 'Godless!'

Fen sipped the warm brew and let Estelle bubble down to her normal simmer. She could have risen to her jibes against the English, or spoken up about Estelle's own feelings towards the priest, but Fen knew it would do no good. Crosswords are never solved by screwing them up and throwing them in the fire, after all.

'Do you know where Pierre is?' Fen said as nonchalantly as possible.

'No, I'm not his keeper!' Estelle was indeed back to her usual simmer. 'In fact, I do not know who was coming or going at all after the fête last night. It was as if wraiths and ghouls were letting themselves in at all hours. I even saw one, you know? Last night, in the moonlight. Walking through the vines. But did I make a fuss and scream? No. Estelle is brave like the French army.'

Fen didn't want to cast any aspersions on the bravery of the French and decided to stay quiet. She lifted the warm mug to her chest and breathed in the chicory aroma as Estelle continued.

'But then I suppose spirits wouldn't need to come through a door, so I suspect it was that man, that murderer, who left the door unlocked – it was unlocked, you see, this morning and I am always the first one to open it.'

Fen thought for a second. 'I thought I was up before you. Well, downstairs at least.'

'Before me? I was up before dawn getting the wood in and fetching the milk from the early market. Excuse me if I like to wash after that, before you are even out of bed!'

Suitably chastised, Fen took a few more sips in silence. She couldn't help it though, she had to say what was on her mind. 'I don't think we should assume Captain Lancaster is a murderer quite yet,'

'He had the capsule, didn't he? So it must be him. It couldn't be anyone else in this house. Madame Sophie wouldn't accuse someone she is so fond of without cause.'

Fen restrained herself from touching on the subject that Estelle herself had been rather cheesed off with the priest when they spoke about him last night. *Thwarting lovers could be a strong motive for murder?*

Rising from the table, she washed up her cup and bade goodbye to Estelle, who was now filling a bucket with water in readiness to wash the kitchen floor.

As she headed up the stairs to their shared bedroom, Fen phrased what she'd heard into a hastily thought out crossword clue, 'Fourteen across: Spirits walk through a big hostel, five letters… *GHOST.*' Not her best work, and Arthur would have laughed at it, but it got her thinking. She was so sure she'd heard James bolt the door last night when he, Hubert and Clément had started their drinking session, and Estelle swore that it was unlocked this morning? Perhaps Estelle *had* really seen something – or, more likely, someone – roaming the grounds last night, using the moonlight to find their way. And that someone might well be another important 'six down' for her. That settled it. She had to find Pierre, and she *had* to try and talk to James again.

Talking to James wasn't going to be so easy though. Never one to look too scruffy, she felt that today of all days, she should represent her co-patriots to the best of her ability. What she had to work with wasn't tip-top, especially as she hadn't had a chance to wash out last night's blouse. However, her finished outfit of a knee-length brown tweed skirt, sensible shoes and a nice cream blouse, covered up by her Sunday-best cardigan, at least looked smart, if not straight out of *Life* magazine.

She pouted in front of the mirror and applied her favourite red Revlon lipstick, reasoning that although it may mark her out as a Godless Englishwoman, it may also catch the policeman's eye long enough to grant her an interview with the detainee.

She looked over to her nightstand, remembering that she hadn't put her cameo brooch safely away after wearing it last night.

'What on earth… where is it?' Fen reached the nightstand in a few steps and swept her hands over it. The brooch wasn't there. She lifted the oil lamp up, although it was futile to think it would be hidden under it. Then she pulled the bed away from the nightstand to see if it had fallen down the side – but found nothing save a small rusty tin, with an Art Nouveau-style black cat on the lid, that might have once contained pins.

Fen was right down on her hands and knees peering under the nightstand when she heard the click of the doorknob. Red-faced and slightly anguished, she peered up to see who was coming in.

'Oh Estelle, it's you.' Fen pulled herself up from the floor, placing the old rusty tin on the nightstand as she did so.

'What is that?' Estelle sounded so accusatory that it threw Fen off for a second.

'What? Oh this? I don't know. Look, I've lost my brooch, the little cameo one I was wearing last night. Have you seen it?'

'Give it here.'

'Oh, right. Yes.' Fen handed over the box to the other woman. 'Have you seen my brooch, Estelle?' Fen didn't want to accuse her of stealing it, but the thought was hovering very close to the top of her mind.

'Of course I have seen it. You left it there in plain sight of everyone. So, luckily for you, I hid it before a thief could find it.'

Fen let out an audible sigh, she was so relieved at Estelle's words. She followed her across the room like a puppy and watched as the other woman delved into her drawer in the chest. Moments later, the drawer was pushed shut with a sudden shudder and Estelle turned round and handed Fen her brooch.

'Oh thank you, Estelle, I would be so upset to lose this.'

'Remember, do not leave your things lying around.'

'No, of course. Thank you.' Fen smiled at Estelle as she bustled out of the room and was left there alone once more. She pinned the brooch to her cardigan and smoothed down her skirt.

In the quiet of the bedroom, two things occurred to her. *Why was Estelle obsessed about there being a thief in the house, and why hadn't she told me she'd hidden my brooch while we were talking earlier?*

A few moments later and Fen was on her way to the gendarmerie. Luckily, she remembered seeing the signpost to the police station when she had first arrived in Morey-Fontaine and knew roughly which direction to take. She followed the château's terrace down past the vegetable patches, noticing as she went that little blond Benoit and his brother Jean-Jacques were still tearing around, chasing each other. *Benoit couldn't have been that black-haired priest's lovechild,* Fen thought to herself naughtily, thinking back to the night before and Sophie's possible tryst.

She waved to the young boys and made a grandiose gesture of pointing at her wrist to indicate that she was still timing them. They waved back but kept chasing each other and their simple joy made her smile.

She walked towards the Place de l'Église deep in thought. Without anything positive in the way of evidence to hand to the chief of police, Fen was going to have to rely on her womanly wiles alone to ensure she was granted an audience with the prisoner.

She paused in front of the glass-fronted village noticeboard and checked her reflection. Lips still red… *Perhaps it would help if my nose and eyes were a bit too?* The policeman might think she was crying over James and maybe the deceit would be a good one; they'd assume the English pair were lovers and, as the French were a passionate bunch themselves, allow her to see him.

'Sorry, Arthur,' she murmured as she rubbed her eyes and pinched her nose. *Darling Arthur,* she could feel him so close to her. She was sure the priest might have known something about him, if only he was still alive! The thought crossed her mind that perhaps the two deaths were linked, and the poor priest was killed just as the foreign woman comes along poking her nose into Resistance affairs… But no one in the small town, apart from James, and possibly the dead man, even knew she was looking for Arthur; although even she had to admit that her excuse of being a travel writer had been a rather poor one.

Perhaps, Fen shuddered as she walked up the steps to the police station, *James – the one connection between Arthur and Marchand – is the murderer after all?*

*

'I didn't do it, Fenella, I didn't.' James rubbed his hand over his face as they sat opposite each other in the little, exceedingly claustrophobic, interview room. The duty officer had taken pity on – or a shine to – Fen and allowed her no more than five minutes with the condemned man.

'Condemned?' she'd asked, not needing to fake her concern.

'He's as good as! I hope he likes jazz, because it is swing time!' The desk sergeant had laughed as he'd jangled the keys to the cell and opened the door. James had been cuffed and pushed towards the room in a manner that made Fen realise the young policeman really wasn't joking.

'I didn't do it.'

Fen couldn't bring herself to agree with him and offer reassurance, not yet, and not while her thoughts of a few minutes ago were still rattling around in her mind. Instead, she acted the advocate and asked him to explain himself.

He sighed and picked up the story from when he'd left the kitchen immediately after Father Marchand's death.

'It was cyanide, that was obvious.'

'To you maybe.'

'Look, the capsule that Estelle found was mine all right. It was my kill pill.'

Fen leant back in her chair, stunned at the frank admission. 'Kill pill?'

'Standard inventory, special forces.' He paused, then carried on. 'When you're captured, if the enemy try to get more out of you than your name, rank, and Ministry of War number, then it's an option for you. Having one means you can control the manner of your death, before you're forced, by torture, to betray anyone or risk the mission.'

Fen shivered. She desperately wanted to ask James if Arthur had had one too and, horror of horrors, had he been forced to use it? But James, more conscious perhaps of the ticking clock, carried on.

'When I left you all in the kitchen, I had to go and check that mine was in my strongbox. But, of course, it had gone. *Stolen.*'

Fen was brought back from her sombre thoughts. 'So you think you've been framed?'

'Yes.'

'But…' Fen tried to work out the possibilities. 'Estelle was no fan of Marchand's, she told me that at the fête.'

'Oh yes?'

'He refused to marry her and Pascal. Said they were getting hitched for "all the wrong reasons", whatever that means. Oh, and he's a chemist, isn't he? And Hubert was drunk as a lord, but then did you notice, this morning, Marchand mentioned something about him at least "having a clear conscience" as opposed to Hubert?'

'No, I didn't hear that. Interesting. Carry on.'

'Well, Clément and the boys are above reproach and Sophie was immobile, she couldn't be waltzing around the château stealing things from strongboxes. But I do think Pierre had the best opportunity to poison the croissants, as he was the only one alone with them at any time.'

'Pierre wouldn't…'

'Why not? I did wonder if Marchand and Sophie were having an af—' Fen stopped mid-word when she saw the look of horror on James's face.

'No, no, no. Look, keep your wits about you.' James's eyes broke contact with hers – he'd seen the shadow of the guard at the grille on the door. He spoke quickly, meaningfully, 'Fen, I promise you, it wasn't me. Watch out though, because someone in that house is a murderer!'

'Time!' The young gendarme strode into the poky interview room and picked James up underneath the armpit, hauling him back to his cell.

'It's to do with the church, Fen! Marchand and Setter.'

James's last words hung in the grey, airless corridor and she wanted to cry, she was so confused. All of his words seemed jumbled to her, like the very worst puzzle, where nothing made sense.

She ran out of the police station, barely able to see through the fog of tears and confusion, she couldn't work any of it out, but she knew as well, deep down, that James wasn't the killer, but someone, perhaps someone under the very same roof as her at night, was.

CHAPTER TWELVE

Fen rubbed her eyes and forehead as she walked back towards the château. She hadn't even had the sense to ask the young gendarme how long James had before trial and she admonished herself accordingly. She felt sick to the stomach, though, as it seemed that her quest to find out what had happened to Arthur was all at once both tantalisingly within her grasp and yet so close to being stripped away from her. If James swung – a thought that brought her up short and made her sick to the stomach – then she'd never have anything else to go on than 'look to the church'.

'Better go look there then, I suppose,' Fen said to herself and walked towards the handsome old stone building that had kept the confessions and heard the prayers of the townsfolk for centuries.

The vast wooden door creaked as Fen opened it. She slipped in, not wanting the sound to break the unearthly silence within the old church. As her eyes adjusted to the dark, she breathed in that unmistakable smell of a Catholic church; the lingering incense mixed with wood polish and dust mites, the wax of candles and the musty fabric of long-ago embroidered altar cloths and kneelers.

'Look to the church,' Fen wondered out loud, in a whisper, so as not to break the trance-like atmosphere in the building. 'Well, I'm here and I'm looking.'

She didn't close the door behind her, aware of how sacrilegious the scraping creak of the door sounded against the holy quiet of the sanctuary. And the light it let in was helping her see the interior of the church, as many of the windows were boarded up, their glass removed. *Or shot out?*

The church itself was large and the artworks within it were vast. All around her were depictions of saints and sinners, some kneeling, their hands reaching up towards the heavenly clouds or pointing in condemnation at their fellow men.

Fen remembered the churches in Paris that her father had dragged them around on Saturday afternoons and suddenly this country church felt more familiar; the Parisians and Burgundians may be worlds apart in some ways, but the Catholic Church, more so even than the German occupation, united them all.

She walked down the centre of the nave. There were no pews like in English churches, but there were a few chairs dotted around.

She glanced over at the side aisles and got quite the start when she noticed Pierre standing there, his back to her as he stood in front of one of the tombs in a little side chapel. His head bent low too, looking like a marionette yet to be pulled up by his invisible strings.

Fen decided to take her moment and called out to him. His head jerked up and he studied her as she walked towards him.

'Pierre, what are you doing here?' Fen was glad she'd finally caught up with him, though she was intrigued as to why he was passing the time of day next to a tomb, instead of checking over the grapes and overseeing the harvest with Hubert.

'*Mademoiselle.*' His formal greeting reminded Fen that she barely knew the man, with the only thing she'd ever really noticed about him being that he was rather quiet. She hoped he wouldn't be even more tight-lipped than usual now.

'*Monsieur* Bernard…' Fen replied with the same formality and was relieved when Pierre shook his head and gave her a wry grin.

'That is my father's name… and his father's…' The tall, dark-haired Frenchman traced the family name with his finger across the dry stone of the old tomb.

'Oh,' Fen moved closer to him, her natural curiosity taking over as she found the *memento mori* of the living man touching the carved names of his dead ancestors desperately macabre, while at the same time fascinating. *If only the dead could talk…*

'Generations of Bernards.' Pierre's voice was calm and Fen relaxed a little; this was no murderer – or at least at this moment she felt he had no murderous intent.

'And you have ensured at least a generation more.' She thought of the two young boys, probably still playing chase around the topiary and fruit trees.

'But I am the last of this one.' He paused. 'My two brothers are buried here. We had to do it at night, so the Gestapo would not see. We had to steal their bodies from the cart on its way to the shallow grave so that we could give them a decent, Christian burial. Father Marchand risked his life, like always, and helped.'

'Were they Resistance?'

Fen knew the answer must be yes and the thought tingled that in and among this family's own sadness hers was also intertwined.

Pierre nodded an affirmation and then slumped down, his back shaking with sobs, muffled as he hid his face in his arms, resting against the tomb of his brothers.

She gently placed a hand on his shoulder but made no pointless attempt to shush him. His sobs echoed around the cold stone church and Fen closed her eyes and listened, offering a prayer to the archangels themselves to bring this man some peace. His sorrow spoke to her as clearly as if he'd been making a testament in court; he simply could not be Marchand's murderer, as he owed a debt to the brave priest, who had helped him bury his two brothers in the most desperate of circumstances.

Fen was itching to ask him about Arthur, but she couldn't bring herself to disturb this poor man's grief. She gently backed away and wiped a tear of her own from her cheek as she left the small side chapel and walked slowly back towards the nave of the church.

She gave a slight bow of her head as she approached the altar, on which rested the same carved gilded coffer that she'd seen Father Marchand carry through the square the night before. She hadn't really noticed it then, but one side was made of glass that would have showed its sealed-in contents off to the worshippers who came to pay homage to it. Its lid was open now and, of course, there was nothing within. The relic of the True Cross really had been stolen.

She'd heard of Herr Hitler's obsession with collecting religious artefacts; his quest for the Ark of the Covenant had been splashed all over one of the rags that Kitty had brought back to Mrs B's farmhouse once and it had provided them all with a jolly half-hour laughing at how silly his plan for world domination via God was. It didn't seem so silly now, and the fact that the Gestapo had forcibly removed this poor village's piece of the True Cross seemed almost as cruel as the deaths that must have surrounded it.

Fen turned from the altar and her heart almost leapt out of her chest. Estelle was standing there watching her.

'*Bonjour*, Estelle,' Fen collected herself and tried to look non-chalant as her heartbeat gradually returned to normal. 'I thought you'd still be up at the house.'

'Why? Because I am only a housekeeper?' Estelle replied, sounding and looking more than a little annoyed at Fen.

'No, no. I just, I mean, I must have lost track of time. What have you there?'

'Curiosity killed the cat.' Estelle sounded no less annoyed, but instead of shielding the basket she was carrying, she made its contents more obvious – it was full of wild and cut-garden flowers.

'Those are so pretty.'

Estelle ignored Fen's compliment. 'And what are you doing here? Gloating over our loss perhaps?'

'Of course not, no. I'm as saddened at anyone over the theft.' Fen tried quickly to explain herself as Estelle seemed more and more rankled by the conversation. 'I was, er…' inspiration struck, 'getting my eye in, there will be so much to write about this beautiful church. And praying for Father Marchand's soul, of course.'

This seemed to appease Estelle, who shrugged her shoulders and started to move towards and then past Fen to the vestry, which was situated next to the chancel.

'My mother used to "do the flowers", as they say. Are you on the rota?' Fen said to the nursery maid, indicating the flowers in her basket.

'Mind your own business.' Estelle was not easy to draw out, but then Fen thought silence was often the best interrogator.

She was right, when, a few moments later, Estelle reappeared from the vestry, her basket emptied of flowers, but the cotton cloth that had cushioned them was still there, scrunched up in the bottom.

'Fine, to stop you from questioning me more… Questions, questions, it is always with you!'

Fen smiled at Estelle, trying not to feel too self-satisfied that she was about to get some sort of answer.

'Blue asters, white cosmos, red dahlias, or, in this case, a very dark pink, but beggars can't be choosers. They are the colours of our mighty *Tricolore* flag!'

'That's awfully clever.' Fen paused for a second, confused as to why Estelle would be bringing them into the church. Then it struck her, what Pierre had said about Father Marchand being a member of the Resistance alongside his own brothers. 'Oh I see, to commemorate the priest. To show everyone who attends his funeral that he was, well, a patriot.'

'We were all patriots! *Liberté, égalité, fraternité!*' Estelle raised her fist in a sign of solidarity with her countrymen. 'But yes, some were more willing to take the war into their own hands. And it was an act of defiance to our occupiers to dress in the colours of our flag! Father Marchand…' she suddenly seemed overwhelmed by sadness, 'oh, I didn't mean what I said last night! He was so good to us. So honourable. He grew flowers, these flowers, in his garden, so we ladies could always have a bouquet.'

It was all she needed to say. Fen understood. The heart of this town's Resistance network had centred around the church and Father Marchand had bravely co-ordinated the whole thing, from burying comrades to growing seditious flowers. 'Look to the church,' James had said, and Fen thought she could now see why.

Estelle had gained her composure and bustled out past Fen. Fen followed her but took the opportunity to check if Pierre was still next to his family's tomb. He wasn't. As the two women got to the door, Estelle's wicker basket knocked against the thick wood and made a dull clanking sound. She huffed and puffed, ushering Fen out, and shut the creaking door behind her, all the sounds merging into one as Fen pondered the new information she'd been given.

CHAPTER THIRTEEN

The next day dawned and there were still hundreds of bunches of grapes to harvest in the vineyard. Unlike the previous day, Fen was the last one down to breakfast that morning, even though it was early. The evening before had been a quiet one, and Fen realised quite how much she'd missed having James in the house.

The mood around the dinner table had been unsurprisingly sombre last night, and Fen had slept badly, her dreams interspersed with garishly coloured flowers, nooses dancing wildly in the wind and a church she couldn't escape. Today, however, was a new day and, unlike yesterday, she was due back among the vines, the harvest taking priority over housework. And she was pleased of the brisk walk on this fresh autumnal morning and thought it would do her good and help her put all of those crazy dreams to bed so that hopefully she could sleep better tonight.

'Bonjour, monsieur,' she said to the cat, who was preening himself by the door to the kitchen, obviously having feasted well on breakfast scraps. He didn't look up at her, but Fen smiled anyway and walked around the château's internal courtyard and then under the tower arch, through the trees and down the gravelly track towards the winery.

The winery rose out of the morning mist, its cinder-block walls the perfect camouflage against the dispersing fog. Its vast doors were closed against the chill, bolted shut. The stark modernity did not compare well to the ancient stone barns that were more typical of the area. Other winemakers nearby had made do converting old threshing barns into homes for the wine presses and barrels, but this winery must have been renovated or built from scratch, perhaps before the war, when this was a flourishing high-end vineyard, used to sending the fine wine to Paris, London and Vienna and wherever else had a taste for expensive Burgundy. Fen remembered her father extolling the virtues of the Pinot Noir grape, its fineness of taste and elegance in the glass.

The thought of her dear Pa, beavering away in his study in Oxford right at this very minute no doubt, cheered her as she hugged her arms around herself. She could imagine knocking on his study door, entering and see him lean back in his chair and remove his glasses, these simple actions being her cue to tell him all about her day or, in this case, the diverting fact that she was now so close to Gevrey Chambertin and Nuit St Georges, some of his favourite winemaking villages.

'A bottle of your finest Domaine Morey-Fontaine,' she enunciated the words in her most RP vowels as if she were ordering wine at the Ritz. Pa would love that. Her breath hung in the air, momentarily suspended in the chill mist. The sun was not yet high in the sky, in fact it wouldn't get too high at all now that the trees were turning golden and the dew clung heavy to the grasses. There was a breeze today and more clouds in the sky than yesterday – the season was definitely on the turn.

Fen took in a deep breath of the damp air and walked towards the vines. A dash of colour caught her eye among the dank greys and concrete blocks of the walls. Someone had draped a quilt over the inside of a small ventilation window; its red, white and blue geometric patterns making a stark contrast to the grey exterior.

Fen paused, wondering if she should go and investigate this oddity, especially with Estelle's words from yesterday about patriots and the colours of the *Tricolore* still echoing in her ears, but the sound of the church bell prompted her to hurry away to the vineyard itself to get to work.

*

'Hey, where's Hubert?'

'Who knows, probably off in that deathtrap truck of his.'

'*Ooh la la*, he'll cause an accident one day!'

Fen smiled to herself as she heard the other workers talk about Hubert. At least she wasn't the only one who thought his truck, or his driving, was a bit beyond the pale.

She'd found a grape hod near the entrance to the winery a while earlier, and with no one around to tell her what her to do she'd followed some of the more experienced workers into the vineyard and had started harvesting. The cart was slowly filling with grapes as the workers laboriously selected, cut and hauled the bunches of fruit over to it. The large Shire horse that was used to draw the cart to and from the vines and winery snorted occasionally, his whiskery nose twitching as flies circled while his forelegs shifted the weight now and then.

Fen was about to try and take stock of what had happened over the last day or so when her thoughts were interrupted by snippets of conversation she heard among the vines. Clearly she was not the only one thinking about Father Marchand's death.

'They say his head was as purple as an artichoke.'

'Three different poisons apparently…'

'*Bof*, poison? No, he accidentally drank some Bordeaux wine and it killed him!'

'*Zut alors*, Michel, you are wrong – it was German wine!'

Their voices carried across the vines and Fen wondered how much of their crass humour was to hide their grief, as from what she'd seen, he really was a very popular local priest. And one who really *might* have choked on German wine, judging by his role in the Resistance.

Her reverie was broken by the sound of Hubert's engine, and as Fen looked up from her vine, she saw a dust cloud follow the sound as the old Citroën drove at some considerable speed towards the winery from the main road.

'Now where are you coming from so quickly, Mr Hubert?' Fen said to herself as she stood upright and walked with her heavy hod towards the waiting horse and its cart full of grapes. She heard the truck's engine cut out and wondered if it would be terribly unsporting to put some of her knowledge of farm vehicles to the test and somehow tinker with it – not permanently, but just to serve him right for a day or two. The thought was possibly a little too gratifying.

She was about to upend the hod into the cart, picturing in her mind the point in the engine where she could disconnect the cambelt, when there was a yell that pierced the air around them.

CHAPTER FOURTEEN

'Whoa, whoa!'

Fen heard the carter behind her trying to calm down the large horse, but instinct told her to run towards the scream – someone obviously needed help, urgently. She dropped the hod, and its precious cargo, and ran in the direction of the screams straight towards the winery. The doors were now flung open and other workers, summoned by the yelling, were milling around the entrance.

'He's in there—'

'How did it happen?'

'Why didn't he raise the alarm?'

'This shouldn't happen in this day and age…'

The voices passed judgement on the situation and Fen, instinctively curious, headed into the darkness of the building. Once her eyes had adjusted to the poor light, she saw that she was now standing in a vast room full of grape presses, each one topped off with a massive screw that was used to slowly but surely crush all of the juice from the fruit. Fen could well imagine a grisly accident happening here, but it wasn't to the presses that anyone was paying the slightest attention. Instead, like the other workers who had heard the commotion, she hurried past them to the next room, the room that held the vast barrels used to ferment the juice from the presses.

Fen elbowed her way through a cluster of men who were blocking the one doorway that separated the rooms. To her shock, she saw Hubert, pale as a sheet, kneeling next to Pierre. His body was lying in the foetal position, his eyes closed and his cap still grasped in his fingers. He looked like he had just curled up for a nap.

'What has happened…? Pierre, is he…?'

'Dead. Quite dead.' The worker standing next to her removed his cloth cap and held it to his chest, his words barely audible, but prayer-like in their tone.

The eerie quiet of those left standing in the winery had been broken by the arrival of the town's doctor. He had taken control now of the situation and was examining the body.

Fen, who had become a little shaky after the initial shock, had regained any composure she might have lost, adjusted her headscarf and, after a brief introduction of herself to the medical man, asked him pointedly, 'Was this an accident, Monsieur Docteur?'

'Sadly, I think it might have been.'

'How did he die? I… I don't want to sound ghoulish, but I can't see any wound. Poison?' Fen couldn't help but draw a parallel to the very recent death of Father Marchand at the kitchen table – a table that Pierre had been dining at too.

'Of a sort.' The doctor studied the position of the body once more and went through the motions – he raised Pierre's lifeless eyelids and checked for a pulse one more time. He continued talking, correctly assuming Fen was still listening. 'It's a rare, but not unheard of, death in these parts. Though, in truth, I thought Pierre Bernard would have known better.'

'I don't understand?'

'Carbon dioxide poisoning. It's a natural by-product of the fermentation process. These great *barriques* churn out hundreds of cubic litres of it, but, generally, this room is well-ventilated. Of course, it's a heavy gas, so Pierre may have accidentally walked into a "cloud" of it, if you will.'

'A heavy gas? Heavier than normal air, you mean?' Fen barely remembered her classroom chemistry lessons, but something the doctor was saying rang a few bells.

'Yes, and it can build up on top of the liquid and if it builds up too much, or if the barrel is too full, well, like a waterfall, it bowls over the top, and if it hits you before it's dispersed, you become overwhelmed and can die.'

'Gosh.' Fen thought about it for a second.

The doctor must have seen her grimace as she looked down at the dead man. 'If it makes you feel better, mademoiselle, it would have been a very gentle death. He would have felt sleepy and drifted off, never to wake again. How many of us dream of such a peaceful end for ourselves, especially after what our countrymen, and yours, have been through.'

'Well, yes,' Fen agreed but wondered, briefly, if the doctor had a penchant for amateur dramatics or Gothic literature as she saw him cross himself and elegantly kneel to pray over the dead body. She couldn't help but interject, 'Dying peacefully is one thing, but dying tends to not be on the cards at all when you're in your prime, due to inherit a château and have a wife and two young children.'

The doctor stood up. 'Quite so, mademoiselle. Death wields his scythe indiscriminately, I fear.'

Fen turned away from the doctor and Pierre's lifeless body. 'I'm not so sure *Death* had as much to do with it as a common or garden murderer,' she mumbled to herself, remembering the thick quilt she'd seen pressed up against the closed ventilation slats earlier that morning. The very same window she was now looking at quite clearly, with no multicoloured quilt in sight.

Fen tuned back into the wailing and general hubbub that was still going on outside the winery door. She let herself out of the smaller fermentation room and headed towards the daylight, recognising, as she got nearer to the entrance, the voice of Estelle outside.

'We are cursed! We are cursed!'

'Come, come,' Fen found the housekeeper on her knees in the dirt and helped her up and to dust herself off. 'You have to be stronger than this, Estelle, think how Sophie will feel.'

Miraculously, this seemed to buck Estelle up and, along with a couple of the other workers and the town's doctor in tow, they formed an incredibly sad and sombrely slow procession back to the kitchen, where they found Sophie playing marbles on the kitchen table with Benoit.

Fen was relieved that the burden of telling Sophie about the death of her husband didn't fall to her, but as the doctor uttered the words, she felt the full force of the newly widowed woman's grief. As with Father Marchand's sudden demise, Fen's first thought was to protect the innocent boy, who was now looking petrified as he gazed at the sobbing face of his mother.

'Come, Benoit,' Fen practically pulled him away from his mother's skirt, his feet kicking her as she grasped him tightly to her and carried him into the courtyard. It took all of her powers of negotiation to convince him to stay put once she put him down and she sat there with him, out by the washing line, until she could no longer hear the shouts, cries and sobs from the kitchen. The little boy looked up at her occasionally, annoyed at how distracted she was from their game of throwing wooden clothes pegs into the washing basket.

'Papa?'

'It will be all right, little one.' Fen couldn't break the news to him herself, unsure of how much a small child could take in.

In his stammering childish French, he answered, 'Mama sad. Papa gone away.'

Fen couldn't bring herself to do much more than nod and scruffle his blond hair. Luckily, before the peg-throwing game had lost the child's interest, Estelle, herself now recovered enough to look after the child, came to relieve her.

'She's taken to her bed,' Estelle told her. 'And unless you want to come into town to pick up Jean-Jacques from Madame Grignon, I suggest you get back to the vines. It's what Pierre would have wanted.'

Fen took her cue to leave and headed out of the courtyard, back along the track, towards the vineyard. Estelle was right, it wasn't even mid-morning and there was still work to be done. Far from being out, alone, in the vineyard, Fen wanted desperately to talk to someone, but who could she trust with her suspicion that Pierre's death was no accident?

Estelle, as far as Fen knew, was nowhere near the winery when Pierre was found. Sophie, the grieving widow, was safely back at the house and, in any case, she could barely put weight on her ankle, let alone have the strength to climb a ladder and fit a quilt to the window. Hubert's innocence was in question, he had 'discovered' the body after all, although what motive he would have to kill his employer, Fen couldn't say, but Marchand had commented on Hubert's conscience before *he* had died, had Pierre perhaps done something similar?

Clément… where was Clément, and did he know his last remaining son was dead?

James was locked up, which made her sure now that he couldn't have killed Father Marchand either. She was sure this was the work of the same person and Fen knew that if her suspicion was correct, she needed proof that Pierre had been murdered.

'Right, old girl,' she talked to herself as she walked along the dusty track, 'you know the score. If you're struggling with your ten across, which in this case is who murdered Pierre Bernard, then you need to fill in your five down,' she paused and thought. 'And the answer to five down is that quilt, or at least where is it, who removed it, and could it really have stopped the ventilation working in that winery enough to kill Pierre?'

Fen entered the building, empty now of people, including the lifeless body of poor Pierre. There was something even fishier than the isinglass used to fine the wines going on and Fen had a hunch that she'd find more clues than just her 'five down' in this industrial building.

She took a deep breath and walked back into the room where Pierre had died. She double-checked the window, partly to ensure the room was well-ventilated now but also to see how or where the quilt could have been strung up. Somehow, that innocuous piece of fabric, that she'd happened to notice that very morning, was responsible for Pierre's death, as why else would it have been there then and not now?

She cast her eyes around the room. The barrels were massive and some must have been ten or twelve feet tall. They weren't like normal barrels, though, not in their proportions or finish. They were wider and less curved from top to bottom. Towards the base of each barrel, there was a little hatch cut into the staves, with a metal door that was firmly shut. Fen trailed her fingers across the smooth wooden surface as she walked around one of these massive structures. It was easy to see how that many grapes, fermenting away in the warm autumn temperatures, could create an overload of carbon dioxide. She subconsciously took a deep breath and filled her lungs. She was about to return to her search for the quilt when she spotted a stepladder.

'Interesting,' she said to herself, clocking that a ladder would have been very useful to a potential quilt hanger. She had to admit, though, that a ladder was no evidence of wrongdoing, as it was also legitimately used by Hubert no doubt to look inside the toweringly high barrels to check on the ferment. Still, she hitched it open and checked that it could be used to reach the window. As she pulled it out to its A-frame, a fluttering caught her eye. There it was, now on the floor. A shred of fabric in blue and red.

'Bingo.' Fen reached down and picked it up, studying it for a moment before folding it carefully and popping it in her pocket. She pushed the ladder back to its closed position and hid it behind the barrels where she found it.

She was turning to leave when a noise behind her made her stop. Footsteps were heading towards her, albeit soft ones, and although she knew she wasn't doing anything wrong per se, instinct took over and she darted behind one of the large barrels, praying that she wouldn't be the second person that day to be overcome by the falling fumes of carbon dioxide.

Fen crouched and listened as the footsteps came nearer. Then they stopped. Fen prayed she hadn't been seen. Explaining why you're in a room where someone has recently died was one thing; explaining why you're now hiding behind a massive barrel in that room was quite another. She tried to hold her breath, but it only made her panic and imagine how Pierre must have felt as he ran out of oxygen.

Hoping her breathing would go unnoticed by the interloper, she risked exhaling and sucking in more air. Any noise she might have made was luckily disguised by a clanking sound. Then a sort of scraping and shuffling. Finally, as Fen's breaths normalised, there was another clank and she heard a lock being engaged – the sort of tinny lock on ammunition cases or strongboxes – then the swish of fabric and retreating footsteps.

Fen risked being seen and poked her around the side of the barrel she'd been hiding behind. She could see through the open door of the fermentation room the retreating figure of Estelle, her old-fashioned worsted skirt sashaying out of the door.

Fen stretched herself out and let the blood flow back to her feet, now stinging with pins and needles. She adjusted her headscarf and was reaching for her lipstick in her pocket when she noticed what it was Estelle must have come in for. She hadn't clocked it in the upset and commotion after Pierre's death, but there, hanging on the wall next to the door that opened back into the main barn with its grape presses and what have you, was a tin cabinet, like that of a first-aid kit. But instead of a green or red cross on it, there was a skull and crossbones in a yellow triangle and the French words that sent a chill down her as she translated them to herself: *Warning: POISONS.*

Poisons? In a winery? And why had Estelle been helping herself from, or putting something into, the cabinet?

Fen slipped her hand into her pocket and reassured herself that she still had the scrap of fabric. As she felt it, she looked up towards the metal chemical safe on the wall. Another piece of fabric caught her eye, this time it was white and delicate. Fen, in stealth mode, tiptoed towards the old metal box and pulled the scrap free of the ragged corner of the closed door.

'Of course,' Fen whispered to herself. 'It must be from Estelle's apron, or one of those frilled sleeves of hers.' Fen pocketed it too. 'And now to find out where she's going with whatever is in this horrible cabinet.'

Fen crept out of the building and peered around. Sure enough, there in the middle distance, she saw Estelle with her basket over her arm walk down the track back towards the château.

CHAPTER FIFTEEN

'Bonjour, Monsieur,' Fen whispered to the cat as she passed him, almost pausing to try and stop him biffing bees with his furry paws. 'No time to parlay, I'm afraid.'

She trotted on at pace to try and catch up with her quarry. Estelle kept to the track alongside the château, but instead of going in, she made her way through the gardens, past the orchard and towards the church. But Fen lost sight of her as she turned a corner out of the Place de L'Église.

Fen paused by the church, using one of the large stone buttresses as a shield in case Estelle looked behind her to see if anyone was following. 'She wouldn't be wrong,' Fen mumbled as she watched the other woman head towards the little road that passed as a sort of high street. Unlike in England, where there would have been more of an obvious central trading road to a town, here in France the roads were mostly residential and peppered with commercial buildings. Yes, there was a main square with a cafe and the greengrocer, but Fracan's *boulangerie*, again on the square, was sandwiched between two houses, while the butcher was almost on the outskirts of town and the pharmacy belonging to Pascal Desmarais was a few streets away.

'Of course, the pharmacy!' If Estelle was heading anywhere into town, perhaps with some chemicals to hand, her pharmacist lover was the obvious port of call.

Fen peered into the glazed noticeboard outside the church. There was just about enough light to see her reflection and she adjusted her headscarf and slicked on a quick dash of Revlon's finest.

It wasn't much of a disguise, but at least if Estelle found her 'following' her now, she looked less like a furtive investigator and more like a tourist heading for an aperitif before lunch. She tried to walk as nonchalantly as she could down towards the pharmacy and it took almost all her effort to retain her composure when a few yards away from her destination she heard the familiar sound of a shop bell and Estelle came bustling out of the pharmacy, slightly flushed.

'Bonjour, Fen,' Estelle greeted her. Was she more flustered than usual? Fen couldn't decide.

'Bonjour, Estelle.'

There was an awkward impasse as the two women blocked each other's way on the narrow pavement.

'Are you going to see Pascal?'

Fen should have had an answer prepared, though, in her defence, the last twenty minutes or so had mostly been run off sheer adrenalin. Not wanting a repeat of the embarrassing 'I'm called Churche and like visiting churches' debacle, Fen hurriedly thought on her feet.

'You know, Estelle, I'm so terribly upset about the deaths in the château that I'm worried I won't sleep and I don't want to keep you awake with my tossing and turning…' Fen was rather pleased with herself for coming up with her instant excuse.

'Keep me awake? As if I could sleep? It is I who have lost a friend and a priest.'

'Yes, of course. I'm sure you won't sleep a wink either. Still…'

'Of course, of course, please spend your money in Pascal's shop! Though you are lucky he hasn't yet closed for lunch.' Estelle grinned, and it seemed to Fen very unlike the smile of someone who had just lost a friend.

Perhaps there was something truly horrid in that cabinet after all? Thinking about it, Fen subconsciously lowered her eyes to look in Estelle's basket. Which was a mistake…

'You know what I said about curiosity?' Estelle pulled the cloth covering her wares further over the edges of the basket, then, in a quick motion, ran her own finger across her throat before flouncing off, leaving Fen to go into the pharmacy on her false errand. She didn't know how much sleeping pills would cost, but she'd better buy some in case Pascal was the sort to ignore client confidentiality and spill all to his girlfriend.

'Bonjour, mademoiselle, how may I help you?' The tinkling of the pharmacy's doorbell had barely stopped before Pascal welcomed her in.

Fen reintroduced herself and Pascal nodded in recognition of their last meeting.

'I was what the Americans call a *swell bopper*, I think,' he laughed and did a little re-enactment of his energetic dancing from the night of the fête and Fen couldn't help but smile at him. He seemed gentle and well mannered, if a bit eccentric.

'Sadly, dancing's off the cards at the château now.'

'Yes, Estelle has just told me of the terrible death of our friend Pierre.'

'Did you know him well?'

'Of course, he was Pierre Bernard, of the family Bernard. But I hadn't seen much of him lately. Not in a professional sense, in any case.'

Fen wanted to ask why, but she felt like it was too nosy a thing to enquire about. Luckily, much like with his lady friend, the pause led Pascal on and he kept talking.

'It was poor Madame Bernard that I used to see more often.'

'Oh really? I hope Sophie didn't have cause to visit you too often? The boys always seem healthy enough?'

'Ah, I see you do not understand, Mademoiselle Churche. Madame Bernard used to visit me not for ailments so much, but for the chemicals that I dispense for the winemaking. Now, of course, she is much tied up with the house and children, so I get to see more of my dear Estelle as she runs the errands.'

'I see. Of course.' So it was confirmed, both Sophie and Estelle had access to the chemicals. *Poisonous* chemicals perhaps?

Pascal carried on talking. 'It is natural, as she's the one with the degree in petrochemical engineering.'

'Oh, yes, I remember someone told me that at the fête.' Fen paused, that *someone* had been James. 'Monsieur Desmarais, can I ask your opinion on something else?'

'Of course, what can I help you with?' Fen couldn't help but notice that the pharmacist had developed a light sheen over his forehead.

'Captain Lancaster is in jail, you know, for killing Father Marchand with cyanide.'

The pharmacist crossed himself.

Fen continued, 'And I wonder, how long does it take for cyanide to kill you?'

'What a question!' Pascal Desmarais took a handkerchief out of his pocket and mopped his brow. 'And not one a humble pharmacist can answer. But, let me see...'

He disappeared through a doorway behind the counter and was gone a few minutes before he returned.

'Here, I cannot let you have it, as it's my only copy, but it's a guide to gases. We were issued them in the last war.'

Fen leaned over the counter at the tattered old leaflet he had produced. She flicked through it as he peered over her, but one paragraph caught her eye. *Prussic acid... Hydrogen cyanide... ineffective in warfare... 1916...* She read the information, nodded to show she had taken it in, then Pascal pulled the pamphlet back across the counter and slid it under the varnished wood.

'*Prussic* acid...' Fen pondered the word, ignoring Pascal's apparent unease as he stood behind the counter. 'The sound of it, well, it's almost pretty, isn't it?'

Pascal looked at her. 'Prussian blue – the paint colour – comes from it. It is hard sometimes to equate such a beautiful colour with such a lethal chemical. Anyway, mademoiselle, how can I help you? One of our Provençal soaps perhaps, or I can see if I have some lavender oil still in the back?'

With the discussion now firmly back to being a transactional one, Fen asked for something to help her sleep and she was only a little concerned at the sheer amount of options Pascal had on offer. She was sure that many of these drugs would be prescription-only back at home, or not available at all. In the months since Fen had received Arthur's coded letter, she'd been given Mrs B's cure-all for insomnia several times: and it was nothing stronger than cocoa laced with some brandy and a strict instruction to count sheep. Now, however, she left the pharmacy with a neat little packet filled with six sachets of powder, each one guaranteed to knock out an elephant.

CHAPTER SIXTEEN

The next morning dawned and Fen awoke. She'd had to dispose of one of the sleeping powder sachets last night as Estelle had been there to witness her supposedly taking it. She'd made the switch when she feigned having to refresh her glass of water and had flushed the concoction down the lavatory. She had then endured a strained night of pretending to be asleep and keeping utterly still when all she really wanted to do was toss and turn with her troubled thoughts.

Although she had fallen asleep eventually, she woke up with all the same problems dancing a jig around her mind. *Where was that brandy-laced cocoa when you needed it!*

She rolled over in her bed, aware that the creaking springs could wake Estelle, but she simply had to change position. Once slightly more comfortable and happy that she could hear the heavy breathing of her somnolent room-mate, she got back to the task of thinking things through. There had been one murder already, she was sure of that, and she was also pretty positive that poor old Pierre had been the victim of a rather unsporting plot to finish him off too.

Time to go through the evidence: a couple of scraps of fabric, a handy ladder, an empty ampule that might have contained cyanide, but which was in police custody so she couldn't even examine it, a furtive housekeeper, if you could class Estelle herself as a clue, and a few more motives besides – oh, and James suggesting she 'look to the church'. She thought about the church and if there had been anything in the old building that could point to the recent deaths, excepting that of the priest himself and Pierre, who only two days ago she'd seen staring at his family's tomb. If this was a crossword, she'd be stuck without… well, without Arthur to help her work it out.

Fen sat up in her narrow little bed and pulled the blanket high up around her neck, huddling her knees with her arms underneath it. Without Arthur, the next best thing would be a thesaurus. And when it came to these murders, her thesaurus was going to have to be James. He could help her make sense of some of the clues, surely, and it might give the poor man some hope that *something* at least was being done to save him from the hangman.

Despite the household being deep in mourning, there was still work to do. Fen washed and dressed and although the temptation was there to run into town straight away and try to see James, she knew that in the long term that would get her nowhere. It simply wasn't done to leave the grapes mid-harvest and she suspected scary old Hubert would report her to Sophie and then she might lose her lodging as well as any more clues as to what was going on around here. Only yesterday afternoon, once she'd returned to the vineyards, having seen Pascal, she'd had Hubert breathing down her neck.

'Where have you been?' His interrogation of her had caught her on the hop. Wasn't he even the least bit sad about his employer – his friend even?

'I had errands in town.' And because she couldn't resist, 'Luckily, no one tried to run me over this time.'

'Well, if you will walk on the wrong side of the road, what do you expect?'

This had left Fen feeling a bit confused. Had his dangerous driving actually been caused by her lugging her suitcase down the left-hand side of the road? By the time she'd tutted to herself and realised that he was being purposefully obtuse, he had disappeared back into the winery and she'd spent the rest of the afternoon mumbling curses to herself as she picked the grapes.

The evening meal had been a quiet and exceedingly sombre affair, with Sophie taken to her bed and refusing to eat, Clément trying not to cry with every mouthful of dry bread and cheese and the two young children silently chewing on their own portions. Estelle had disappeared off as soon as the young boys were put to bed and only reappeared as Fen was changing into her nightdress.

She left Estelle lightly snoring and was about to descend the spiral stairs down to the kitchen when she heard a sniffling, followed by more of a sob. Tracing the sound back down the corridor, Fen gently turned the handle of the door that she believed the noise was coming from. To her slight surprise, it was the boys' room and Jean-Jacques and Benoit were both sitting upright in their iron beds, Benoit in floods of tears and Jean-Jacques trying to comfort him.

'Boys, what's wrong?'

'No one has come to wake us.' Jean-Jacques was obviously trying to put on a brave face in front of his little brother, but Fen could see his bottom lip starting to quiver.

'Do you usually get woken up? I thought young boys like you were the alarm clocks for the rest of us?' Fen was trying to sound jolly and thought a joke might cheer up the upset children.

'Mama, Papa or Essie usually come and help us dress.' The little boy looked so serious that Fen realised that no amount of joking would cheer him up.

'Well, you've got me this morning. Essie is still snoring...' She couldn't help it, she was desperate to see their sad faces smile, and it worked with Benoit, who stopped crying and started honking like a pig. 'Exactly like that.'

Fen chuckled too as she helped Benoit out of his tangled sheets. Something brightly coloured on his bed caught her eye, however, and it took quite a lot of restraint to keep her attention on the small boys rather than investigate it immediately. Their cries of needing 'a peepee' kept her on mission though, so she shepherded them to the bathroom and then helped wash their faces in the cold water of the jug and basin that was on their chest of drawers. Once both boys were dressed and looking vaguely acceptable, she ushered them out of the room, finally taking the chance to look behind her back towards Benoit's bed. There it was, she was sure of it. The same quilt that she'd seen hanging at the window of the winery. Its geometric shapes and bright blues and reds so recognisable.

'Jean-Jacques, Benoit, go downstairs, I'll be there in one minute!' She didn't care if her call down the landing alerted Sophie or Estelle to the fact that she was in the boys' bedroom, she just had to check to see if the quilt had a piece missing. In the act of making the small boy's bed, she pulled the quilt fully off the sheets and held it up. As she flapped it out and laid it flat across the bed, she saw, clear as day, a small tear on one of the corners and the exact same shape of material missing as she had right then at that moment in her own pocket.

Fen was about to leave when Benoit popped his head back around the door.

'Hungry!'

'Yes, yes. Benoit, can I ask you something?' Fen was thinking on her feet again. The boy nodded. 'Is this quilt always on your bed?'

'Yes.' He thought for a bit. 'My special blanket from Weenfluffer.'

'I see. Well, let's be off with us downstairs, we can't keep Jean-Jacques from his breakfast.' Fen walked towards Benoit and was a little surprised, but incredibly touched, when the young boy reached his chubby hand up to take hers, and then led her authoritatively down the landing towards the stairs.

*

Clément had been seated at the table when she'd got downstairs with the two boys and they'd made the old man smile, briefly at least, as they'd clambered onto his lap and demanded stories from their grandfather. Much like the meal the night before, breakfast was a sombre affair, and Fen was pleased to leave the children and Clément in the dark, tomb-like kitchen once she'd eaten and head out to the mist-covered vines. The day was going to be a warm one, she decided, as she watched the vines gradually appear once the sun burned off the morning dampness.

Autumn always was her favourite season, and not just because she celebrated her birthday in September. It was the perfect season, with no expectations of having to be sunny, and there was no risk of chilblain-catching cold or the seemingly endless wait for spring. No, autumn simply did what it did well, and today looked like it was going to be one of those days, with the smell of woodsmoke lingering in the air, the leaves in the trees catching their first tints of gold and yellow and the bees buzzing around harvesting their own local treasure.

Fen worked through until midday, when Estelle appeared with her lunch and something for Hubert and the other workers who weren't heading home for a brief rest.

'Thank you for getting the boys dressed this morning,' Estelle said, and Fen wondered if that was a look of sheepishness. 'I overslept, but then you should have woken me!'

Fen didn't know whether to accept her thanks or apologise so did both and the nursery maid moved on, serving the other workers with their bread and cheese.

When she'd finished eating, and had gulped down fresh water from the tap at the end of the vines, Fen adjusted her headscarf and braced herself for talking, once more, to Hubert.

*

'I don't understand how you think you can help him.' Hubert shrugged in a very Gallic way as he inhaled the smoke from his stubby Gauloises cigarette.

Fen had been worried he might say that, but carried on, trying to ignore the deep cream colour of his stained teeth. 'It's not help as such, rather support. It must be terrible for him in that cell and I think we both know he wouldn't have committed that murder.'

Hubert stared at Fen, making her feel distinctly uncomfortable, and she wondered if he did actually agree with her. Luckily, he spoke before the situation got too awkward.

'He was with us, side by side with Marchand and the Bernards in the war. I agree, he is not the murderer, but don't get your hopes up that you'll get him out.'

'I won't, but would you allow me to visit him this afternoon? I don't think they'll let me in if I wait until this evening – they might even ship him off to the gallows before then!' Fen hoped that wasn't true, but the thought of James doing the hangman's jig had been one of the worries that had plagued her sleep last night.

'Fine, fine.' He took another deep inhalation before flicking the stub away from the vines and grinding it with his foot.

Fen thought it best not to tarry and instead to take the win of Hubert agreeing she could leave. She nodded a goodbye and took herself back to the château to change out of her work clothes.

'I have evidence of his innocence,' Fen was standing on one side of the counter in the old gendarmarie, a rather officious junior officer was on the other. She'd been arguing with him for over half an hour and it was like pushing water – or wine – up a hill. He point-blank refused to listen to her.

'The evidence was found and logged already, mademoiselle, and the prisoner is awaiting relocation to Beaune for the court session.'

'But I can prove it wasn't him. How can a murderer be a murderer if a second murder happens in almost the same place when the *murderer* is behind bars? Unless you're telling me that your cells here are as flimsy as your Vichy government!'

Fen wondered if she'd gone too far, insulting the Frenchman like that, and in the distance, down the corridor, she was sure she heard a faint laugh.

'Mademoiselle, I assure you our cells are strong and firm, as if presided over by Pétain himself!'

Nice recovery, Fen thought to herself, relieved that she hadn't just been banged up for contempt or some such.

She pressed on with her advantage. 'Then how could Captain Lancaster be the murderer of Father Marchand,' she stopped to cross herself, hoping this would endear her to the Catholic police officer, 'if he couldn't have murdered Pierre Bernard?'

'But Monsieur Bernard,' he crossed himself, 'wasn't murdered. He was the victim of an unfortunate accident.'

'I say he,' Fen crossed herself again, 'was. And, what's more, I have proof.'

'Proof?'

'Yes. Sort of.'

The Frenchman snorted in the way only the French can.

'I have this.' Fen triumphantly pulled the piece of quilt out of her pocket. 'I found it in the hinge of the ladder in the fermentation room and I believe it belongs to a quilt – a rather nice one actually – that I saw hanging at the ventilation window of that same room on the morning of the murder.'

'The *death*,' the policeman corrected her and then crossed himself.

Fen rolled her eyes.

'I believe it was murder,' she paused and almost made the sign again herself, but then thought all of this crossing was getting quite silly. 'And I believe that the same person, whomsoever they may be, was the perpetrator. You see both men were poisoned, in a fashion, and both the murders took place in or around the château, so they have to be linked. Stands to reason then that if Captain Lancaster has been locked up in your cells, he can't have killed Pierre Bernard… and therefore not Father Marchand either.'

The policeman merely shook his head and handed the piece of quilt back to Fen. 'Please, mademoiselle, take your haberdashery home with you and do not waste any more of my time.'

Fen sighed, knowing she was defeated and took the scraps from him. 'Fine, monsieur, but I will prove to you I am right.'

She did her best French-style huff, learnt during her Parisian schooldays, and turned on her heel, head high. But inside she felt utterly defeated as she headed out into the autumn sunshine, unsure of what to do next.

Fen walked back to the château and found herself alone in the vast kitchen when she returned. The house was eerily quiet. The two young boys were nowhere to be seen and, of course, their mother was very possibly taken to her bed, both with grief and injury. *Poor Sophie*, Fen thought. *Her husband, her brothers-in-law. It must feel like her family is dropping all around her.*

Fen helped herself to a drink from the flagon of well water that always stood full by the great stone sink, then thought about the puzzle in front of her. Two deaths, one innocent man locked up for one of them, but the other couldn't have been an accident, could it?

'What would Arthur do?' Fen wondered out loud to herself and was surprised when a quiet voice answered her rhetorical question.

'He would have spoken to Father Marchand.'

'Monsieur Bernard!' Fen turned in time to see the elderly man carefully sit himself down in one of the wheel-back armchairs, the one at the head of the table. He laid his large hands on the wooden tabletop and lowered his head.

Fen walked over to where he had sat down and pulled out the chair next to him. She desperately wanted to know more about how Clément knew Arthur, but also knew that this was a man, a father, who had not long lost his third son.

'Monsieur Bernard, Clément… I'm so sorry for your loss.' She hoped she didn't sound too awkward, comforting people was never her strong suit, and she'd not known what to say to him at all the night before as they'd sat in silence, chewing over supper. Now, though, she placed both of her hands over one of his and sat like that for a while until Clément could reply.

'Your Arthur was a brave man.'

'Was…' Fen's heart broke all over again. 'You knew him?'

'He was here. With James and—'

'The Baker Street Irregulars…'

'Yes.'

The two of them, both wrapped up in their own grief, sat in silence for a while.

'I don't know what James has told you…'

'Barely anything, Clément.'

'He takes a long time to trust people. Perhaps that's why he's still alive.' He paused and drew his hand away from Fen's. 'Arthur was known as Setter. He was a marvellous agent. Sabotaging communication lines with nothing but an old pair of secateurs…' the old man almost laughed at the memory. It came out as a cough instead.

'Our local network of Resistance fighters had been noticed by the British command and Baker Street saw fit to send us help. The British agents hid here in plain sight, as vineyard workers, all of them speaking perfect French and keeping their heads down, but all the while sending communiqués back to London and sabotaging the occupiers whenever they could.' He sighed and took his handkerchief out of his pocket and blew his nose. Fen hadn't realised she'd been holding her breath while he'd been talking and the anticipation of what he might say next was almost too much to bear. The old man carried on talking as she quietly exhaled.

'Arthur was the radio man and intercepted messages about the Gestapo's orders to steal the relic from our church. He and Marchand were determined not to let it go, but instead of a gunfight, they fooled the Nazis by swapping the real one for a fake and hiding the true relic here.' Clément's eyes were full of sadness as he stopped speaking.

'Go on, please,' urged Fen, though in truth she wasn't sure if she was ready yet to hear what might come next.

'One night we were raided. The Gestapo had been tipped off, by the Weinführer we think, and they came and arrested Arthur and ransacked the house. They found the relic,' he nodded to the fireplace, 'hidden up there behind a loose stone.'

'He was arrested…' The colour had drained from Fen's face and she felt a chill come over her. *Why was it only Arthur who was in their sights that night? Where had his so-called friend and colleague been?* 'And James?' She asked Clément, her voice almost a whisper.

'He wasn't here that night.'

'Where was he?' Suddenly Fen wondered if she'd been wrong about James. *Why hadn't he been by Arthur's side?* But Clément leant over to her, tears in his eyes.

'He was burying my sons with Marchand,' he pulled back and crossed himself.

'I'm so sorry, Clément.' *So that was why…* 'And Arthur?' She was desperate for him to continue; she needed to know if there was any hope at all of finding him still alive.

'He was meant to be planning a safe route out for the relic and creating another decoy. He was setting a clue in a letter in his room upstairs. But the Nazis arrived and dragged him away. There was nothing we could do. Guns to our heads… They would have killed us too.' His expression implored her to understand. 'We never found the letter and I don't know if he swapped the relic for the second decoy…' the old man paused. 'We have to assume not. And we never saw him again. I heard from Marchand a few days later that Arthur had been taken to Dijon… and shot.'

At that last word, Fen choked, the emotion that she'd been trying to restrain throughout their conversation suddenly erupting from her throat, her grief spilling over as she rammed her hands over her mouth, trying to stop her gasps, stop her heart from coming right out and beating its last on the kitchen table.

'There, there,' Clément, himself the one so recently bereaved, was up and out of his chair, his arm around her. 'He was a brave, brave man.'

Fen couldn't reply to say 'I know', all she could do was weep.

As she wept, she felt the strong but gentle arm of Clément help her from her seat and the old man accompanied her up the spiral staircase to her bedroom.

'Why don't you take the rest of the afternoon off,' he suggested. 'You've had a nasty shock. Plus, we could do without the salt from your tears getting into our wine.'

Fen knew Clément was trying to cheer her up and she gave him a weak smile as she turned to face him in the doorway of her room. She felt empty, and as fragile as an eggshell. She wanted to fall onto her creaking bed and never get up again.

'Thank you, Clément.' She grasped his hand and held it tight.

'I'm impressed that you came all this way to find him. He was a lucky man.'

Clément's kindness was almost too much and it was all Fen could do to nod a goodbye to him as she turned the knob on the bedroom door and let herself in. She kicked her shoes off and sat down on her bed, the creak breaking the silence. She lay down and stared up at the ceiling. Her eyes stung from crying and her throat ached from the sobs.

She closed her eyes and wanted the darkness to envelop her forever. She was attuned to the silence and if she didn't move, her bed wouldn't creak. There were no sounds in the room, or in the grieving house at all. She lay like that for hours, drifting in and out of sleep, her eyes adjusting to the gradually darkening room as the sun set outside. And whenever she did close her eyes and begin to fall asleep, it was Arthur's face she saw, smiling at her, his eyes twinkling behind the thick tortoiseshell of his spectacles.

'I love you,' she whispered, as she finally succumbed to a deep and now dreamless sleep.

CHAPTER SEVENTEEN

If you are reading this, then in all likelihood I am dead.

His words from his last letter to her repeated themselves over and over in Fen's mind as she lay awake in the quiet of the early morning. She had let them give her hope that he might yet be alive, and she now felt an emptiness where that hope had lived inside her for so long. She lay still for a while, chasing the dust motes around in the air with her eyes, each one illuminated by the thin strips of early-morning light coming in through the shutters.

She could hear the rhythmic snoring of Estelle coming from the bed next to her. Otherwise the house was quiet and she was alone with her thoughts. She had done what she had set out to do, and yet she didn't feel like her mission, if you could call it that, was yet complete. She thought about what Clément had said. *Why would the Weinführer have tipped off the Gestapo? Who had tipped off him?* Fen thought about it a little more and gradually the emptiness inside her started to fill with a new sense of purpose. No, her mission wasn't finished yet, not by a long shot. The difference was that now she was determined to find out *who* had betrayed Arthur… and if it was the same person who had a penchant for murder round here.

The sound of footsteps on the landing caught her attention and she listened as they paused outside her bedroom door. But the doorknob didn't twist and, within moments, Fen heard the footsteps walk away down the corridor towards the staircase.

Her bed let out an almighty creak as Fen sat upright. She glanced across at Estelle and was pleased to see that she was seemingly dead to the world. There was enough light coming in through the shutters for Fen to notice a white envelope on the floor by the door. Whoever had hovered outside her bedroom door must have slipped it under.

With another hideous creak, Fen got up from her bed and walked over to the door and picked up the envelope. It was clean and new, unused. There was no postmark on it, let alone a name or address. Safe in the knowledge she wasn't opening anything specifically addressed to Estelle, Fen slid the letter out. It was very obviously a much older and more often-read letter than the envelope had suggested, and calling it a letter was overstating the fragment of writing that Fen was holding in her slightly trembling hand.

'What the blazes?' Fen mumbled as she tried to grasp the meaning of what had been posted under the door. The letter was merely the bottom half of one sheet of writing paper, torn at the natural crease where it would have originally been folded. And the writing itself was in German. And, more importantly, the signature – just an initial letter – signed at the loving and really quite sentimentally emotional end, was an S.

Fen held the letter tight and crept back towards her bed. She was sure that the letter had been given to her specifically, but why? And who was S? She looked over to the bed next to hers and remembered what Benoit had called Estelle yesterday, Essie. S. Or S for her surname, Suchet.

Then there was Sophie Bernard. But neither of them had shown any love for the Germans…?

Or was it someone completely different altogether?

Still, in crossword terms, she had that all-important clue now – a proper capital letter to slip into her answer. Holding that thought, she crouched down by her bed and pulled her suitcase out. Tucked into the silk lining of the lid, in a little pocket, she remembered she had a pencil. She took it out and stashed her case away. Sitting back down on the creaking bed, she studied the letter. On the back of the envelope she started writing out a few words, crossing them over each other as if they were in a crossword grid. When she finished, it looked like this:

```
                      G
           C Y A N I D E
           H           R E L I C
         Q U I L T     M
           R   E       F A B R I C
     T     C   T       N
     H     H   T
     I         E
 O P E N D O O R
     F
```

Fen heard the church bell clang the hour, so she folded up the envelope and slipped it into her pocket. Estelle started to stir and Fen wasn't at all surprised that her own stomach was noisily demanding something to eat. She went to her drawer and slid it open. She pushed her underclothes and a woollen jumper out of the way and, much to her relief, her hand rested on the cameo brooch that her mother had given her. She wrapped her fingers around it and held it to her chest. Oh, how much did she wish she were home right now, and not in this murderous château. But she knew what her parents would say if she cried on their shoulders. *Finish what you've started…*

'Or you can't move onto the next thing,' she whispered the end of the phrase to herself.

As she closed the drawer, she noticed the packet of sleeping draught sachets. It was slightly opened and Fen fished it out and opened it up properly. She counted the sachets: one, two, three, four… she was sure there had been six in there when she'd bought them and she was also sure she had only flushed one down the lavatory. She looked over to Estelle, who was now rubbing her eyes.

Yesterday morning had been a different story, though, hadn't it; Estelle had been very late to rise. If she'd stolen one of the sachets and taken it after Fen had fallen asleep, it would have still been having an effect come morning.

Before Estelle could start quizzing her on what she was up to, Fen closed the packet and lodged it at the very far back corner of the drawer. She placed a bunched-up woollen sock in front of it, in such a way that if the box were moved, the sock would be too, and closed the drawer. With her back to Estelle, Fen quickly got the envelope out and added another word alongside the grid before putting it back, safely, in her pocket. The word was D R U G G E D.

The next few days passed by, accompanied by a certain numbness for Fen. She got up, dressed and worked in the vines and harvested the grapes and emptied her hod and stopped for lunch and then did it all again in the afternoons before heading back to the château to wash, change and sit at the table, nodding along to the chatter from Estelle and the boys and smiling at Sophie and Clément when she could bring herself to smile at all.

All the time she was awake, she looked at the places where Arthur had been. He'd sat at this table, he'd hidden in these vines, he'd spoken to these people and he'd laughed with his new-found friends as they'd plotted their ingenious ways to foil the Nazi occupiers. He'd been a secret agent after all. She should have guessed from his way with clues. And even his letter to her. *No wonder his code name was Setter.*

By the evening of the third day since Pierre's death, the glum crowd were sitting around the old wooden kitchen table having supper. Sophie was still limping, her ankle swathed in bandages, and she winced every time she was expected to move it, even for her elderly father-in-law to sit down or for her boys to scramble onto her lap.

'You should call Dr Laurens to look at that, it might be broken,' Clément urged his daughter-in-law.

'I don't want a fuss, it'll heal in its own time, I just haven't given it a chance to rest. I've been talking to Father Coulber...' she went on to describe the new priest, who had miraculously agreed to take on Morey-Fontaine along with his own parish, that of Vougeot, which bordered it. 'He is a very pleasant man,' she said to the table, her face a picture of pure martyrdom as she moved her leg from its stool so that she could lean over and help herself to more bread.

'I have heard very good things,' agreed Clément. 'He's no Marchand though.'

'I know, I know. I'm only saying that he is a pleasant man and he will do Marchand and our Pierre a very good joint service.'

'He should not be dead.' Clément lamented. 'And all my sons, my three strong boys.'

Fen felt awkward and wondered if she and Estelle should make eye contact and mutually agree to leave the grieving pair to it, but Estelle wasn't looking anywhere near Fen's direction, instead she was chewing loudly and helping Benoit to some more gratin.

'Clément,' Sophie continued, 'do not forget that you still have me, and my sons. Your grandsons. *They* are your boys now.' She leant back away from him.

'Yes, yes, dear boys. They are so young though.'

'They will learn from you as Pierre, Thierry and Jacques learnt from you. They are bright boys and they will be your heirs.'

Fen looked over at Benoit as he shovelled gratin into his mouth and then glanced at Jean-Jacques, catching him mid nose-pick enjoying a particularly satisfying excavation. *A lot to learn indeed.*

'The funeral plans are all set,' Sophie seemed to have changed the subject. 'Tomorrow at ten. My poor darling Pierre...' Her shoulders shuddered and it was Clément's turn to lay a comforting hand across them. And so the meal carried on, awkward silences giving way to staccato bursts of planning, with Sophie making sure by the end of the evening that they all knew to meet in the kitchen at 9.30 a.m. in their Sunday best, ready to give Father Marchand and Pierre their heroes' send-off.

The church of SS Raphael and Gabriel was heaving with townsfolk the next morning. Fen had given up her seat multiple times to those who looked more in need, or at least more in mourning. Old ladies crept into the church hunched over their sticks, supported by their daughters, or some with sons and grandchildren, their mourning-clothes-clad backs as black and bent as the carapace of beetles.

Clément and Sophie greeted them all at the door, only proceeding to the front row of chairs as the large wooden doors were closing and the service about to start. Father Coulber had been every bit as pleasant as Sophie had said and after the service she had taken his arm as he walked her to the side chapel, where the Bernard family tomb had once more been opened. Fen saw the tears in Clément Bernard's eyes and thought she heard him mouth, 'one, two and three' as the coffin was taken down into the vault, the entrance to which was next to the tomb.

After the interment, Father Coulber helped Sophie limp to the church door, where she and Clément and the young boys were greeted by the autumn sunshine and various members of the community. Pascal Desmarais the pharmacist and Sylvestre Fracan the baker were both there – Fen still wondered if the latter was culpable for poisoning the croissants – *and his name did begin with an S...* She also noticed how many mourners were carrying the same types of flowers that Estelle had left in the church the other day: blue asters, white cosmos and reddish dahlias.

A few townsfolk had roses, in white or red, and there was one woman with a lovely blue hydrangea head. *They're showing their respects to them as patriots as well as friends.* Fen was just thinking what a touching display it was when she saw, crushed on the floor next to where Sophie was now standing shaking hands with Monsieur Martin, the local clockmaker, a bunch of dead blooms, wilted and broken-stemmed. They were in the same colours as the flowers of the other mourners, yet they were obviously days old and almost rotting. *Who would have dropped those there? And so close to the grieving widow?* Fen was about to flit over and pick them up before Sophie could notice them when she heard a familiar gruff voice in her ear.

'What ho, Fen.'

'James!' Fen was relieved as hell to see him and, in an uncharacteristic display of affection, flung her arms around his neck. 'Gosh, I'm so glad to see you! They let you out?'

'I think your taunt about the Vichy government swung it.'

'So that was you I heard laughing down the corridor?'

'Yes, gallows humour, to be sure, but actually I think you were on to something. I think someone in a higher place might have had a word.'

Fen instinctively looked towards the church.

'Not that high, but something like it.' James nodded towards the retreating back of Father Coulber, who was climbing into a smart, black Citroën.

'Well, He moves in mysterious ways and all that. I'm just so relieved that you're free.'

'Me too. Look, let's get out of here. We need to talk.'

James led Fen past the church towards the small orchard of fruit trees. They walked in silence for a few moments until James stopped and looked around. They were alone under the trees.

'I'm sorry I didn't tell you that I knew Arthur.'

Fen looked up at him. She couldn't work out if his face, tanned still from the summer in the fields after the war, but tired now, from too many days in a cold cell, comforted her or not. He was a real and living link to Arthur, but she was jealous that it was him, and not her, who had spent Arthur's last days with him.

'Why didn't you?' she asked.

James looked at his feet, scuffing them into the dirt of the terrace. 'We've met before, you know.'

'Really?' Fen looked puzzled. Her powers of recognition were usually pretty strong, and she cast her mind back over the last few years – even into her youth – but she couldn't place him. 'I'm afraid I don't recognise you at all.'

'Well, I say "met", it was more of a crowded dance hall. And the odd occasion when I would pick Arthur up and take him back to our digs.'

'You were in Sussex…?' *The straw-haired man in the Land Rover…* 'Of course, now I remember!'

'That night at the Spread Eagle in Midhurst, when you met—'

'You were there too?'

'We were training together. There were a few of us, Elsie and Jack, and then Arthur and me.'

'I'm sorry, I suppose I…'

'… Only had eyes for Arthur? That's OK.' James rested a hand on Fen's shoulder. 'That's how it's meant to be, isn't it, when you fall in love.'

Fen's lower lip started to tremble. *Since when did gruff old James Lancaster turn into some Hollywood screenwriter with his way with words?* She took in a deep breath and sighed it out, trying desperately not to start crying again.

Luckily, James pulled his hand away, shoved both of them into his pockets and kept talking. 'It was called the Special Operations Executive, the SOE. Though we rather brashly called it the Stately 'Omes of England as we were all based in some rather decent digs. Down that way, near you. I think Arthur wanted to recruit you into our circuit at one point, what with your language skills, but—'

'But I used to make it pretty clear that I felt my duty was in the fields.'

'Yes. He said if you mentioned the Crisis in Paris one more time, he was going to ship you back there with a sack of turnips for the poor.'

Fen snorted, she remembered their many discussions about how the underclasses were always the worst affected by war and subsequent financial depression, and how she felt duty-bound to help them.

'You must have thought I was a real old goat!' Fen looked up at James and saw him smiling too.

'Maybe, but Arthur loved you for it.'

Fen wanted to cry those wracking great sobs again, but settled for a hiccough as she tried to stay focused on all the information James was giving her. She drank it in, news of Arthur, even just talk of Arthur, like a desert traveller finally finding an oasis.

'Why didn't you trust me, when I first arrived, I mean? If you recognised me?'

'It wasn't that I didn't trust you. I simply couldn't fathom what you were doing here. It takes a certain amount of bravery, and a whole lot of crazy, to travel all this way through... well, through war-torn lands to find your fiancé.' James's foot was scrubbing all the dirt off one of the paving slabs that began the pathway back to the church as he spoke.

'Not my usual style, to be sure,' Fen said gently.

'Ha, Arthur was right, you would have made an excellent agent. Although not if you go around insulting the Vichy government to every jobsworth junior officer of the Republic!'

Fen huffed out a sort of laugh. It was true, her Land Army work aside, would she really have lasted two minutes out in this very different sort of field?

'Plus, and don't get cross with me here for not saying anything before, but I've been tasked by the powers that be to find out who betrayed Arthur. And suddenly having his betrothed turn up from back home… well, you put a real spanner in the works. I had to keep my distance a bit, sorry.'

'Fair enough.' Fen wasn't sure it was entirely fair, but then cringed at the thought that her grand plan of finding out what had happened to Arthur had actually gatecrashed *official* and much more subtle investigations. *Still, onwards…*

'I need you to keep all this a secret: our connection through Arthur, everything. I can't tell you more right now, but promise me. Service as usual, yes?'

Fen sighed. She felt quite deflated, what with expending so much of her energy recently trying to get James freed – only to find him now pulling rank on her like this. After speaking to Clément, she knew Arthur was dead, but she hadn't come all of this way not to find out who had betrayed him and why. Not to mention the recent deaths. What choice did she have though but to work with James now?

'Fine, yes.' Fen thought for a moment. 'It might be too late though. There's someone in the house who knows I'm poking my nose in.'

'What do you mean?' the concern playing across James's face was clear to see.

'A few days ago this was pushed under my door.' From her pocket, Fen removed the letter written in German, still in the envelope she was using to write her word grid on, and passed it to James.

'Interesting...' he scanned it quickly and handed it back to her. 'Thoughts?'

'Not really, only that someone might have been more friendly with the Germans than we thought. But there's no date, this could be decades old. Or it could be faked, or it could be from, or framing, anyone with the letter S in their name: Sophie, S for Estelle Suchet, Sylvestre Fracan...'

'Best keep it to yourself for now.' James frowned. 'All of it, like we just discussed.'

'Yes, of course.' Fen wasn't sure who she would talk to about it all anyway except James.

'Good. Thank you. Look, I have to dash. See you around.'

At that, he briefly touched her on the shoulder and then turned and strode into the château.

'How rude,' Fen mumbled to herself, not really meaning it this time. Her interest was piqued, and even though she and James were supposed to be nothing more than recent acquaintances, she felt the subterfuge would be worth it, or at least she hoped so.

CHAPTER EIGHTEEN

It was a day of mourning, to be sure, but it was also mid-harvest and, in honour of Pierre, the team of workers from Château Morey-Fontaine went back to the vines that afternoon. Fen was surprised when Hubert, instead of pointing her in the direction of the fields, tasked her with cleaning the winery. She'd been in there, of course, since Pierre was found, but still, the fact that she was sluicing down the floor where his body had lain was very much giving her the heebie-jeebies.

She kept glancing up to the window, checking it was open and the room was well-ventilated and it crossed her mind more than once that perhaps Hubert had a murderous reason for asking her to work in the room of death. Luckily, the comforting sounds of winery life around her calmed her and Fen even managed to cheer up a bit when she discovered there was a little mirror nailed to the wall by the fermentation barrels and she could check her headscarf was just so. She knew looking her best wasn't her priority at the moment, but there was a reassurance in the familiarity of checking one's appearance, habitually adjusting one's headwear and reapplying one's rouge, that Fen really appreciated.

Her washdown complete, Fen stashed her mop and bucket away and was about to leave the winery when the white metal cabinet that she'd seen Estelle take something from a few days ago caught her eye. And, what's more, it was very slightly open.

Fen closed her eyes and took a deep, decision-making breath. Before she had even opened her eyes again, she knew what she was going to do. Yes, it might be none of her business, and yes it might be cat-killing curiosity, but she was damned if she wasn't going to take this opportunity to see what was inside that cabinet.

She moved towards it as naturally as possible, keeping an eye on the door to the main pressing room as she went. Checking once more that she was alone, she opened the door. Fen had been prepared to find boxes of chemicals perhaps, even those chillingly macabre hexagonal brown and blue poison bottles, and she did indeed find all of those in the cupboard. More intriguingly, though, she found a tortoiseshell hair clasp, a small silver frame with… yes, that was who it was, a photograph of Pascal Desmarais in it, a curled-up length of red silk ribbon and a silver cigarette case.

Fen gingerly picked up the cigarette case, praying that it might be what she thought it was. She turned it over in her hand and opened the clasp. There were three cigarettes in it and the elastic that held them in place was the exact colour she'd remembered it being when she'd last seen Arthur take a cigarette out and put it to his lips. She ran her fingers over the case and there it was, in small, modest type, A M-H in the bottom right-hand corner. *Arthur Melville-Hare.*

She held the case so tightly that her knuckles whitened and then she brought it to her lips and closed her eyes. Two breaths later and the case was back in the cabinet and the door was back to being slightly ajar, just as it had been when she'd found it. She'd known in an instant that she couldn't take the cigarette case. Whoever had placed it there, stolen it from Arthur even, would know she'd been snooping. And although she had a good idea who that someone was – someone who framed a photograph of their lover perhaps – she didn't know to what lengths that someone was going to at the moment to protect their secret.

*

Later that day, once work was ended and the winery was cleaner than it had ever been, or at least Fen thought so, she started working out how she should act towards James. No one else at the château had seen her talking to him after the funeral, so it was left up to her to play her role as she wished. Should she be icily cold or Britishly chummy? The thought only occurred to her as she was leaving the fields that the family themselves might be wondering how to react to him, too. Word had swept around the town, or so she had heard from some of the other vineyard workers, of James's innocence and that Clément had made it clear that he was still welcome to live and work there.

As it happened, the atmosphere in the kitchen that evening was somewhat leaden. Fen walked in to see Sophie standing by the stove, leaning on a cane as she stirred a pot, while Clément and the two young boys played dominoes at the table. The heavy tread of boots on the stone steps announced the arrival of James and Hubert into the kitchen and Fen noticed that Sophie's back stiffened while she stirred.

'Evening all,' James greeted the room and accepted a warm handshake from Clément as he sat at the table.

'It's good to have you back,' the old man let his hand go, but before he turned his attention back to his grandsons, he added, 'I was sure it wasn't you.'

Fen looked at Sophie, who seemed to be glaring at the casserole in front of her as if it had personally insulted her. She turned and caught Fen looking at her.

'What was I supposed to think?' the Frenchwoman muttered, directing her question to Fen, who couldn't do much more than shrug. 'I found his capsule, broken and used!' She passed a pewter dish of cabbage and ham to Fen to place on the table.

'You could have given me a chance to explain,' James spoke up from where he was sitting. 'If you'd asked, I could have told you that it had been sto—'

Sophie raised her hand to silence him. Fen looked from one to the other and wondered if any sort of apology or truce would be forthcoming. Before either James or Sophie could say another word though, there was a clattering in the hallway and moments later Estelle walked in.

'Where have you been?' a fractious Sophie asked, leaning heavily on her walking stick as she stirred the pot of beans and mutton with the other hand. 'I had to get the dinner on myself!'

'I'm sorry, madame, I was waylaid.'

'By that pharmacist?'

'Madame, do not be cross with me. It is your fault I am late. I had to wait while he wrote this note to you.'

'To me?' Sophie's interest was obviously piqued, so much so that she ignored Estelle's rudeness towards her, and Fen watched as she took the proffered note from the maid's outstretched hand.

Estelle bustled around thereafter, putting her pinny on and rubbing the cheeks of the little boys, who were already stuffing their faces with bread crusts.

'Just a bill.' Sophie needlessly declared to the room, as no one present, excepting the naturally curious Fen, could care less about the note between the pharmacist and his client. Fen tried to concentrate on laying the table but saw how Sophie slipped the note into her apron. Bills, like death and taxes, seemed to stop for no man, or war, or period of mourning, and despite her frosty countenance towards James, Fen felt sorry for the widow, who now had the world, or at least the running of the estate, resting squarely on her shoulders.

'I think we need something to cheer us up,' Sophie announced later that evening as she pulled a thick thread through the toe of a sock. The early-evening meal was over and Clément, James and Hubert had decided to go and visit Hubert's house in the town to see if it was in need of any repairs since the Weinführer had left. Fen wondered if that was only a pretext to escape the obvious atmosphere in the kitchen that had built up over the meal, but, whatever the reason, the ladies were left to amuse themselves in the château. Estelle was back downstairs, having put the quarrelsome pair of boys to bed, and was now washing up the supper dishes in the old ceramic sink, stalwartly ignoring the obvious yelps and shouts coming from the boys' bedroom, the noise echoing down the spiral stone stairs of the tower.

'Good idea, madame,' Estelle was the first to go along with Sophie's suggestion, wiping her hands dry on her apron as she turned to face her mistress properly.

'What do you propose?' Fen was tending to the stove, using a cast-iron riddler to help the ashes fall down to the collecting pan that sat at the bottom.

'If I get us some blackberries and apples, we can have a proper pudding tomorrow night. Maybe Fen can make us an English-style, what do you all them? A croo… a crube…'

'A strüdel?' Estelle ventured.

'No.' Sophie gave her an odd look. 'It's an English dessert… croom…'

'A crumble?' Fen guessed it. 'Yes, of course.'

'That's it! I'll find the ingredients tomorrow. I think we could all do with a treat.'

'How will you manage, madame?' Estelle pointed towards Sophie's foot, which was hoiked up on a stool, alongside several pairs of socks waiting their turn to be darned.

'*Eh la*, you are right, Estelle. I forget that I am completely useless now.' Sophie emphatically put her darning down into her lap, as if to show how stapled to the spot she was. Then she started sniffling. 'It's just that, since Pierre died, I have only been out of the house to go to his funeral and I feel so stifled here.'

Fen started to feel a bit awkward, never one for being the best at comforting people, especially crying women. Still, she decided a mere twisted ankle shouldn't stop Sophie from getting some fresh air. 'I'll help you. I mean, tomorrow, you can lean on me and we'll go together?'

Sophie looked up at Fen and smiled beatifically. Estelle, on the other hand, had a face like thunder and Fen realised that the other woman had wished *she'd* had the idea first and had won herself a morning away from her chores. Fen thought it suited no one for the atmosphere to remain so strained, so suggested a quick game of cards before bed. She hadn't banked on the two French ladies being so keen on some very competitive whist and soon Fen was twenty matchsticks down and staring down the barrel of the second consecutive rubber with no tricks to her name at all.

'I fold. Honestly, you two are card sharks!'

'What does that mean?' Sophie asked, while not taking her eyes off the cards in her hand.

'It's an American saying. It means that you're very good at this game. Here, you two fight it out and I'll feed the stove, see if I can't get this kitchen nice and toasty.'

Fen left the two Frenchwomen bidding against each other and stoked the stove. She noticed a dead bee on the floor and deftly flicked it into the flames, though it gave her no pleasure to do so. A sure sign of the end of summer. Then she wandered around the kitchen for a bit as the ladies fiercely collected tricks of cards and defiantly trumped each other again and again. Fen paused in front of one of the large kitchen dressers and pulled down from one of the shelves, which was mostly full of copper jelly moulds and Danish blue and white china, a ledger of sorts.

'What have you found there, Fenella?' Sophie's voice came across the kitchen from the table.

'Oh, I'm sorry, I really shouldn't have been so nosy.'

'No, you shouldn't.' Estelle seemed almost gleeful in her chance to chastise Fen. 'I've told her so many times, madame, that she should be less nosy.'

Fen started to slide the ledger back into the shelf when Sophie stopped her.

'No, bring it here, I will show you.'

Fen carried it carefully, its battered hardback cover not doing much of a job to contain the sometimes loose pages that were contained within. She placed it on the table and Sophie put her playing cards face down next to it. Estelle followed suit.

Sophie picked up the book and held it tenderly. 'This is our ledger of how much wine we managed to hide from the Germans.'

Fen waited for the traditional spit on the floor, but it didn't come from these women.

'You mean the Weinführer?'

'Heinrich Spatz,' Sophie clarified.

'He was meant to live here, wasn't he?' Fen asked.

'*Meant to?*' Estelle looked indignant on the château's behalf. 'He wasn't even meant to be in our country!'

'Calm down, Estelle, it's all over now,' Sophie soothed her. 'Heinrich Spatz decided, with my help, that it would be better for him to lodge in the town. He stayed at Hubert's house – it's not so bad, you know? He has a nice house, a large one in the centre of town. I told Spatz he would be better able to liaise with all the local vineyards from there and he believed me.'

'And Pierre's boot in his arse had something to do with it too!' cackled Estelle.

'Estelle, you are too coarse at times, you know?' Sophie's ticking off made Estelle bristle and she picked up her cards and sucked her teeth in. Sophie continued, 'And having him lodged in the town meant that Pierre and his father, and the other men here, Hubert and so on,' she paused and briefly touched Fen's hand, 'well, they decided to hide what they could from the Germans. So that this château, this business, would still have stock to trade once the war was over, they logged each wine that they hid, or that they siphoned off into different bottles, you know the sort of thing. They were up late at night in this kitchen, sometimes until dawn, changing labels and faking bottles.'

'All to fool the Weinführer?'

'Yes, of course. But also the Gestapo and the ordinary soldiers, all the Germans. They were looters, thieves. They would crawl all over this house and never find what they wanted! They must have thought we were the least profitable vineyard in the whole of Burgundy!'

Fen let Sophie laugh to herself and thought back to the fragment of letter she had in her pocket and doubted that the S in question could be this patriotic mother and thorn in the side of the German high command. She glanced down at the ledger again, but Sophie quickly closed it.

'Here, be a dear and put it back where you found it. Clément would not like us to be looking through it and laughing, not on a day like today.'

'Of course, madame.' Fen begrudgingly did as she was told.

'And now, Estelle, you can finish taking me for all the matchsticks in the house!' Sophie eased a smirk from the other Frenchwoman and the game continued until the rattle of the outer door announced the men were home from the town and bedtime was decided upon all round.

CHAPTER NINETEEN

'Hubert, you can do without her, for a little while at least.' Sophie was filling in the winery manager with her plan to collect fruit that morning, with Fen's help. She'd prepared herself for her first day out since Pierre died by teaming her widow's weeds with a headscarf, albeit the pattern on it was a sombre purple one. Her ankle was tightly bandaged, but Fen noticed the swelling still bulging from the top of it.

'We're in the middle of harvest, Sophie, and down a pair of—'

'You don't need to remind me,' Sophie snapped, and Fen wondered if she might start crying again right here at the kitchen table.

'Of course, madame, I understand.' Hubert bowed his head at her, his cap grasped between his hands, and then he was off and out of the kitchen, but not before giving Fen what she thought was a pretty snide look.

Sophie must have noticed as she turned to look at Fen. 'You mustn't pay him much attention, Fenella. He's a man's man, you know? I think he always felt that this vineyard should by rights be his, not the Bernards', you see.'

'Why's that?' Fen was genuinely interested.

Sophie waved her hand in the air as she explained. 'Oh, generations ago, Clément's father's side of the family, I think. Yes, that's right. The Bernards have always been here, but Clément's father was a nephew rather than a direct descendent – the Bernards at the time had only had girls. One of whom married another winemaker from a local family near here, the Ponsardines, and Hubert is their descendent. It's why he has such a nice house in the town, he's not a bad catch, you know. But a bit… what's that word the British use… *chippy?*'

Fen smiled, pleased that she wasn't the only one who found Hubert tough-going, and she was intrigued by this new information about the grumpy winemaker.

'Ooh ouch.' Sophie winced with pain as she hobbled to the door of the kitchen.

'Here, let me help.' Fen went to Sophie's aid. She caught up with her employer by the door and helped her stagger through it, then through the small hallway and out into the autumnal morning. The poor woman looked wracked with pain, even though she was trying to mask it. 'Gosh, look, Sophie, I don't want you doing yourself in just to get us some fruit. Let me go instead.'

'No, Fen, Hubert is right really, you are needed in the vines as soon as you've seen me to the village. Harvesting really is something I cannot manage at the moment, but slowly and carefully, I can get to the square and, from there, cousin Sybille will meet me and take me to her farm for the fruit. It will keep me occupied, you know. I cannot stay in this house, thinking about…'

'I know… I mean, I understand. Here, let me take your basket for you.'

Sophie tried to argue, but Fen had it from her so she could use her stick with one hand and lean on Fen with the other.

'Gosh, feels like you've already got half a pound of apples in here!' Fen wasn't as rude to look under the gingham cloth that was draped over the wicker basket, but she could feel that it wasn't empty.

'Just a dish of leftover casserole for Sybille,' Sophie replied.

Fen nodded and then slowly helped Sophie across the courtyard and terrace and then over the old lawns to the fruit trees.

'I could as easily make a plum crumble out of these,' Fen offered, seeing the pain Sophie was in with every step.

'No, no. I spoke to Sybille at the funeral yesterday and she was keen to see me today. She'll meet me in the square and take me to her orchard. It will be better for your English crumble, yes? Blackberry and apple?'

'Delicious, yes,' Fen agreed but was unsure of this whole plan and the strain it was putting on Sophie's injury.

They made idle small talk as they walked and although Fen thought it a little strange that two such recently bereaved woman should avoid the topic altogether, she knew grief was a curious thing. She would have loved to have spoken about Arthur and heard what Sophie might have to say about him, but she heeded James's request and kept quiet. Sophie was obviously coping with her own grief by dealing in pleasantries and Fen let her chatter away about the town and its surrounds.

'You must visit Clos de Vougeot while you are here.' Sophie was telling her about the local monastery that had been making wine for hundreds of years. 'I'm sure you will find all sorts of interesting local history there. Perfect for your article. How are you doing with that by the way?'

'So-so,' Fen couldn't bring herself to lie, so changed the subject. 'Are they a vineyard too?'

'Yes, a very good one. Our German friends were so impressed at the wine there that they took the lot!'

'Oh,' Fen wasn't sure if Sophie was joking. Fluent in French she might be, but not for the first time Fen felt rather less fluent in *being* French.

An agonising – for Sophie at least – twenty minutes or so later, both ladies and the basket were in the Place de l'Église.

'Here, let me sit for a while.' Sophie was almost panting as she heaved herself down onto a stone bench. 'You can go now, Fen, if you need to, I mean, thank you so much for helping me, but Sybille will be here soon.'

The bell in the ancient tower of the church struck nine and Fen smiled at Sophie, who pointed up at the sound of the bell, indicating that it was when she was due to be picked up.

'If you're sure, madame?'

'Quite sure, Fen. You've been most kind.' Sophie placed her hands either side of her on the bench and closed her eyes, her face pointing up towards the sky. Fen took this as her cue to leave and headed through the grounds of the church and the fruit trees, across the old lawns and bypassed the château itself to get to the vineyard and start her day's work.

When Fen found Hubert, he was up a ladder, scratching his head and leaning over one of the old basket-style grape presses. The presses were all full of grapes now, and more were coming in all the time from the harvested vines.

Hubert looked up when Fen entered the winery and rolled his eyes, mumbling something about England always showing up too late.

'What's the matter, Hubert?' Fen asked, pretending she hadn't understood or heard his slight.

This time, Hubert didn't look up from the old press, and Fen stood a moment watching the Frenchman lean over the edge of the vast basket, which was full of red grapes. He shifted his weight on the ladder and scratched his backside.

Fen looked away and whistled a few notes, not wanting to interrupt him but keen to know what her morning's duties would be. She was just about to go and find something to do for herself when he started muttering again.

'It's jammed, it's stuck.'

'I'm sorry, what is?'

'The plate, it won't screw down.'

'Can I have a look?'

'What can you do? Some expert?' He looked crossly at her and Fen wondered what she'd ever done, except not fall into a ditch fast enough, to inspire such grouchiness from him.

'I'm rather a dab hand at engines and the like,' she thought back to her impish scheme to sabotage his old truck. 'I might be able to fathom out what's—'

'Go away, there are grapes to be harvested, even if we can't damn well press them…'

Fen didn't need yelling at twice and shrugged her shoulders. 'Fine,' she mumbled to herself and then a very quiet 'how rude!' for good measure.

She headed out of the winery and towards the fields. It only took her a few minutes to be back in sight of the château as she followed the rough track that edged the vineyards.

The grapes had all been picked from these near fields and all but one of the other south-facing slopes further away and the pickers were active in the middle vineyards, a good fifteen-minute walk from where she was now.

'Time to stretch the old legs.' Fen hummed a tune to herself and started the walk. Out of the corner of her eye, she noticed Estelle running from the winery towards the château, holding her skirts up to her knees so she could get a fair pace going.

'Now what are you up to?' Fen said to herself as she watched the figure take the steps up to the terrace two at a time and dash round to what Fen assumed would be the kitchen door. With Estelle now out of sight, Fen continued walking towards the vines, following the sounds of the pickers' voices and the odd whinnying of the cart horse.

'Where is Hubert?' one of the other workers asked her when she got there and picked up a spare hod.

'He's in the winery, and acting like a bear with a sore head.'

'Typical! Why though?' the local worker asked.

'Why indeed. Well, I don't know. Something about one of the presses being stuck.'

'*Ooh la la*,' the worker shook his head and looked worried and went on to tell Fen in great detail about the need to get that press fixed as quickly as possible as it was well known that the Bernards were running a shoddy enough winery with their old and cranky presses, far too few of them too, and to have one out of service when these next hods of grapes came in... 'The Englishman is very good at fixing machines,' he continued. 'He should be around here somewhere, send him to help.'

'Good plan,' Fen nodded and looked about her, hoping to see James among the pickers. She knew he wanted her to act all nonchalant about knowing each other, but she still felt a certain comfort in having him near – a link to Arthur now that she knew she'd never see him again. Some women kept their lover's tokens close at hand, but Fen liked the idea that James could tell her so much about Arthur, and she could really talk to him about her fiancé – much better than a lock of hair or an embroidered handkerchief.

But James was nowhere to be seen and Fen clasped the hod to her and joined one of the working parties, looking up every now and then to check the landscape for the familiar blond hair and almost permanent, but not wholly unwarranted, scowl.

Estelle brought the lunch rations round, but her thunderous face made Fen think twice about asking her why she'd been dashing away from the winery earlier. And she was just finishing off the chewy end of a piece of cheese, more rind than goodness – Estelle really couldn't be her biggest fan she thought – when she saw the black-clothed figure of Sophie slowly hobbling along the farm track.

'Madame! Sophie!' Fen called to her and trotted over to her, with the intention of helping her home.

'Ah, Fenella, you angel.'

'Can I help you, Sophie?'

'Yes, that would be kind, thank you.'

Fen reached over to the basket, but Sophie held it close to her and instead motioned for Fen to help her by holding her arm. 'It's easier for me to lean on you.'

Fen did as Sophie requested and let her lean against her as they limped back towards the château, through the gatehouse and into the courtyard. Once Fen had seen Sophie into the kitchen and helped her to a seat, she bade her employer a goodbye and turned to leave.

'Oh, madame.' Fen suddenly turned to face Sophie. Something had been bothering her and she'd finally noticed what it was. 'You've lost your scarf.' She pointed to her own red and white spotted one on her head.

Sophie's arm flew up to touch her bare head. 'Ah, *zut*. I must have left it at Sybille's. No matter. Goodbye, Fen.'

Fen felt very much dismissed and walked back to the vineyard with one thought going round in her mind. Cousin Sybille... could this be a new contender for the S of the German love letter?

A few hours later, the sun started to fall behind the treeline to the west of the vineyards and Fen heard the church clock strike the hour in the town. It was the signal to the workers to down tools and, along with the rest of them, Fen picked a couple more bunches of grapes to fill her wicker hod before heading back towards the gently whinnying horse and his cart. Her fellow grape pickers dusted themselves down and some took a long thirst-slaking drink from the tap at the end of one of the rows, while others mounted their bicycles, which had been left there since the afternoon shift had started.

'*Zut alors!*' She heard one of the workers exclaim, as he clambered off his bicycle saddle and looked carefully at his front tyre. He prodded it a bit and gave the old rubber wheel a squeeze. Tutting to himself, she saw him scrub around in the dirt next to his tyre and throw a couple of shards of pottery into the vines, away from the path. 'Such mess!' He tutted as he decided to push his damaged bicycle away from the vineyard.

Fen was intrigued as to what could have caused the gash to his tyre and walked over to where she'd seen him toss the offending shards. It didn't take her too long to spot a few pieces of creamy white porcelain. She bent down and picked them up, running the smooth ceramic over in her hand, but being careful of the sharp, knife-like edge where it was obviously cleaved from another similar shard. In all, she found three pieces and neatly fitted them back together into a sort of incomplete bowl shape.

'How odd,' Fen wondered to herself, but rather than drop them back into the path, she pocketed them in her dungarees. Something told her, like a marker in a crossword clue, that there was more to this than met the eye. Why would a small bowl be broken and discarded in the vineyard? It struck her as odd, like the shreds of fabric she'd found in the winery, and she patted her pocket to make sure they were safely inside.

'Ah, Fenella,' Sophie greeted Fen when she entered the kitchen, having taken her work boots off in the hallway. 'Just the person. So' – she indicated the ingredients she'd picked up on her trip out – 'where do I start? Is it like clafoutis? Or frangipane?'

Fen couldn't help but chuckle and was relieved when Sophie smiled back at her. It was so hard in a house that had seen so many recent deaths – and one wrongful arrest – to know if you'd walk into somewhere with the atmosphere of a morgue, or to somewhere a bit more 'make do and mend'. Luckily, this evening, it seemed to be the latter.

'Well, madame, I don't think we need to get as technical as that.'

'You know what they are?' Sophie looked up at Fen from her seat at the table, half in admiration but also, Fen wondered, a tiny bit annoyed that this Englishwoman had such a cosmopolitan palate.

'Of course. I grew up in Paris, you know?'

'Ah, of course, I thought I could detect some of the city in you.'

As Fen set Sophie off peeling the apples and sorting through the blackberries, she rubbed the smallest amount of fat – she couldn't tell if it was butter or lard or something in between the two – into the flour and rationed sugar.

'Ideally, this should have about quadruple the amount of good brown sugar,' Fen mused as she set about the mixture, using the very tips of her fingers to rub the flour and fat into a breadcrumb-like consistency.

'Oh, sugar! How I miss it!'

'Those croissants from Fracan were exceptional,' Fen said, though instantly regretted bringing up a subject so close to that of the murdered priest. Luckily, Sophie didn't seem to connect it, or mind, and carried on with her reminiscing about her own time in Paris.

'Did you ever go to the patisserie in Rue Champollion? It's a few streets away from the Sorbonne.'

'No, I don't recall—'

'The strawberry tarts were…' Sophie kissed her fingers like a happy chef. Then she sighed. 'Those were the days, you know.' She paused as she peeled some more of the apples and then passed them to Fen, who, having made her crumble topping, was now able to cut them into slices and place them in a pie dish.

'Did you meet Pierre in Paris?' Fen hoped her question wouldn't spoil Sophie's seemingly contented mood, but it seemed an innocent enough question.

'No, not Pierre. Believe it or not, I had a German boyfriend then.' Sophie had almost whispered it.

'Gosh. I don't suppose you know what happened to him?'

Sophie thought for a moment, her eyes glazing over slightly, and Fen worried that tears might be about to come and inwardly scolded herself for possibly upsetting Sophie. 'No, no, I don't. But I don't know what happened to that girl back then either, you know?'

The war had changed them all and Fen would be the first to agree that the happy-go-lucky kid she'd been in Paris in the 1930s was a stranger to her too, now she had weathered so many winters since then. Fen shivered and wanted to change the subject before it all got too maudlin.

'Shall I go and find Estelle?' She asked the question of Sophie, who seemed to be completely unfazed about the lack of her boys' nursery maid, even though the little ones were starting to whine for their dinner and Benoit was climbing up her sore leg to get onto her lap, in order to be even closer to her ear to whine into. For once, Sophie wasn't wincing in pain and Fen had a moment of grief pour over her as she imagined what her and Arthur's children might have been like. It seemed a far cry to believe she might ever have that perfect motherly relationship, now there was no one who could ever be the father.

Fen turned towards the stove to hide her tears from Sophie, who was appeasing Benoit by popping juicy blackberries into his mouth. She wondered where James was, and if Hubert had found him and got help with that press. Dry-eyed and recovered enough now to turn around and speak, Fen was about to tell Sophie about the damaged wine press when the kitchen door was flung open.

Benoit gave an involuntary squeak and slipped off his mother's lap, leaving a purple smear down her sleeve. Sophie tutted and turned to see who had made such a violent entrance, as did Fen, and both ladies were greeted with a face as white as the ash from the stove. It was Hubert, standing in the door, his work boots still on and dirty from the soil between the vines, one hand pressing against the door frame, keeping him from falling over. Sophie turned back to Benoit to give him a ticking off for getting blackberry juice everywhere, so it was Fen who stepped across the kitchen to ask the estate manager what was wrong.

'Is it the press? I was just telling madame—'

Hubert shushed her with his free hand and then wiped it across his brow. 'It's not the press that's the problem now. It's the body.'

CHAPTER TWENTY

'The body?' both Fen and Sophie exclaimed. Fen had a ghastly thought of a crumpled human body being the cause of the press not working, its screw coming up against bone and flesh rather than grapes and seeds. 'Oh dear Lord…'

Putting her feelings of dislike towards the man aside, Fen urged Hubert into the room and bade him sit next to the sheet-white Sophie. A pair of bright and wide blue eyes looked up at her from under the table and Fen mustered all her self-control to calmly pick up the small boy and, with nodded consent from his mute mother, take him to the doorway and send him out to play with his brother. Fen watched him run towards the older boy and only when they both seemed content building mud patties in the last of the early-evening sunshine, did she let her forced smile drop and turn back to the adults sitting, ashen-faced, around the kitchen table.

'Stabbed.'

'Stabbed?'

'Through the heart.' Fen caught the end of Hubert's explanation to Sophie.

'And then dumped in the wine press?' Fen couldn't help but make that assumption.

Hubert turned to look at her as she sat down opposite him, on the other side of Sophie, who was now holding her head in her hands and mumbling, 'So much death, so much death.'

'No.' The estate manager held Fen's gaze. 'Not dumped in the wine press. No Frenchman would pollute our national treasure this way.'

'Perhaps it wasn't a Frenchman?' Sophie looked up from her hands and her eyes darted from Hubert to Fen, who remembered it was Sophie who had accused James a few days earlier of Father Marchand's death.

As they sat in contemplative silence, another figure appeared at the kitchen door. Clément, wringing his oily hands inside a rag. He solemnly walked in and Fen sighed in relief that the elderly man wasn't the body that had been found, be it in a wine press or not.

'Have you heard, Clément?'

'Heard what now? James and I…' he looked around and seemed perplexed that the Englishman wasn't with him, 'have just fixed that bloody press. The grapes are wasted, and those from the best field too. You know what the problem was?'

'Clément, not now,' Sophie beckoned him over and Fen, being the closest to him, offered him her chair. Sophie reached across and held the old man's hand as Hubert continued.

'When you and James came and relieved me from that bloody press,' Hubert said, 'I went to go and manage the pickers in the far vineyards, the Pinot Noir.'

'Yes, yes, I know my own vineyards,' Clément chuntered and Fen could feel him getting agitated. Hubert, in a display of sensitivity that Fen had never seen before, placed his hand on the elderly man's arm. 'I'm so sorry, Clément, but we found a dead body there.'

There was a silence.

'From the war? A shallow grave?' Clément pulled his hands away from Sophie and shrugged off Hubert too.

'No, not from the war. From today.'

Before Hubert could say anything else, Estelle bustled in, whistling to herself, holding what looked like Sophie's basket.

'Good evening,' she called out to the people around the table, obviously not feeling the tense atmosphere in the room. 'Madame, I found your basket in the courtyard and rescued it from being used as a helmet or some such.' She looked around the faces of the stunned people around her. 'I suppose it's up to me to get the dinner on? Unless we only want English pudding, eh?' She clocked the mess of apple peelings and mixing bowls on the table and chuckled to herself, placing the empty basket down at the far end of the table.

'Estelle, sit down.'

'Sit down? Like I have time to sit down with you all sitting down, yourself excluded, madame, of course.'

'Estelle!' Sophie's command stung through the air and Estelle shrugged and came to sit down next to Hubert and opposite Fen. Fen tried to meet her gaze, but Estelle was huffing, and had folded her arms, not wanting to show how upset she was at her employer's sharpness.

'Fine I am sitting, now what?'

'Hubert...' Clément had found his voice. 'Hubert has some terrible news for us. A man...?'

'Yes, a man,' Hubert confirmed Clément's query.

'Has been found dead, in the furthermost vineyard.'

Estelle gasped and crossed herself.

'He was stabbed, through the heart, though there was no weapon nearby.'

'Who was it?' Fen dared ask the question that she knew must be on everyone else's lips.

Hubert's reply shocked them all.

'Pascal Desmarais.'

Fen gasped and was about to reach across the table for Estelle's hand, when the grief-stricken woman, who was repeating 'no, no, no' over and over, pushed her chair away and fled from the table and out of the kitchen door into the twilight.

'Pascal Desmarais? The apothecary?' Clément seemed struck by the randomness more than the terrible nature of the news.

'The pharmacist, Clément, yes.' Sophie was breathing slowly, staring straight down at the table.

'Why would anyone kill that old softie? Did he have a rival for Estelle's affection?'

'Don't be so foolish, Clément,' Hubert snapped at him.

'He's not so foolish, you know,' Sophie raised her eyes up and looked at all of them for a moment. 'Good men are few and far between and Estelle was doing well to secure the advances of such a professional man, with his own business and all.'

'You don't really think that, do you?' Fen challenged Sophie. 'Stabbed out of jealousy?'

'Through the heart.' Sophie pointed towards Hubert, reminding the table of what he'd said earlier. 'If that is not a *crime passionelle*, then I don't know what is. Now, Fen, please go and find Estelle, we can't have her wandering around in distress in the dark and in front of the boys.'

'Yes, of course.'

Fen wasn't convinced of Sophie's theory and, judging by the look on Hubert's face, he wasn't either. Nevertheless, she left the table and headed out to find Estelle, calling to the boys when she saw them, busy cutting slices out of their mud pies.

'Jean-Jacques, Benoit – go inside and find your grandpa. You can all clean up together.'

A few whines later and they were scurrying towards the kitchen, hopefully, Fen thought, none the wiser about the most recent tragedy to befall this beautiful old place.

'Estelle!' Fen called out in the gloaming, hoping that Estelle's white apron would show up in the half-light.

She saw a figure approaching and waved, before realising that it was James, not Estelle who was coming towards her.

'What ho,' Fen had her hands on her hips and let James come up to her. She scanned the horizon one more time before continuing. 'Heard the news?'

'About the candlesticks?'

'No, what?' Fen asked, confused.

'The problem with the press. Not mechanical, but structural. Instead of just grapes in there, there were a pair of very nice silver candlesticks.'

'Gosh.' Fen paused, remembering the other precious objects in the chemicals cabinet. 'That would be headline news on any other day. Want to know the real top story?'

'Go on.' James looked more cautious than Fen had thought he would and she wondered if he knew more about today's goings-on that he was letting on.

'Pascal Desmarais has been murdered.'

'What?' James looked shocked.

'That's why I'm out here, looking for Estelle. She's just heard the news and is in a right old state.'

'Who would kill Desmarais? Do they know?'

'He's barely cold, James. I don't think anyone back in the house has any inkling what to do right now, let alone form theories about who knifed him in the heart.' Fen wasn't trying to make light of the tragedy, but she could see James looking more and more on edge. What he said next confirmed as to why.

'The last thing I need is the gendarmes back. Let's guess who they'll blame.'

'I hate to say it, but Sophie's already got you pegged for it.'

'Has she now?'

'Fresh out of jail and your killing spree continues and all that.'

'Quite.'

'But you can't disappear, that would look even more suspicious.' Fen had hit the nail on the head and she could see James thinking through his next steps.

'You're right,' he said finally. 'But we have to solve this, and fast. I can't risk the threat of *Madame Guillotine* a second time.'

*

Fen found Estelle, weeping into her apron, under the fruit trees by the church.

'Come now, Estelle, this isn't the place to be, come back inside.'

Estelle snorted and scowled at Fen. '*Come now, Estelle,*' she mimicked, then, whatever she said next, Fen couldn't understand through the bawling. After a long while, Estelle started talking. 'You don't understand. I had been doing so much for us both, for our life. Now he is gone and I will be alone.'

'I'm so sorry for your loss, Estelle, but you're not alone. Lots of us are in the same boat.'

Estelle stopped sniffing and looked at Fen. 'I remember Arthur.'

Fen was so taken aback by Estelle's mention of her fiancé that she started to well up too. Of course the maid would have known him, he lodged in the same house as her. It must have been because of her not-too-friendly demeanour, but it had never really occurred to Fen to ask Estelle about him.

The two women stood in silence for some time, both coming to terms with their losses. Fen wanted to pry all sorts of information out of Estelle; what had happened the night Arthur was arrested, did she know who had betrayed him… A shiver ran over Fen's body as she realised it might be the grieving woman next to her as well as anyone else.

Estelle broke the silence. 'Pascal meant everything to me. All of our young men went off to fight for France, and, yes, other young men came to the town.' She nodded at Fen. 'But, unlike other women, I was not interested in the Englishmen or,' she spat, 'the Nazis.'

'Of course,' Fen murmured.

'I had never looked at Pascal Desmarais before the war, nor he me, I am sure. But with men's work turning to women's work and Sophie sending me to the pharmacy for the medicines for the boys and for the Resistance fighters, and, of course, for the winery chemicals that Pascal had ordered in for us, well, we got to know each other a little better.' She paused for a while. 'Who would kill him?'

'I don't know, Estelle.' Fen laid a comforting, she hoped, hand over Estelle's arm. 'I just don't know.'

'He was a patriot and a good man.'

'If he wasn't a patriot, well, would that be motive to kill him? I mean, are there still grievances in the town?'

'Those who collaborated were run out of town after the occupation ended. I don't think there are any more left. And in any case, my Pascal was not one of them. He had no choice but to serve the soldiers, of course, but he fought in the Great War against the Kaiser's men, so he was no collaborator now!'

Fen thought for a bit. She wished, not for the first time, that she'd never come on this bizarre mission. 'Come on, Estelle, come inside, I know Sophie's worried about you.'

After a brief hesitation, Estelle nodded and started to follow her. Fen suddenly remembered something she'd said and asked her, as they walked across the scruffy lawn towards the terrace, 'What did you mean, Estelle, when you said *you'd* done so much for you both?'

'Nothing. I mean I… I mean a woman does things, yes.'

'Oh, I see. Yes.' Fen felt the flush coming up her cheeks but didn't feel like her question had been answered, not properly anyway, and something was nagging at her. She shrugged it off and flicked on the torch she luckily had in her pocket, guiding them both back to the warmth of the kitchen.

'These are from the church.' Clément was scratching his head, looking at the gleaming candlesticks on the kitchen table. 'How did they get into my wine press?'

'They must have been stolen from the church and hidden there,' Sophie said matter-of-factly.

'What idiot would put candlesticks in a wine press?' Clément carried on.

'Someone not used to making wine.' Hubert seemed equally perplexed.

Fen and Estelle had come back into the kitchen and heard the tail end of this conversation. At the sight of Sophie coming towards her, Estelle had burst into sobs and Fen gratefully handed her over, like a school nurse might hand over a child with a grazed knee to a more sympathetic mother, and joined the men at the table.

James had picked up one of the candlesticks and was admiring its craftsmanship. 'Must cost a pretty penny, these.'

'They are priceless.' Clément was confident in his valuation.

'Not priceless,' Hubert argued. 'But divinely purchased.'

'You couldn't sell these on the open market, they would need to be melted down,' James stated.

'We should get them back to Father Coulber,' Clément declared, 'before they are noticed to be missing and we are found with them.'

'I'll go,' James volunteered, and Fen smiled to herself as she realised James had just found his legitimate way of scarpering from the scene of the murder.

The murder. Why was no one talking about it, and instead harping on about the candlesticks?

'What is happening to poor Pascal?' she asked, hoping it wasn't an insensitive question.

'He has been taken to the morgue,' Hubert answered matter-of-factly, picking up and turning over one of the silver candlesticks in his hand as he spoke.

Not much more was spoken of that evening. The table was cleared of fancy candlesticks and the usual pewter ones were lit. The adults, except Estelle who had decided to stay in her bedroom, only settled down to eat at gone ten o'clock, the supper preparation having taken second place to most other things, and after a rustic mix of lardons and tomatoes with bread, everyone turned in for the night.

'I'll take these to Father Coulber in Boncourt-le-Bois first thing in the morning,' said James to the retreating backs.

Fen wasn't sure but she thought she heard Sophie mutter a 'good riddance' under her breath, while Clément raised a hand in acknowledgement but didn't turn around.

'Good plan, James.' Fen winked at him and went up the spiral staircase to bed.

CHAPTER TWENTY-ONE

Château Morey-Fontaine, France
October 1945

Dear Mrs B, Kitty and Dilys,

Where to start? I have so much to tell you. Don't panic, but I seem to be tripping over dead bodies… In fact, I have a horrible feeling that my coming here might have started a bit of a chain reaction as I can't shake the feeling that they may have something to do with Arthur.

It's so hard to actually put this into writing, but Arthur is dead – I've been told it by two reliable sources. One of whom is Captain Lancaster, who I told you about before, and the other is old Clément Bernard, the patriarch of this dwindling family. They both say what a brave and clever man he was though, so I must dwell on that and not the sadness, I suppose.

Please don't be alarmed about me being caught up in all these deaths. Luckily, Captain Lancaster has been released (he was arrested for the murder of the local priest, before being exonerated, poor chap) and I feel like he's a friend worth having. Can you believe, he was stationed near Midhurst too and was actually at the Spread Eagle the night I met Arthur and Edith ran off with that Canadian boy behind the bins! Anyway, I hope he's not the murderer because I feel like he's a real link to Arthur. I have one more thing to find out about his death before I leave here, and that's who

*betrayed him to the Gestapo. Once I know that, I will let it
rest and come home.*
  Anyway, these murders…

Fen filled her old friends in on what had been happening at the
château, hoping the exercise of writing it all down would suddenly
make the murderer come to light. She closed the envelope and wrote
the address of the old Sussex farmhouse on the front, sadly still as
mystified as ever. She hoped she sounded more cheerful than she
really was, too, as she didn't want Kitty or Dilys thinking they had
encouraged her to come on this trip only to find it a fool's errand.
Well, it had been in a way. Arthur was most certainly dead and,
for whatever reason, three others besides.

She pressed the seal down further on the envelope and slipped
it into her dungarees' pocket. She fished around in there and dug
out the other envelope, the one with the German letter inside and
her grid on the back. She stared at it for a moment and added a
couple more words until it looked like this:

```
                        G
            C Y A N I D E
            H           R E L I C
            Q U I L T   H
            R   E   F A B R I C
        T   C   T   N
        H   H   T
        I       E
O P E N D O O R
        F


                            F
                P A S C A L
                        O
                        W
            D R U G G E D
                        R
                S H A R D S
```

She stared at it some more, running the words over silently on her lips, and then neatly folded it and slipped it into her pocket alongside the letter to Sussex.

Breakfast that morning was bleaker than ever. Sophie was quiet and sombre and Estelle… well, Estelle was nowhere to be seen. Fen had heard her leave their bedroom at the crack of dawn and wasn't quite *compos mentis* enough to ask her where she was off to. Fen suspected it might have been to the church, or perhaps to the pharmacy, somewhere she could be alone but close to her memories of Pascal.

Fen chewed on the last of the bread, her plate now empty, bar a few crumbs, which she decided would be a treat for the birds, even if those birds then became a treat for the fluffy old cat.

'Speak of the devil,' Fen said to herself as the cat yawned at her from its place in a sunbeam in the courtyard. 'I'll not lead them into your temptation…' she muttered as she walked a little further away from the kitchen door, before emptying the crumbs from her plate near where the boys had been playing mud pies the evening before.

Those poor young things, Fen thought to herself. *Much of their lives have been shrouded in war and even now they are surrounded by death.* As the thought tripped across her mind, she saw something glinting in the morning sunshine. Whatever it was, it was half buried by several failed mud pies and what was visible was mostly covered in dirt.

Fen crouched down to get a better look. Putting her plate on the cobbles, she used one hand to steady herself as she pulled a long, steel blade out of the mud. It looked like a knife, but over a foot long, and incredibly thin. The handle had an odd fixing to it, including a round opening, and the blade itself, as Fen turned it over in her hand, revealed the word 'Enfield' on it.

'Oh dear,' Fen dropped the rifle bayonet back to the ground, as she realised that it wasn't just mud that dirtied the blade. Dried blood covered the wooden handle. She shuddered to think that this was what the boys must have been using to mix and then cut up their mud pies last evening. Carefully, she picked up the blade and put it on the plate, and then used both hands to carry the weapon and its platter back into the kitchen.

'Oh no!' Sophie exclaimed as Fen brought the bayonet to the table.

'I'm sorry, madame.' Fen felt personally responsible, as if she had left the blade outside to be played with. 'I think your boys might have been playing with it last night. I hope they're not hurt. I think it might be…'

'… The blade that killed Pascal?' Clément had appeared and was standing over her shoulder now, looking down at his old weapon. 'It's mine, of course.'

'When was the last time you saw it?' Fen realised too late that her words could be construed as being slightly accusatory, but she hoped her tone was gentle enough. She just needed to know how this *murder weapon* got into the courtyard.

'I haven't seen it since I put it away after our last skirmish with the,' he spat on the floor, 'Gestapo.'

'Could the blood be, well, I mean, did you use it that night?'

'I am an old soldier, and I respect my weapon. Whether it saw action or not,' Clément paused, and Fen inferred that indeed it might have been used against the occupiers, 'I would never put it away… dirty.'

Hubert entered the kitchen and Clément beckoned him over. Fen sat down next to Sophie, who was sitting by the fireside, her ankle raised up on a stool.

'You think it's the weapon that killed Pascal, don't you?' Sophie half whispered to her.

'I do.'

'It's an agent's weapon, you know. A knife. Like poison.'

'What do you mean?'

'I mean, accidents do happen in wineries.' She crossed herself as the memory of her very recently buried husband hung between them. 'But poison, knives... they are agent's methods of killing.'

'You mean...?'

Sophie shrugged and turned her face away from Fen. 'I will see that it gets to the gendarmes. They need this important piece of evidence.'

James... Fen thought to herself. *James...* the only agent left in this neck of the woods, or so she thought. It was, after all, his poison capsule that had been used to kill Father Marchand. He had free run of the winery so could have blocked off the ventilation to the fermentation room. And he was nowhere to be found at the exact time that Pascal was murdered. *Had she been a fool to put her trust in him?*

She shook her head. It didn't make sense, and Fen hoped more than anything that she wasn't yielding to some sort of patriotic bias, or was being blind to something merely because James was a friend of Arthur's.

She stared at the blade on the kitchen table while her thoughts vied for attention in her mind. But what about the white fabric fragment she'd found? Or the mysterious poisons cabinet in the winery? She shook her head, wanting to dislodge something that she'd seen or heard, some subconscious thought that would help her make sense of it all. She knew it was in there, she just needed to work it out.

Fen made an excuse to return to her bedroom. Finding the bayonet did not excuse her from her daily toil, and she promised

Hubert she'd be in the vines as soon as she could. The fragment of white material was snatching at her thoughts, however, and she needed to put that little niggle to rest.

She knew Estelle had been up and out early and wasn't surprised to find their bedroom empty when she got there. She closed the door firmly behind her, hoping that the sound of the knob turning the catch would forewarn her of any interloper as she started to search through Estelle's clothes. She'd assumed the white cloth must have come from one of Estelle's aprons – she wore them almost every day and Fen was sure she'd been wearing one when she saw her, albeit from behind, when she was leaving the winery the other day.

She found two freshly pressed ones in the top drawer of the chest of drawers and although she didn't dare take them out and shake out the creases to examine them, she could peel back the folds and inspect them fairly well there and then. Nothing. They were intact and, Fen had to admit, not really the same texture as the finer fabric that she'd retrieved from the cabinet. *I suppose the starch might have worn off.* But it was evident to her now that unless Estelle had a better quality pinny than these two, then she had drawn a blank in linking Estelle to the cabinet, save for her own eye-witness account. Fen patted down the aprons and closed the drawer.

Out of sheer curiosity, she opened the second one down – it was still one of Estelle's and she felt incredibly deceitful having a peek, and then terribly silly too as all it contained was a jumper or two and her undergarments. Fen was about to close the drawer when she caught sight of something poking out from under one of the jumpers. It was a letter. Fen gently pulled it out from under the heavy thick wool and turned it over so she could see who it was addressed to. To her absolute horror, the black ink spelled out her name, care of Mrs B's farmhouse address.

*

'Why does she have a letter addressed to me, and, I assume it's her, a stash of objects, including Arthur's cigarette case, in the lockable cabinet in the winery?'

The fluffy cat didn't reply, but Fen kept stroking his head in the hope that his furry little ears would provide inspiration. She'd been desperate to keep the letter, it was hers by rights after all, but in the same way she'd put the cigarette case back the other day, she instinctively knew that now was not the time to repossess this most precious of belongings. She gave the cat another stroke and then walked quickly towards the vines, not wanting Hubert to have any excuse to shout at her for shirking her duty.

When she arrived, the working party was already in the last of the far fields that needed harvesting, the one that Pascal had been found in. *Had been killed in.* Fen shuddered but picked up her wicker hod and took her position in a row of vines and started picking. She looked along the row and noted that far fewer workers were out today. Catching sight of a tall man nearby, she put down her hod and slipped under the gnarled wood and fulsome leaves of the vines to go and ask him where everyone else was.

'Everyone else?' He looked at her as if she had a pumpkin for a head. 'Where do you think? Not here! Not when there's a murderer about.'

'But the murders are…' Fen wasn't sure what she was about to say, only that she felt that the murders were linked somehow to the château, the family, the Resistance, not that an indiscriminate mass murderer was on the loose.

'The murderer is someone around here, that's all we know, so watch your back, eh?'

With that ringing in her ears, Fen slipped back through the vines to where she'd left her hod and began working. The monotony of it helped her go into a sort of meditative state and she started piecing together all she knew. The clues hovered in front of her eyes, her envelope grid, one word sliding into another; some corroborating others – like the fact that she knew there was a thief in the house and she had definitely found some stolen objects. Then it came to her: *alibis, that's what I'll concentrate on next.*

Fen poked her head up over the top of the vine she was working on and could see that no one particularly interesting was around, even the tall man was much further along his row now. There was no one else nearby.

'Right then.' Fen put down her hod and crouched on the dry, dusty ground. She pulled the envelope and pencil out of her pocket and started a new tally. She kept it to just initials and started working out where everyone was for each of the murders.

Father Marchand. Well, that was easy in a way – everyone was around the table. But then, that might not have been when he was poisoned. She remembered the pamphlet the now-deceased Pascal had shown her about the gases used in the trenches and how Prussic acid, otherwise known as hydrogen cyanide, which was deemed in the end too light and ineffective a gas for trench warfare, would kill a man in hours rather than minutes. So really, he could have been poisoned that morning, or even the night before, long before breakfast at any rate. So that ruled no one out, apart from the injured Sophie.

She then started afresh with Pierre's murder, for she was still sure it wasn't a terrible accident. Sophie couldn't have got to the winery… but someone took the quilt from Benoit's bed. She drew a big E next to Pierre's name as her thoughts turned less to everyone else's alibi and primarily to Estelle's. She knew her way around the winery and went to the cupboard often. The white scrap of fabric might not be hers, but the quilt could definitely have been taken by her and used to block the ventilation. She was also a dab hand at stealing – and using – sleeping draughts. Fen glanced at the word D R U G G E D that she'd written on the envelope a few nights before. *And Marchand, she'd hated Marchand…*

Fen straightened up and placed the envelope back in her pocket. For the rest of the day, she argued with herself the pros and cons of whether Estelle could be the murderer, but it kept coming back to one thing: motive. Having the slightest reason to kill the local priest was one thing, but to kill her employer and her lover?

'Of course, I'm assuming there *is* only one killer amongst us,' Fen reported to the cat as she trudged back up the pathway after her day's toil was done.

With considerably fewer workers left in the vineyard, and the race now on to get the grapes harvested before they over-ripened or were devastated by birds or the weather, her back and arms were aching almost as much as her head. What's more, although she hated to admit it, to man or beast, she was absolutely no closer to finding out who was responsible for killing the good people of Morey-Fontaine.

CHAPTER TWENTY-TWO

Fen looked at the bath and the hot-water geyser above it. It occurred to her that perhaps she should check the fixings, as there had been one too many 'accidents' around here already, but her shoulders and back ached and she was dusty and sweaty from working the shift of two or more people. She turned the hot tap on and stood and watched as the bath slowly filled with steaming water. Never one to take advantage, she only let it get to an inch or two deep before turning off the tap and sluicing in some cold water from the basin. She gingerly climbed in, hoping the water was still warm enough – and deep enough – to ease her tired muscles.

Fen knew she had to confront Estelle. If only to get her letter and Arthur's cigarette case. It was clear to her now that Estelle was the thief, but was she the killer too?

Fen lay back in the few inches of water and closed her eyes, dreaming of a full, steaming bath, gently scented with aromatic herbs and salts. How easy it would be to fall asleep and then submerge yourself...

'Hang on a tick...' Fen sat upright. 'If Pierre was asleep before he was asphyxiated by the carbon dioxide – well, that would explain why an experienced winemaker didn't spot the danger signs, or indeed the quilt. He must have been drugged.' She looked over to the lavatory, where she had flushed away the sachet of sleeping powder a few nights ago. It had been so easy to come about them, even so, Estelle had almost definitely stolen one from her... *Was it to replace one she'd already used?*

Fen pushed herself up from the bath and grabbed the thin piece of linen she'd found to dry herself with. Wrapping it around her, she walked over to the basin and finished washing, splashing water on her face. All the while, she was thinking. *If Pierre had been drugged, then when does that put his time of death, or at least time of starting the chain reaction? Who had access to sleeping powders and was the pharmacist's death a revenge?*

Back in her room, Fen dressed herself and sat down on her bed. She knew the words would come, but she needed to be a little bit more prepared as to what she was going to say to Estelle.

She got up and went over to the chest of drawers. Her hands hovered over where she knew the letter from Arthur was, but she controlled herself and pulled out her own drawer and fetched out a jumper. She poked around in the drawer for her mother's brooch too, but it only took a moment for her to realise that it wasn't there.

'Oh this is too much!' she exclaimed.

'What are you looking for?' Estelle's voice was alarmingly close. *How had she crept up so quietly?*

'I think you might know full well. Where is it?'

Estelle had the decency to look sheepishly at Fen. Then she pushed her out of the way and pulled open her own top drawer. She reached inside and pulled the brooch out from under one of the pressed and starched aprons.

'Here.' Estelle held the brooch out to Fen, who took it quickly and closed her hand around it protectively. She was desperate to ask why the other woman had so obviously stolen it, but she thought about Arthur's letter and knew that pushing Estelle now on the brooch could make her clam up about what else she might be hiding.

Fen looked over at the opened drawer and asked, 'Anything else in there you'd like to return to me?'

'I don't think so. No,' Estelle sneered.

'What about the letter that Arthur, *my Arthur*, wrote to me.'

'You have been sneaking through my drawers? How dare you!'

'How dare I? I think I had good reason.' Fen tried to remain sounding firm but fair. 'Now hand it over, else I'll shop you in for all this thieving.'

'You can't, I won't let you!' Suddenly the Frenchwoman had her hands around Fen's neck, forcing her up against the wall. 'I have lost everything, if I lose this position...'

'Stop!' Fen could barely breathe. 'Estelle, stop!'

The Frenchwoman glared at her, then released her and, to Fen's astonishment, started crying.

'I'm sorry, I'm sorry. Forgive me.'

Fen rubbed her throat with her hands, wary of the woman who had almost throttled her. It was easy to see how Estelle could become murderous, but now, now she just looked completely beaten.

'I'm not a murderer, I'm not a murderer,' she wept, then suddenly reached out and grabbed Fen's arm. 'I have done bad things, yes. But I have not killed anyone. I am sorry for stealing your brooch.'

'And Arthur's cigarette case?' Fen tried her best to hide the tremble in her voice, as she was still being gripped by Estelle and was more than a little scared.

'How did you know?'

Fen pulled her arm free and quickly moved a few steps away from the other woman, putting a safe distance between them. 'I saw it in the chemical cupboard.'

'Oh.'

'I'll be wanting it back.'

'Fine, fine.' Estelle seemed deflated, downcast. 'I have never been in love, you know, but Pascal was everything to me. He promised me so much. But he asked things of me too. I had to steal back the chemicals that he sold to the Bernards so that they would order more from him.'

'Lumme, that's not exactly playing by the rules.' Fen wasn't at all impressed.

'And he also said if I stole from the English *and* the Germans, we would then be able to save up and be the real winners of this war.' Estelle wiped her nose with her sleeve and carried on, slightly more defiantly than before. 'There are always winners and losers, and I'm fed up of being a loser all my life! "Estelle, will you wipe my children's bottoms? Estelle will you cook for us? And clean for us. And clean up our mess." Ah, this is not fair, no?'

'No, but stealing mementos from grieving loved ones is also decidedly *not* fair.'

'I did not know Arthur would have some fancy woman coming after him.' Estelle's retort made Fen frown. She wasn't a fancy woman, but perhaps the others in the château all presumed it.

'The letter is worth nothing, why steal that?' Fen asked.

'I didn't steal it.'

'Come on, I think we're a bit past that now, aren't we?'

'No, honestly. Arthur gave it to me. Here' – she got up from the bed and advanced towards both Fen and the chest of drawers – 'you can have it.'

Fen let out the breath she didn't realise she'd been holding as Estelle handed her the letter. To hold something of Arthur's, to look at his writing, to read his words. Fen didn't want Estelle to be there when she opened it. It might all be too much for her.

Estelle must have taken Fen's silence as her cue to escape further interrogation. 'I'll leave you to read it,' she said, then followed up with the slightly less friendly, 'but if you tell a soul here that I have been a little light-fingered, I will fence that cigarette case before you can say "Gauloises".'

Fen didn't care at that moment, and nodded without really concentrating. All that mattered to her was the letter, *Arthur's* letter. Perhaps his last. She waited until the other woman had left the bedroom and then started to open it. Despite Estelle's proven track record of being a thief, she obviously wasn't a spy or nosy parker and the envelope was still sealed. Fen uncurled her fingers from the brooch she was grasping and used the pin to gently prise it open. She sat down on her bed, the springs providing the fanfare she really didn't want for the grand unveiling. She read:

France, August 1944

My dearest Fen,

I'm writing this in such a hurry – Estelle is breathing down my neck, but I have to trust her to give this to you. One word of advice, pat her down before you leave – since I've been here, I've 'lost' my cigarette case, five francs, two pens and now, probably my life, although I can't blame her for that. Although someone here has betrayed us, someone in this house is a collaborator. So I only trust you, darling honeypot, to find that holy object that starts off reliable but ends at sea, I hear. I've stashed it, knocked about, in Greater Rutland.

I knew you'd come, my clever darling. I'm so sorry that I'm not here to greet you. The clatter of boots is on the stairs – I love you, I love you, I love you, adieu.

Fen's tears hit the paper before she could move it safely out of the way, and Arthur's last signature was blurred forever.

CHAPTER TWENTY-THREE

Fen had to compose herself after reading Arthur's letter, which she'd done again and again, wiping her tears away each time she reached the last line. *Darling Arthur*, she'd thought, *even with the enemy at his door he'd tried to cheer me up.* And he'd confirmed her suspicions about the light-fingeredness of Estelle too. Fen had put the letter away and then slipped it out of its envelope numerous times, reading and rereading his words, and of course stumbling over the nonsense that hid within it more clues. As she put the letter back in its envelope one more time, she heard the church bell strike the hour and knew she should be getting downstairs to help with dinner.

Closing the bedroom door behind her, she walked along the corridor to the spiral staircase in the old tower at the end of it. In an awful echo of what she'd just read, she could hear the clatter of someone's boots coming down from the floor above and she paused to see who it was.

'James!' she hissed at him, in a whisper, as he appeared around the curve of the staircase. The very man she needed to see. She raised her finger to her lips to indicate that quiet and subtlety was needed and they descended the rest of the staircase together. Instead of going into the kitchen, Fen let them both out of the small turret door so that they could talk somewhere, privately and unspotted by the château's other residents. She led James under the gatehouse and they stood there, beneath the vaulted ceiling so beloved by the local pigeons, listening to them gently coo as they began their roost for the evening.

'What is it?' James spoke when they were both sure that no one was listening. The slight echo of his voice made Fen frown, so they walked a few steps further away, into the light covering of trees next to the path.

'What are you doing back from seeing Father Coulber so soon?'

James sighed. 'Sadly he wasn't there, so the housekeeper took them in with my scribbled note of explanation and told me to trot on. And now I'm back here in the metaphorical frying pan.'

'Well, let's hope it doesn't turn into a fire.' Fen looked up at James and saw a hint of the same concern pass over his face too. 'I don't know if anyone's told you yet, but I found Clément's old bayonet this morning.'

'No, and that means…?'

'It had,' Fen lowered her voice even more, 'blood on it. We think it's the weapon used to kill Pascal.'

'Really? Where did you find it?'

'Over there,' Fen pointed back through the gatehouse to the courtyard. 'Sophie's taken care of it, but I don't know if the gendarmes have it now. Oh, and I've found the letter by the way.'

'You have had a busy day. What letter?'

Fen subconsciously touched her neck – she really had had quite a day of it. She was quick to answer James, though. 'Clément told me about it while you were in prison. The one that Arthur wrote to tell you, or rather me, where the real relic is hiding.'

'Clément told you about that, did he? He obviously trusted you.'

Fen exhaled and frowned a bit. She didn't know who to trust, especially with the contents of this letter, but she had no choice but to confide in James.

'And Arthur obviously trusted Estelle, as he gave her this letter, even though it was addressed to me…'

'What, and she never gave it to you? Isn't that case in point as to why you can't trust Estelle?'

Fen sighed. 'Yes, and that she's admitted to me,' Fen rubbed her still aching throat, 'that she's the thief in the château.'

'Arthur always had his suspicions.'

'Yes, he said as much in his letter.' Fen paused, trying not to well up with tears as she thought back to Arthur's tender words. She took a deep breath and continued. 'It's more than a few francs and trinkets though. She and Pascal were pilfering from everyone here, including the Bernards by stealing their chemicals and reselling them back to them…'

'Dirty rascals.'

'Quite, but not murderers. Or collaborators. Anyway,' Fen handed the letter over to James. 'Read this. Well, maybe not the last bit.' She felt her nose fizzing as she remembered Arthur's loving sign-off.

James carefully took the folded letter out of the envelope and, much to Fen's surprise, pulled a pair of spectacles out of the top pocket of his shirt.

'What?' he questioned her as she stared at him.

'I didn't expect you to be a bit of an old four-eyes, that's all. I thought glasses were Arthur's thing.' She smiled at the memory of Arthur's thick tortoiseshell frames.

'Him the brains and me the muscle, you mean?'

'Something like that, I suppose, yes. Anyway, read it, what do you think?'

James took a moment to take in the odd sentences. 'I take it you've had a stab at working it out?'

'Yes. Not much to report so far, except that I assume he's talking about the relic. And not just because Clément said there was a clue-filled letter about it. If you take the start of reliable, well that's your R E L I and then with the bit about "ending at sea, I hear"; well that means it sounds like sea, which is the letter C. So that's your RELIC spelt out. The next sentence looks like it should be so simple, although I've never heard of Greater Rutland.'

'Hmm, "I've stashed it, knocked about, in Greater Rutland". *Multum in parvo* and all that.' James studied it a bit more.

'Rutland's motto?'

'Yes, from the Latin meaning "a great deal in a small place". Seems apt for a holy relic in a small casket, assuming it's pointing us to where it is.'

Fen shivered and James indicated that they should probably head back to the house.

'Will you let me keep this, to keep working on it?'

'Of course.' Fen hesitated. 'May I... I mean, you will give it back to me, won't you?'

James smiled at her and, as they walked across the courtyard towards the kitchen door, rested a hand on the small of her back. 'Of course.'

'Ah, Fenella, can you chop that onion please?' Fen and James had barely stepped inside the warm kitchen before Sophie had asked her to help with the family's dinner. James had taken his leave before Sophie could scowl at him any more and headed towards the stairs. 'Always so furtive!' she had said, raising her eyebrows in a conspiratorial way to Fen, who was of the opinion that James had very good reason for avoiding Sophie. She was sitting at the head of the table, her leg perched up on a stool. Benoit was curled up on his mother's lap, playing with a piece of old string and a twig, and Jean-Jacques was writing in his tatty schoolbook. Fen felt a sudden pang of pity for Sophie and her children; husband and fatherless now, and no uncles either.

Husbandless... Fen wondered for a second if perhaps the sudden absence of a man about the house was rather convenient for Hubert, who may benefit from moving into the position of lord of the manor once Clément was dead. He could do a lot worse than marry back into the family and retake what he might view as his rightful place at the head of it.

And Estelle… she was obviously upset about Pascal, but were her tears, like Fen's were right at this moment from the chopped onion, not flowing due to sadness at all? Hadn't she been part of a troupe of travelling performers before she settled in Morey-Fontaine? Maybe she was a better actress than she had let on…

'Now put them in the pot and move on to the potatoes,' Sophie's voice carried across the table and Fen did as she was asked, but her mind was still on the possible murderers here in the house. So far, Hubert seemed to have the best motive; jealously of this branch of the family taking what he might see as his inheritance and perhaps greed enough to drive him to claim possession of the château. Could James even be tarred with the same brush? A lost soul of a soldier could do worse than kill his way to the top of a ready-made family. Fen shook the idea out of her head. Sophie would be the last person to accept an offer from James, and besides, it didn't seem like his style. Plus, there was something about his accent and demeanour, if not his scruffy clothes, that made Fen wonder if James could simply buy this château if he wanted to.

And Estelle, well perhaps she had been blackmailed by Pascal into helping him scam the Bernards, although why she would kill the priest and her employer, she couldn't fathom. Sophie had that clandestine meeting with Father Marchand the night before he died – a lovers' tryst or had they met for quite a different, and less loving, reason? But surely she was beyond suspicion, as her swollen ankle put her out of action for the time of all three deaths.

'And add the stock now,' Fen heard the instruction and brought her concentration back into the room.

'Yes, Sophie, like this?' She helped finish off making the vegetable soup and checked the prove on the freshly made bread rolls in the larder.

'They will only take twenty minutes or so,' said Sophie once the rolls were in the oven, 'why don't you go and find the others? I know no one has much of an appetite these days, but they must eat.'

Fen smiled at her and ducked out of the room. She was only halfway up the spiral stone staircase when she bumped into James. This time, it was him who put his finger up to his lips and beckoned her to follow him up the stairs, past the landing that led to her and Estelle's room and up to the top attic floor. He led her along the much smaller, lower-ceilinged corridor and Fen was about to remind him of the impropriety of them being seen together up here when he turned around and starting talking at her, thirteen to the dozen.

'I've had an idea, you see, how we can flush out the murderer. It should be relatively easy, but we'll have to work together.'

Fen opened and closed her mouth a couple of times and took Arthur's letter, which was being thrust at her while James was speaking.

'Here take this too, so Estelle doesn't think you've shopped her in. We can't have anyone suspecting what we're planning.'

'Which is?'

'A trap.'

The soup was bubbling away when Fen returned to the kitchen and she heaved it off the hotplate and onto the warm cast-iron surround. Sophie had managed somehow to cajole the children into laying the table, although Benoit was insisting his mother play with him, chasing him round the table. He was roundly shushed by his harried mother and told not to be so silly, as she leant down and massaged her swollen ankle.

'That still looks so painful,' Fen reached across and brought the water jug to the table and poured Sophie a glass.

'*Eh la*, it's getting there. If only hearts could mend as quickly as ankles.'

Fen looked at Sophie and nodded. 'If only, indeed.'

'I'm sorry you've come to us when there's so much…' Sophie sighed and couldn't complete her sentence, but Fen knew what she meant. This beautiful old château had the potential to be a wonderful home, a splendid place to come and stay, if only they could catch the killer in their midst. Fen was tempted to ask Sophie what it was like having the British agents lodging with her, and find out more about Arthur's last months, maybe even eke out a little more as to who might have betrayed him, but before she could speak, James came downstairs and Clément, Hubert and Estelle appeared and took their places around the table.

The conversation was muted, with Clément leading the meal with a grace, but not mentioning too much in the way of thanks to their Father in heaven.

'How is the harvest going, Hubert?' Sophie asked as she passed her bowl across to Fen, who was standing up and ladling out the hot soup.

'Despite it all, it's not too bad. Maybe not quite up to 1937, for the whites at least, but it's got potential.'

'And the wine press is fixed?'

'Yes, we are full steam ahead.'

Fen noticed that James was still quiet, waiting for the right time to lay his bait. She had been unsure of his idea about tempting the murderer to show themselves, but she had begrudgingly agreed that the only way to stop the gendarmes from pointing the finger at him would be to find out who had killed the others and, even better, catch them about to kill again. 'Then it will be irrefutable', he had said, and she'd had to agree. But even so, she was nervous as she waited for him to set the trap that would lead perhaps to another attempt at murder.

'And, James, we are glad to have you back.' Clément reached out an arm and clapped James on the back. 'From Boncourt-le-Bois and from prison! I knew you would not have killed our dear Marchand.'

Without wanting to make it seem too obvious, Fen turned towards Sophie, interested to see what her reaction would be. Unsurprisingly, her face was stony.

'It's good to be back,' James confirmed, before spooning some of the broth into his mouth.

'We'll be pressing the grapes from the eastern fields tomorrow, I'm glad you're here to put your back into that screw. Rather you than me.' Hubert seemed to be trying to lighten the mood, but Fen could see Sophie's face and it was like thunder.

'Why *did* they release you?' Sophie blurted out, ruining Hubert's best efforts at manly *bonhomie*. Her resentment towards having James back in her house must have been simmering away since his return. 'Are we all now expected to believe that you *lost* your capsule?'

'Sophie,' Clément chastised her.

'It's all right, sir.' James put down his spoon and looked across the table at his accuser. Fen was speechless. She thought James was going to try and lay some bait for the murderer, but he seemed to be back to defending himself. She stared at him as he continued. 'Father Coulber was able to secure my release.'

'On what grounds?' Sophie had a determination about her that Fen hadn't seen before. But then grief always did come in stages and Sophie may have been through sadness and denial and was now bordering on anger.

'Sophie...' Clément seemed keen to keep the peace, but James was ready to put up a defence.

'On the grounds that the cyanide capsule – lost, stolen or otherwise – was only circumstantial evidence and I have an alibi for the morning of the murder. I was here, with you all.'

'But cyanide can take hours to kill if administered in a small enough dose.' There was silence around the room. 'What?' Sophie questioned the eyes staring at her. 'I do have a chemistry degree, you know. Anyway, I was laid up in my bedroom all morning before Marchand came to breakfast, it couldn't have been me.'

'No one is suggesting that at all,' Clément again tried to keep the peace and calm his daughter-in-law down.

'I was with her too,' Estelle piped up. 'So I am in the clear. And none of you seem to care that I have also lost the love of my life!' She got up to leave, but Clément pleaded with her to stay and finish her supper.

'We have all lost loved ones. Please, let us at least eat together and try and heal these wounds. We are all we have left now.' He reached across and squeezed Sophie's arm and then looked at Estelle, the young boys and back to Estelle. 'Please?'

'Fine, fine.' The nursery maid sat down and silence once more took over the dinner table.

Fen felt awkward, sitting as a comparative newcomer in this room full of people who had been through years of occupation, war and hardship to now be faced with a killer in their midst. Not that she didn't have her own grief to dwell on, but she raised a silent prayer that this horrible situation would soon be over.

James broke the silence. 'I have an idea who might be responsible too. Father Coulber and I have been talking.' He kept his eyes down, looking into his bowl as he spoke.

'For all three deaths?' Fen asked him, knowing full well his trip to see Father Coulber had been utterly unfruitful in that respect.

'Please, not in front of the children,' Sophie said with a pleading look in her eye.

'Of course, I'm sorry,' Fen felt terrible, but couldn't deny how on edge she was with the atmosphere around the table being far from jolly and James about to walk right into the lion's den.

No one said anything for a few moments, then Estelle looked up from her soup bowl and levelled a demand at James. 'If you know who did the… *the things*, then why don't you tell us?'

'Shh, please,' pleaded Sophie, trying to distract Jean-Jacques with a chunk of bread spread thinly with what butter was left from the crumble making the day before. Benoit had already excused himself from the table and was playing on the floor by the stove with his twig.

'Father Coulber is in Beaune until the day after tomorrow; he's checking a few details out for me.'

'A few details of what?' Estelle, to Fen's mind, was looking as shifty as ever. Did the thief have an even guiltier conscience?

'Why get the priest involved now?' This time it was Hubert, and Fen could see James's annoyance brewing.

'Because—'

'Enough!' Clément interrupted James. 'That is quite enough. For goodness' sake, let us talk of grapes and wine. Hubert, are the tanks ready for the juice that will come from tomorrow's pressing?'

Much to Fen's relief, the conversation moved on and the supper was eaten between bouts of uncomfortable silences. Finally it was over and Fen cleared up the dishes as Clément helped Sophie to her feet and up the spiral stairs. The two little boys had run on before them, and the household all started to slowly prepare themselves for bed. Fen wondered, as she wiped the last of the water from the drying bowls, if James had been successful in routing the killer. One thing was for sure, he'd been successful in just about ruining everyone's evening, but had it been enough?

Once in bed, Fen took Arthur's letter out and read it over to herself. The light of the oil lamp on the bedside table glowed on the thin, almost translucent paper. *Arthur must have rushed this one off,* thought Fen as she identified the clues as not being his best work. Still, she rubbed her thumb gently over the ink and then kissed her fingertip and pressed it to the last of his words – *adieu*.

'You're not going to cry on me, are you?' Estelle, with her hair in a net, pulled her blanket up to her chin in the bed next to Fen.

'No. Goodnight, Estelle.' Fen wasn't sure if Estelle deserved any sort of niceties, not after what happened this afternoon, but her good manners always seemed to prevail, even with suspected murderers.

She turned the lamp off and let the bedsprings creak her into a comfortable position. Sleep came more easily than she would have expected after the upset of the day, but she awoke a few hours later to the sound of Estelle rustling around the room.

Luckily, Fen's wits were about her and as she became aware of what was happening, she realised she would have to stay absolutely still so that her bed didn't creak and alert Estelle to her waking. After a few moments, Fen's eyes adjusted to the dark and she dared to turn her head very slightly on her pillow, to get a better look at what Estelle was doing. To her surprise, and quite some relief, she was praying silently, going through her rosary, as she looked out of the window. Fen decided that Estelle seemed less murderous than yesterday, so let the bed announce the fact she was awake.

'Shhhh,' the Frenchwoman hissed, then beckoned Fen over to the window.

Fen sat up as quietly as she could and slipped out from under the blanket, aware now of how cold the nights were getting. She would have done anything to have had one of Mrs B's warm rubber bottles to nestle her feet against when she got back under the covers.

'What is it?' Fen had put thoughts of cosy Sussex farmhouses to one side and was now standing next to Estelle by the large, unshuttered window.

'There, do you see it?'

'What? Where are you looking?'

'There, you numbskull,' Estelle pointed to the far edge of the lawns, where the moonlight illuminated the grass.

Sure enough, Fen squinted and saw what Estelle was looking at. A white figure passing through the hedge, disappearing and appearing.

'It is a ghost, a phantom. I told you all that I had seen one last week, the night before—' Estelle broke off and crossed herself, gripping the rosary in her knuckles so tightly that Fen thought the thin rope would be crushed. 'It is a portent of doom, an omen!'

The Frenchwoman carried on saying almost-silent prayers and Fen, more intrigued than superstitious, squinted into the dark night to try and catch sight of the phantom. The moon passed behind a cloud and the whole garden was dipped into darkness once more.

'Come, Estelle, let's sleep. There's nothing we can do, standing guard up here.'

'I must check on the children.' She paused. 'First thing in the morning, perhaps.'

The two women climbed back into their own beds and Fen, wide awake now, wondered if the figure was indeed a phantom, and if that ghostlike shroud, so bright white in the moonlight, might have left a very real scrap of earthly fabric in the winery last week?

CHAPTER TWENTY-FOUR

Fen took extra care getting ready the next morning, as she wanted to make sure she kept all the little clues she had been gathering close to hand. After she'd put on her usual headscarf and a dash of lipstick, she stood back from the mirror and collected her thoughts, and her evidence, together.

In her right pocket, she had the two scraps of fabric. The one she knew came from the quilt, the other she highly suspected might be something to do with Estelle's moonlight phantom. She had Arthur's letter, partially decoded, in her central front pocket, along with her mother's brooch; she was pretty sure Estelle wouldn't make another attempt to steal it, but she wasn't going to take any chances. And, in her left pocket, she had the envelope containing the fragment of German writing, and also her word grid, which she'd updated to look like this:

```
                        G H O S T
            C Y A N I D E
            H           R E L I C
        Q U I L T       H
            R     E   F A B R I C
    T       C     T       N
    H       H     T
    I             E
O P E N D O O R
    F
```

```
                                F
                S C A L       L
            P A S C A L       O
                                W
            D R U G G E D      R
                                R
                        S H A R D S
```

Estelle had promised, before she left the room that morning to check on the boys, that she would return Arthur's cigarette case to Fen. As Fen had suspected, Estelle was using the winery's chemical cabinet as her stash. So, the women had arranged to meet at the winery directly after breakfast. From the sounds emanating from the nursery down the corridor, the boys were not only alive but very awake and very alert – sounds of wooden blocks being hurled at each other suggested to Fen that, omens or not, nothing seriously bad had visited the château in the night.

The winery was in full flow when Estelle and Fen got there shortly after breakfast.

Estelle raised her eyebrows to Hubert, who was monitoring the sluicing of juice into one of the barrels. Cries of '*whoa!*' and '*oop-la!*' peppered the air, creating a sense of busyness.

All hands on deck, Fen thought to herself, remembering how depleted the workforce was now, with many of the local workers seeking harvesting jobs in other vineyards until the Morey-Fontaine killer was apprehended. The workers who were left were too preoccupied to notice the pair of women heading into the fermentation room.

Fen stood behind Estelle as she placed the key in the lock of the chemical cabinet and clinked open the bolt. She opened the door and reached inside, fishing out the silver cigarette case and passing it to Fen, who did her best not to snatch it away and clasp it to her. She could so easily have spent the next few moments just taking in the sight of the precious object, but something Estelle was doing caught her attention.

'Four, five, six, seven… *Zut alors*,' she muttered, beginning counting again from one with a very purposeful finger tracing over the contents of the cabinet.

'What is it, Estelle?' Fen was intrigued. Was she counting money? She hadn't noticed much else in there when she'd found the cabinet open the other day.

Estelle ignored her question and kept counting, finally slamming the cabinet door shut and locking it.

'Estelle?' Fen repeated.

'There's not enough there…' Fen could sense the agitation in her voice.

'What do you mean?'

'Blue fining. No matter. I must have lost count. Anyway, you have your memento back. That is all now, yes?'

'Yes, thank you, Estelle.' Fen felt slightly defeated, *thanking* the thief who had stolen something precious from Arthur, but she couldn't help it, plus she was turning the name of that chemical over in her brain – *blue fining*, why did that ring a bell?

Pocketing the cigarette case, she followed Estelle out of the fermentation room and almost collided with Hubert.

'Sorry, I—'

'Watch where you're going, *tsk*.' He sucked his teeth in and dismissed Fen from the winery, suggesting she was better off doing 'women's work' back at the house. In no mood to argue with him, and all too delighted to be away from him, Fen headed back to the château's kitchen, where Sophie was more than pleased to make use of her.

'Take the ash out of the stove, then black the grate. After that, you can finish the washing and Estelle can take the boys out for a play and then help me with dinner.'

Fen had got on with all the tasks and was only distracted once by James calling her to one side as she hung up the boys' clothes on the washing line.

'*Psst.*'

'What?' The whispers were almost stage-like.

'I'm still alive.'

Fen rolled her eyes at James and threw a peg at him.

'I suppose I should say that I hope you stay that way…'

'Ha,' James laughed at her. 'But there is always tonight. The trap is set.'

'James, I am a bit worried about all of this.' Fen finished hanging a small shirt on the line and crossed her arms. 'I mean, how will you defend yourself if you're knocked unconscious or something?'

'Ah, so, I've thought of that. I'm afraid that's where you come in.'

'Me?'

'Yes, you've got to help me, be my eyes, as I'm pretty sure I'm going to have to do some West-End-worthy acting to lure the killer in.'

Fen stared at the Englishman and shook her head, not to say no, but to indicate her doubts over the plan. 'I can't see how I can be your shadow all evening, or all night, without it tipping off the suspicions of the killer. I mean, if you were thinking of doing someone in, seeing their bodyguard next to them might put you off.'

'Not sure I'd go as far as to say you look like a bodyguard.' James ducked as another peg flew through the air at him.

'You know what I mean.'

'Well, I should imagine we only have tonight to get through. I said Coulber would be here tomorrow and hinted that between us we knew who the killer is, so that gives us a narrow window of opportunity.'

'Or at least it gives the murderer one.' Fen thought for a bit and then said, 'When Arthur and I used to do our crosswords together, it was always the most satisfying bit when a clue fitted in with the letters you already had – so that if the answer was *murderer* and you already had the D and an R… Well, it was just very pleasing.'

'And this is relevant, how?'

'We have those letters, in the form of our clues. Look here,' Fen knelt down on the cobbles and turned the now empty wicker laundry basket over to create a rudimentary table. On it she placed the two pieces of fabric and the piece of paper with German writing on it. 'Hang on a tick!' She bade James stay where he was and ran off to where one of the old trees grew in the courtyard. Soon enough, she was back and crouching by the upturned basket again. 'This twig can represent the bayonet that I found out here in the courtyard.'

'Right, I see.' James leant back and rubbed his chin. 'Pop two of those clothes pegs on, Fen, they can represent the candlesticks stuck in the wine press.'

'Will do,' Fen reached behind her and did as James asked. 'Plus, there's this little ceramic bowl that I found in the vineyard. I don't know if it means anything, but, well, here it is.' She added the shards to the collection. They both looked down at the ragtag bunch of items on the upturned bottom of the basket. 'So, who matches all these clues?'

They both considered the objects. James was the first to speak. 'Well, the fabric suggests to me that it's one of the ladies of the house.'

'Ah, but I've already rather sneakily checked Estelle's aprons and they're all present and correct. And Sophie doesn't seem to wear white like this, not that I've seen anyway.'

'Fair enough. Next we have the bayonet.'

'Clément's, by his own admission.'

'And the candlesticks?'

'Well, obviously the church's, and it could explain why Father Marchand was killed? Maybe he knew who had stolen them,' Fen voiced the theory. 'And you're the one who told me to "look to the church" when you were arrested. I forgot to ask what you meant by that.'

'I don't know really. I just have a feeling Marchand knew more about what might have gone on during the occupation. I can't shake it, but I think he was killed to stop someone being exposed.'

'A thief? Surely a thief would be fairly secure in hoping they would be forgiven, asked to say a few Hail Marys and then set free. I don't think stealing from the church should be a motive to murder the priest.'

'No, but collaborating with the Germans is now a capital offence.' James held his finger up and then looked around him. His eyes alighted on a squashed daisy among the grasses and he added it to the basket table. 'The dead flowers. Thrown towards the mourners at Pierre's funeral. And maybe something to do with whoever has been corresponding in German.' He pointed to the letter signed by the mysterious S.

'Estelle told me about this. Flowers, I mean, they're a symbol, a sort of code. Wearing the *Tricolore*, albeit in the colours of your clothes, was a sign of resistance. And women would give red, white and blue flowers, or receive them, to make a sort of point.'

'So someone could have been suggesting that one of the mourn-ers at that funeral was, what? A dead patriot? A terrible gardener?' James paused in case another peg came his way, but Fen was lost in concentration. He continued on a more serious note: 'Not exactly a damning piece of evidence, is it, when you think of it. Dead flowers on a warm autumn day, at a funeral.'

'No,' Fen agreed. Then a thought occurred to her. 'Something else Estelle told me is that one of the chemicals used in the winery – and I presume one that she used to steal to return to Pascal – is blue fining.'

James looked at her sternly. 'Blimey. Why didn't you tell me? How long have you known that?'

'Only since this morning, when Estelle took me to her stash of stolen trinkets in the chemical cupboard. And it's annoying me, as I know I've heard of it somewhere before…'

'It's another form of cyanide.'

'What?' Fen looked up at James. Suddenly the collection of clues looked no more serious than a children's game, not now they had concrete proof that there was cyanide in the winery. Then it came to her. 'Of course, Pascal had a leaflet on poisonous gases from the last war. We talked about Prussic acid, which was hydrogen cyanide.'

'Well, blue fining isn't quite that bad, it's a different compound. And this doesn't help us narrow it down; Estelle, Sophie and Hubert, probably even Clément, could all access that cupboard.'

'At least it makes the discovery of your capsule very circumstantial.'

James took in a deep breath and let out an audible sigh. 'Yes, at least there's that. Tell you what though, Arthur was right: it will be damn satisfying when we fit it all together!'

'Until then, we need to disable you in some way. Some public way, in readiness for tonight.'

'I don't much fancy a cosh to the head...'

'And I don't fancy being hauled in front of the beak for doing it to you either. No, I was thinking more subtle than that. You see, rather than me stand bodyguard over you all night, you need to be the one who's alert and awake, but without the murderer knowing. If you're sure that the murderer will act tonight, then I have an idea...'

Dinner that night was a sombre affair. Everyone seemed to have a bone to pick with someone else. Sophie was upset that James had trodden mud into the floor and had still obviously not given up on her initial accusation that he had killed Marchand. Hubert was cross that the juice pressing had taken longer than it should and kept asking James where he had been. Fen knew he'd snuck back to the house to talk to her but had to reassure Estelle and

Sophie that she'd been working all afternoon. It was only Clément who praised his daughter-in-law and Estelle for the food they had managed to rustle up, including another fruit crumble, this time using a windfall of plums from the trees by the church.

'I think Jean-Jacques and Benoit deserve our thanks tonight for dodging the wasps and bees to save us these delicious fruits.' Their grandfather smiled at them and the boys glowed with the praise.

'And thank you to Fen for teaching me the recipe,' Sophie generously credited her, before turning back to wipe some mushed fruit off her younger son's face.

'I think I've sprained a muscle,' James chipped in, changing the direction of the conversation.

Fen knew this was her prompt. 'Will it hurt you all night? Will you be able to sleep?'

'I'm not sure. The mattress is hard enough at the best of times.'

'Well, forgive me for not providing you with goose down and silk!' Sophie interrupted, obviously taking James's criticism personally.

Fen rescued the situation. 'James, two birds and all that, why don't you take one of my sleeping draughts? It'll knock you right out until morning.'

'Do you mind? I'd appreciate that, thank you.' James set about his fruit with gusto, and Fen wondered where on earth he'd learnt such hammy acting. Still, the stage was set and someone else around that table had been given their cue.

CHAPTER TWENTY-FIVE

By the time the church bell had clanked its way through ten chimes, the château was in silence and Fen lay in bed concentrating on trying to hear anything beyond her own breath. She could make out the light scratch of the woollen blanket catch slightly on the rough wood of the bed, but beyond that; nothing.

She had gone to bed that night having made a show of giving James one of her sleeping draughts. She'd given him one of the sachets in the kitchen, having run up to her room to fetch it, and he'd poured a glass of water from the large jug by the sink. He hadn't drunk it there and then so they'd made a small commotion on the first-floor landing, so that everyone knew he had taken it. What he'd actually done was throw the contents of his glass out of one of the tower's windows and substituted his drugged water with Fen's. She quickly replaced hers with water from the bathroom.

That had been a few hours ago and Fen lay now, wide awake with adrenalin coursing through her body – she felt like a stoat or ferret, trying not to twitch as the fox circles.

Then she heard it. The faintest of noises from the bed next to her. Estelle was stirring and slowly getting out of bed. Fen lay still, scared to even open her eyes in case some moonbeam escaped through the shuttered windows and showed her up. Instead she pretended to sleep and monitored Estelle's movements with her ears alone. She was dressing, or so it sounded, as she was opening and closing her drawers and the large armoire doors. Then the unmistakable sound of the doorknob turning, its heavy click as the catch slid away from its surround and into the door.

Fen counted to ten, slowly, trying to calm her breaths as well as give Estelle time to get along the corridor before she tailed her.

Eight... nine... ten... Fen breathed out and slowly raised herself up and out from under her blankets, careful not to let the bedsprings announce her movement too much to the world. She decided against putting any socks on, surmising she'd be more sure-footed and agile without, but she paused to pull her navy wool jumper on over her nightgown. She didn't want to look like a ghost wandering about the château, but without pulling on trousers, she'd have to hope that the jumper would camouflage her enough against the dark of the night.

As Fen skirted along the edge of the landing, a clock somewhere in the house chimed the hour, only a few minutes behind the church bell. It stopped as she got to the stone spiral stairs and tiptoed up them to the top floor of bedrooms, where she now expected to see Estelle trying to kill James.

Much to her shock, there was no sign of Estelle at all and James's door was still very much closed. Fen reached it and bent down, pressing her ear against the wood to try and hear something. There was nothing at all coming from the inside of the room. In a sudden panic, fearing she was too late and James had fallen prey to his own trap, Fen pushed open the door into the room.

It was pitch black in there and Fen, with no prior knowledge at all of how the room was laid out, was blinder than a mole in a hole. She closed the door behind her and walked forward, but in so doing sprung what appeared to be a tripwire and a tinkling bell was now ringing over James's bed. Fen yelped as a force was thrust against her, pinning her to the wall. A torch light was suddenly shone in her face.

'You!' James said, but not letting her go at all. 'I thought I could trust you?'

'It's not me, you idiot!' Fen flustered, pulling at the strong arm that had her pinned against the wall, closing the air off at her throat. 'Stop, get off! It's Estelle!'

'What?' James pulled away.

Fen appeared to deflate as she collapsed slightly against the wall. 'I was following Estelle. I thought I was too late, I…' Fen couldn't help it, but tears sprang to her eyes. Tears of frustration that she'd ruined the trap so carefully set and so hastily ruined, by her.

'I've not seen her.' James held out a hand to Fen and helped her stand upright. 'There's not been a soul here all night.'

'Where has she gone then? I thought I heard her dressing.'

'Doesn't take an overcoat to slip upstairs and kill someone.'

'I suppose so. Oh James, I'm so sorry, I've ruined everything.'

'Shhh. Hear that?'

They both stood motionless and James turned his torch off but not before illuminating the bed quickly to show Fen that he'd actually made a dummy out of straw and sacking, to look like he was still fast asleep.

Quietly they stood and, once again, Fen did all she could to control her breathing. Her eyes became accustomed to the darkness, there was enough moonlight coming in through the gaps in the shutters for her to vaguely make out solid objects, like the bed with its dummy in it. Then there it was, the click of the handle and the slow opening of the door, which by pure luck now, both Fen and James were hiding behind.

A ghostlike figure, its whiteness almost glowing in the barest of moonbeams, moved across the room towards the bed. The faux James was obviously doing its job and this new intruder didn't actually touch the supposedly somnolent body. Instead the figure leant over the glass of water that sat on the bedside cabinet and gently stirred in a powder.

As the figure turned towards them, James flicked on the torch and shone the beam directly at the intruder. The blinking, scowling face looking back at them was that of Sophie Bernard.

CHAPTER TWENTY-SIX

'Get out of my way!' Sophie screamed as she tried to push past James and out of the room.

'Not so fast, madame!' He grasped her by the shoulders and pushed her down onto the bed, where she sat awkwardly with the scarecrow James underneath her.

'What were you doing?' demanded Fen, who felt useless without any sort of weapon, so instead used the light from the torch to find the oil lamp and matches and lit it so that she and James could clearly see that it was their landlady and employer who was caught in their trap.

'What's going on here?' A sleepy Hubert appeared at the door, wiping the sleep from his eyes with his big, farmer's hands.

'We've caught the murderer, Hubert,' James confidently told him, but before he could answer, Hubert was being begged and pleaded with by Sophie.

'Oh Hubert, Hubert, it is not me, it is them! It is these English ghouls who have come into our home and our family and destroyed everyone we love. They have set me up, they are plotting to kill me!' The words spilled out of her like a gush of wine from a barrel.

'Calm down, Sophie, I am still half asleep.'

'Then wake up to this!' she screeched, and launched herself at him.

In the nick of time, Fen saw the flash of steel as Clément's old bayonet caught the light of the oil lamp. Reacting as fast as she could, she launched herself at Sophie and caught her off balance so that they both crashed against the thin plaster wall of the bedroom.

The shock woke Hubert up properly, realising that he had just been saved from a nasty injury.

Fen felt dazed and the only thought going through her head was *Where is that blade?*

Suddenly she felt it, the thin steel tip pressing into her side as Sophie stood above her, about to thrust the long, sharp bayonet into Fen.

'No!' roared James, who dropped his torch and bore down on the woman, now revealed beyond doubt to be the murderer. He pulled her off Fen just as the blade was easing itself through the thick blue wool of her hand-knitted jumper.

Thank you, Mrs B, Fen sent a little prayer Sussex-ward, grateful as she thought of Mrs B sitting in her armchair knitting in that dear farmhouse.

'Are you hurt, mademoiselle?' Hubert was kneeling next to her as James pinned down Sophie on the bed.

'Yes,' Fen gingerly probed where the bayonet had begun to penetrate her skin. 'But it's not too bad I think. It doesn't smart as much as falling in a ditch, so I'm all right.'

'*D'accord*, I'm sorry, I'm sorry.' Fen let Hubert whisper his apology, finally, and pull her upright and she sat, knees up to her chest, back resting against the wall as another person appeared at the door.

'What's this commotion?' The booming voice of the patriarch, Clément Bernard accompanied him into the room. 'James? Hubert? Explain yourselves.'

'Dear Papa, help me!' Sophie started the pleading again, but in unison James, Hubert and Fen all said, 'Oh shut up.'

'I laid a trap,' James started the explanation, still pinning down the scowling Sophie. 'I said very publicly that I was due to see Father Coulber tomorrow and discuss the murders and, thanks to Fen, I let everyone believe that I would be drugged up to my eyeballs tonight, dead to the world, if you will.'

'What's that got to do with Sophie?'

Fen could tell that Clément wasn't at all happy with the fact that his daughter-in-law was tied up in this.

'We've just caught Sophie in the act, trying to poison me.'

'And if that wasn't enough,' chipped in Hubert, 'she then tried to stab me, and managed to hurt Fenella.'

Clément was looking more and more bemused. 'She is unarmed now, yes?'

'Yes.'

'Well, get off her, man, and let's all talk about this downstairs. I can't have the boys and Estelle hearing all this going on. Come on.'

'That's a good point, where is Estelle?' Fen let Hubert help her downstairs as James held Sophie by the wrists and they all walked down the stone spiral staircase into the kitchen.

With the dying embers of the fire stoked, the four adults sat around the large table and glared at each other.

Clément started speaking first. 'So explain to me again how Sophie came to be in your bedroom, James.'

'It's nothing like that, sir,' James started and Fen almost wanted to laugh, the thought that this could be something so simple as discovering a secret love affair was light relief indeed. 'For a few days now, Fen and I have been trying to work out who committed the three murders...' He paused, catching Clément's puzzled expression. 'Yes, three. I'm afraid that I agree with Fen in believing that your son's death was not an accident.'

'You see, I've been finding some very odd clues,' Fen carried on. 'And as you've probably all guessed, I've been on a bit of a secret mission here – to find out what happened to Arthur.'

'He was a good man,' Clément said. 'And betrayed by someone, indeed.'

'Well, I believe that, like a good crossword, all the clues are connected, and that what's happened here in the last few days very possibly has something to do with what happened to Arthur and your sons,' Fen paused for them to make the sign of the cross, 'and that their deaths also played a role in the fates of Father Marchand, Pierre and Pascal Desmarais.'

'Go on?'

'So I looked at it like I would a crossword, and when I couldn't work out my ten across, I tried to solve my six down.'

'What is she talking about?' Clément looked at Hubert, who replied with a shrug.

'Carry on, Fen.' James made eyes at the two Frenchmen, but Clément nodded and Fen kept on talking.

'So we had no idea who murdered Father Marchand. Except, when Pierre was murdered, we knew it couldn't be James, so he's out of the soup.'

'The what?' Sophie looked scornfully at Fen and then said to the room, 'She makes no sense and you're keeping me here in my nightdress, freezing cold, on this crazy Englishwoman's theories? Come on, Clément, tell them to let me go!'

'*Shh*, Sophie. Let her finish.'

'*Bof!*' Sophie flung her now bound wrists up in the air in frustration.

'So I started to look at things differently. Find some clues. And I found some all right.' Fen rummaged around in one of the copious sleeves of her land girl jumper and pulled out her clues. She laid the pieces of fabric on the table. 'This,' she picked up the white piece, 'I found hanging from the rusty hinge of the chemical cupboard in the winery. I think,' she leant over to where Sophie's arms were resting on the table, and matched the fabric to that of her nightdress, 'this might be yours, Sophie.'

The men all gasped as the piece exactly matched a small hole in the sleeve of Sophie's nightdress.

'I am in charge of the chemicals, what of it?' Sophie shrugged off the accusation.

'Yes, you are. And that's because you have a degree in chemistry from Paris,' Fen continued, undeterred.

'And?'

'*And* I found out that one of the most poisonous chemicals that you keep locked in that cupboard is blue fining – or potassium ferrocyanide, to give it its full name.'

'It's used, in extreme situations, to stabilise the wine,' Hubert volunteered.

'And it would take someone with a background in chemistry to know how to turn the ferrocyanide into common or garden cyanide, yes?' Fen asked him, as much for the benefit of the others as for herself.

'Yes, I suppose it would.'

'Of course, we all thought Father Marchand was killed with James's kill pill from his agent's kit. But, actually, I believe Sophie stole the capsule and destroyed it, using her own cyanide to kill Father Marchand.'

'Why not use my capsule, if she stole it?' James looked genuinely puzzled.

'Because I didn't steal it!' The others turned to look at Sophie. She carried on, 'I am not a thief.'

'So Estelle had stolen it…' Fen wondered out loud. 'The little tin I found down the side of the bed…'

'Did it have a black cat on it?' James asked.

'Yes… maybe…'

'Well, that clears that up then. Estelle must have decided it might have been of some use. Perhaps Pascal told her what it was and disposed of the poison, but she kept it as a useful bargaining tool.'

'Or blackmail. And it was pretty useful for her – getting you banged up for the murder distracted everyone from her thieving too. I wouldn't wonder if she dropped the capsule right in front of your nose, Sophie.'

'Pah!' Sophie butted in. 'I am not a thief, and apart from some hypotheses about my skill with chemicals, you cannot prove I'm a murderer either!'

'Except I found these…' Fen pushed the shards of porcelain across the large old wooden table and placed them into the rough shape of the crucible they had once been. 'A chemist's crucible. Used to heat the ferrocyanide and produce the deadly poison. And don't forget, we all thought Sophie was an invalid, as she had apparently twisted her ankle.'

'Which meant she couldn't have possibly killed Pierre or Pascal. Or even Marchand,' James concluded.

'Or so we thought. Odd how you seem as agile as a mountain goat tonight though, Sophie?'

'It is healing now, I think.' Sophie pouted.

'Hell's teeth, woman!' James thumped his fist on the table and even Fen was astounded by Sophie's ability to keep lying.

'The dead bees that kept appearing in the kitchen – it was you,' Fen thought out loud. 'Stinging yourself to keep the swelling up. I knew it rang a bell. My friend Edith was stung by a bee once and although the swelling on her wrist was immense, she could still use it quite well as she curled her hair later that day.' Fen mimicked twirling her hair with a rotating wrist action. 'So you can quite easily have the look of a painful swelling while gadding about quite quickly.'

'Maybe I was stung too,' Sophie replied.

'*Shhh,*' said everyone else.

'So when Pascal figured out, long before we did, that you had killed Pierre and Marchand…'

'How did he do that?'

Fen thought for a moment. 'I followed Estelle to the pharmacy the other day and I asked a few questions. Pascal and I talked about Sophie and her education. And I asked him about cyanide too. *He* must have put two and two together and then realised she was using the ferrocyanide.'

'*Bof*,' Sophie exhaled in a Gallic show of contempt.

'Something caught my eye in an old leaflet Pascal had from the Great War. Poison gases.' Fen was very aware that all the eyes in the room were focused on her now. She took a deep breath. 'Hydrogen cyanide was used in 1916 apparently, but only briefly as it takes too long to, well, kill unless it's used in vast quantities.' She paused and noticed how Clément's eyes were tearing up. He had served in the Great War and it seemed he must have remembered it well. 'I think that a small quantity wouldn't be an instantly fatal dose. Instead it brings on nausea and dizziness for a few hours before the fatal effects take hold.'

'So you're saying that Marchand wasn't poisoned at the breakfast table?' James was quick to catch on to Fen's theory.

'Exactly.'

Before the news could sink in, there was a clatter outside the door and it was flung open, with a dishevelled Estelle suddenly appearing at the door.

'Estelle, help me please!' Sophie was quick to try, but Clément stood up and glared at her, then demanded to know of Estelle where she'd been at this time of night.

'The winery.' She pulled the door closed behind her.

'Why, Estelle?' Hubert asked.

'I needed to check something. The really bad one, the poisonous one, it was gone, you see. I noticed it this morning but was distracted.' She glared at Fen, as if returning Arthur's cigarette case to her had been the root of all of their problems. She sat down at the table and only then seemed to notice Sophie's bound wrists and look of utter fury. 'What's happening here?'

'Fenella is spinning wild stories,' Sophie spat across the table, but Clément banged his fist on the table and all but snarled at his daughter-in-law.

In the heavy silence that followed, Fen pieced together more of her thoughts before carrying on. 'The kitchen door, and your phantom, Estelle...'

'I was brave tonight, yes, going out even though we know the gardens are haunted!' The housekeeper crossed herself. 'You saw it yourself, Fen!'

'I think you were safe tonight,' Fen reassured her, 'as the phantom was here all the time. The night before Marchand was poisoned, you said, did you not, that you couldn't sleep and you'd seen a ghost walk along the vineyard's edge?'

The maid nodded, in wide-eyed anticipation of an explanation.

'Sophie was that ghost, heading to the chemical cabinet in the winery dressed only in her nightgown, where she tore her sleeve on the metal hinge.' Fen picked up the piece of white fabric from the table and then, once everyone had noted it, laid it back down next to the broken crucible. 'I think she stashed her home-made cyanide there too. It was she who left the kitchen door unbolted as she'd walked to the priest's house across the lawns that night and slipped him some poison.'

'How would I know the priest would drink it?' Sophie asked indignantly.

'I never said he drank it...' Fen pushed her point home and all the others round the table turned to face Sophie, their eyes like Spanish Inquisition pokers, bearing into her.

'Ha! Fine. Yes.' Sophie slammed her bound fists down on the table. 'He was onto me. I had to kill him!'

'Ah...' Another realisation came to Fen. 'The night of the fête, I saw you and Father Marchand leave the church, although I thought perhaps you were having a tryst of some sort, but actually he was—'

'About to ruin everything, all my plans!'

Clément, who looked like the world was crumbling around him, turned to face Sophie. In a voice weakened with emotion, he simply asked, 'Sophie, what have you done?'

CHAPTER TWENTY-SEVEN

The night wore on and between them the whys and hows of Sophie's murderous path were laid out to all. Fen explained how the first murder had taken place, in effect, the night before, with Sophie administering just enough cyanide into the glass of water beside the bed of the sleeping priest so that he would die at some point during the next day.

'That it was during breakfast was a bonus,' James added, 'as Sophie was already laid up by then, with so many witnesses.'

'I think Sophie *had* slightly hurt herself,' Fen allowed Sophie that one small grace, 'during her dramatic and very public fall, but the bee stings kept the swelling nicely puffy so we all absolutely believed she couldn't move, let alone run.'

'Marchand was on our side though, wasn't he?' a slightly confused Clément brought the conversation back to the priest's death.

'Yours and mine,' James agreed, 'but perhaps not hers.' He nodded towards Sophie.

'Exactly,' Fen said, and started to think out loud. 'Marchand had his finger in all sorts of secret agent pies, as it were. He knew all about Arthur, and you, James. Plus he grew the flowers in the Tricolore colours… I think he had a pretty good grasp as to what Sophie was planning all along and threatened to out you, didn't he?'

'Well, what was she planning?' an exasperated Estelle blurted out. Then she turned to address Sophie. 'Why did you kill Pascal? To keep me here? Slaving for you?'

'Don't get hysterical, Estelle,' Sophie sighed.

'No.' Fen laid a hand on her room-mate's arm. The most she felt could do at the moment to comfort her was to explain how and why her lover was killed. 'To solve Pascal's murder, we have to go back to Pierre's.'

'My poor son.' The now openly weeping Clément was being comforted by Hubert.

'Pierre was drugged and left to sleep next to the fermentation tanks.'

'How was he drugged?' James was fiddling with the clues on the table.

'A sleeping draught at breakfast?' Fen ventured.

'It was much easier than that,' Sophie spat out the words, and looked around the table, her eyes inviting suggestions from anyone else. 'No? I followed Pierre to the winery. Fool, he was shocked to see me up and about, but pleased too. Didn't question it. I limped a bit, of course, just to keep the act up in case anyone saw. Then I insisted that he have some coffee and I was all "oh darling, this harvest will be the best and you need coffee to concentrate", and he drank it. Fool!'

There was a mixed look of horror and disgust on every face but Sophie's as they took in how easily she had duped her husband, and quite how unrepentant she was.

She continued, revelling in her cleverness. 'And then, once he was drowsy, I said, "Lie down here" – and like a stupid baby, he did.'

Clément buried his face in his hands, while most round the table simply shook their heads in disgust and sorrow.

'You'd brought the quilt with you?' James asked. 'But not for him to lie on?'

'No.' Sophie flashed her eyes at him. 'No... I had left that outside, though if he'd seen it I would have said that I was feeling frisky, you know?' The looks of disgust amplified around the table. '*Eh, la*, once he was asleep, I fitted the quilt up and bolted the door behind me. He was dead within the hour. Before any of you had even had your breakfast.' She laughed to herself, seemingly oblivious to the pain she was causing to her father-in-law, who was now murmuring 'my poor boy, my poor boy,' over and over.

'Why did you want to kill Pierre though?' Hubert asked quietly, his arm still around the grieving Clément.

'Because,' Sophie's voice was low and almost unrecognisable, 'I did not love him. Not for years. Not since I found my true love again.'

'The letter written in German!' Fen exclaimed. She pulled it out from her nightdress's pocket and opened the envelope. 'You *are* the S.'

'What does this mean?' Clément was shaking with anger and Hubert was doing all he could to keep his arm around the old man, now in restraint as much as comfort.

Sophie sighed. 'Heinrich Spatz…'

'The Weinführer?' Fen was aghast.

'Yes. The Weinführer. When he arrived in this town, I couldn't believe my eyes. My Heinrich! I thought I'd never see him again. We'd been lovers, you see, when we both studied at the Sorbonne. And he was so civilised.' Sophie, though bound and captured, had a dreamy, faraway look in her eye. She continued, 'He was a wine merchant before the war. He wanted to commandeer this château, but I knew we couldn't carry on our affair in front of all the workers, and you,' she nodded to Clément and Hubert.

The old man made to lunge at his daughter-in-law, but the fight seemed to have gone out of him and he sank back into his chair, exhausted, as Sophie continued.

'Heinrich and I stayed in touch after the liberation of Dijon in forty-four. He had to retreat with the army but was biding his time, waiting for us to be together again. When old memories had died…' she spat the words across the table to Clément.

'You did help the château hide its wine though.' Fen nodded towards the journal sitting on the shelf of the dresser.

'But of course I hid the wine from the Germans, I did not want our wine to go to the Eagle's Nest to be wasted on some puff-chested little man from Austria. I wanted it safe, here in the château, for when my Heinrich returned and we could run the business together!'

'The quilt is German, isn't it?'

'Yes. A present from Westphalia.'

'And Benoit is…'

'German too,' Sophie admitted, almost triumphantly. 'Well, half German. He has his father's hair.' She chuckled as if she was merely telling fellow mothers of her angelic little boy.

'But you still haven't answered me!' Estelle was fuming, staring boar-like at her employer. 'Why kill my Pascal?'

'Like she said,' Sophie nodded towards Fen, 'he had found me out. He wrote me a note, the one *you* delivered to me the other day.'

'I did…' Estelle couldn't finish speaking. She closed her eyes and covered them with one hand as she took in the consequences of what she had done, however unwittingly.

Sophie continued, 'He threatened to tell Clément and the police. So he had to die.'

'And you used your ankle as your alibi again,' Fen confirmed everyone's suspicions. 'You pretended to go to your cousin's for fruit…' Fen paused and looked to the ceiling for inspiration. 'Ah, yes, I thought the basket seemed heavy, even before you had collected any fruit. You had the bayonet in it.'

'Easily taken from Clément's unlocked memorabilia cabinet in the library. And when you left me in the square, I waited until you were gone and doubled back to the vineyards. I'd sent a message to Pascal to meet me there, you see. Silly oaf thought I would pay for his silence. Well, I paid all right, but with steel, not gold!' Sophie almost seemed to be enjoying herself, but a frown was still firmly set on Fen's forehead.

'You gave him seven inches of bayonet blade.'

'And hoped the wild boar might hide the cause of death, but there you go, he was found too soon for that.'

'You disgust me!' Estelle snarled at Sophie.

'Ha, I disgust *you*? The thief who was stealing from me? It was self-defence! I was protecting my assets from you thieves! Candlesticks hidden in the wine press – come on, Estelle, what sort of amateur are you?'

Estelle blushed, though it was hard to see through the puce of her anger. 'So what if we stole from the church? It had already lost its relic and its priest, who would miss a couple of candlesticks? But that silver would pay for a new life for me and Pascal.'

'Pascal was no better than a pillaging privateer, and he got what was coming to him.'

'As will you, Madame Bernard.' James stood up and went towards the door. Fen had also heard the sounds of engines in the courtyard.

'Who called the police?' Sophie suddenly seemed afraid.

'I did,' whispered Estelle, who was still fuelled by her fury. 'When I realised the blue fining packets didn't add up.'

'Then you have as much to fear as I do, Estelle,' Sophie started to bargain with her maid. 'Back me up to the police, tell them I've been set up and I'll say you didn't steal—'

'It's too late for that now.' James placed a hand on Estelle's shoulder. 'Father Coulber will understand when we tell him and will forgive Estelle.'

The gendarmes flooded the kitchen of the château as they had done a few days before, but this time it was Sophie Bernard who was shackled and led towards the door.

'One moment, please,' Fen called out as they were about to lead the murderess away. The column of policemen, with the nightdress-clad Sophie cuffed between them, stopped and she turned to face Fen. 'Before you take her away, can I ask one more thing?'

The most senior gendarme nodded at Fen.

'Sophie, did you betray Arthur?'

There was a moment's silence. 'Yes.'

'Why?'

Sophie thought for a moment. 'His mission was to sabotage the Germans. I had no trouble with that, as I said, I had no love for the occupiers in general, just my Heinrich. But Heinrich was being pressured by his superiors. With not much in the way of wine flowing back to high command, thanks to my own bloody husband and father-in-law, he had to show them he could deliver in other ways. When Herr Hitler decided he wanted the True Cross, it was easy for me to get it for them.'

'Except you didn't.' James was standing behind Fen. She could feel the solidity of his body and was grateful for it. Without him there, she felt like she might crumble to the ground.

'What?' Sophie tugged against the uncomfortable handcuffs and looked genuinely annoyed.

'Arthur made sure that you'd found the wrong relic, up there,' he pointed to the chimney breast and the loose stone. 'We don't know where the real one is, not yet, but he did save the relic for the town.'

'You betrayed him for… for nothing.' Fen was determined not to cry.

Sophie scowled as she was pushed through the open door of the kitchen and out into the hall and from there to the solitary police van.

'Her fate will be a bad one. To be a *collaborateur horizontale*, not to mention a murderer.' The voice was Hubert's; he remained seated at the table, resting his arm around Clément's back.

'She is a disgrace to us,' the old man could barely get the words out.

Fen looked over to them. 'Hubert, was it you who…?'

'I found the letter from Spatz, yes.' Hubert anticipated Fen's question. 'I found a stash of letters, mostly burnt or ripped up, in the house that he had commandeered. It was my family home, and Sophie had pleaded with me to let Spatz have it instead of the château. How could I refuse Madame Bernard? She was then only a young woman with a young child, and me, one of the family supposedly. She suggested I move into the château if Spatz had my house. And to my shame, the lure of being able to call this place home, finally, appealed. Even if I was only given a room up in the attic with the Englishmen!'

'Why didn't you tell the others about the letters?'

'The S was only a hunch. Who else would believe me? Everyone loves Sophie.'

'She had asked that I sign the estate over to her and her sons…' Clément's muffled voice, his mouth hidden in the crook of his arm as his head lay on the table, confirmed all of their suspicions about Sophie's motives.

'And I think you would have done, you old fool,' Hubert continued. 'James is too much of a man of action, he wouldn't have known what to do with the letter, and Estelle, well, I knew Pascal called her Ess, but I didn't know if she was trustworthy, if you will allow it.'

Estelle frowned at him but let the accusation lie.

Fen made a mental tally of all the clues she'd collected: the pieces of fabric were now explained, as were the shards of porcelain. The phantom had been unmasked and the thief exposed. One more thing niggled at her. 'Can anyone explain the dead flowers at the funeral?'

James, Hubert, Clément and Estelle all shook their heads.

'Just dead flowers then, I suppose,' said Fen.

'Maybe,' James chipped in. 'Although they do tally with when Father Coulber and I turned up. He had been Marchand's mentor and a lynchpin in the local Resistance group too. Perhaps Marchand had shared his suspicions about Sophie with him.'

'So he was in the Resistance too?' asked Clément.

'Yes, though he ran the groups out of Beaune mostly. He made sure only a few of us knew of his connection, but luckily the Chief of Police was one of them. I didn't want to say this too openly the other day, but it was when Coulber explained to the policeman that I would never have killed Marchand because of our links, well, luckily I was freed.'

Fen smiled at him. 'And there's me thinking it was my taunts about the Vichy government…'

CHAPTER TWENTY-EIGHT

The noise of Sophie's arrest had unsettled the young boys, so Estelle had bowed to duty and gone upstairs to calm them down and help them drift back off to sleep. In the commotion of events, Fen hadn't noticed where James, Clément and Hubert had gone. She walked over to one of the large windows, but it was deepest black outside. The church bell managed to get to eleven strokes, so Fen assumed it was eleven o'clock and not just that the bell had finally given up the ghost.

Ghost…

There it was again, a light glowing on the horizon, a will-o'-the-wisp hovering in the dark, flickering here and there…

Fen blinked and peered further into the darkness. For a moment she was confused. *Sophie had been the ghost, surely?*

'That's no ghost,' she said, looking around for a taper to light a spare oil lamp with, then went to find her coat and boots in the hallway.

She shivered as the fresh air enveloped her but kept her lantern raised up high. She had last seen the flickering light disappear behind the fruit trees by the church, so she headed down the terrace steps and walked briskly across the once formal lawns. There it was again, the light, sweeping the ground this time as if searching for something. Fen felt exposed and crouched, turning down her oil lamp as low as it would go and hiding it, rather dangerously, within her coat.

She kept focused on the light up ahead and watched as it did one final sweep and then disappeared. Quickly, she trotted over to where she thought she'd last seen it shine and turned the oil lamp up to as bright as it could go. To her absolute surprise, she noticed that a paving slab, for she had come through the trees now to the courtyard around the church, was jemmied out of its natural position and lying awkwardly on the ground, revealing below it a steep staircase down to even darker depths.

'What would Arthur do…?' Fen mused, and then answered the question herself as she stepped down onto the first tread of the steps.

She caught sight of the light, and once more lowered her own flame until its glow barely showed her where to put one foot in front of the other, but no matter, the ground seemed firm underfoot. All of a sudden, the light disappeared, most likely around a corner. Fen stopped. Voices carried over the air towards her and she realised that the torch must have belonged to Clément, who was the last to join whoever else was down there. She paused, not wanting her footsteps to give her away, now Clément had stopped walking too.

She listened intently. That other voice… *who was it?*

'Brick by brick, Clément, like how we made it.'

'We had more hands then. Thierry and Jacques were here too.' Another voice, 'Two good men.'

So there were three of them down there; Clément, James and Hubert, of course.

Fen crept along the corridor, feeling her way via her fingertips that brushed the cold stone. The voices were soon camouflaged by the sound of hammers bearing down on chisels and the cacophony made it easier for Fen to move even further along the passage. Her right hand never strayed from the stone wall, her guide, but the other one clenched around the handle of the oil lamp.

She reached the end of the passage and knew the three men were only a foot or so away. What was she doing acting like such a scaredy-cat? She had just helped to uncover the murderer in their midst, she should have nothing to fear from these three…

Fen rounded the corner and cleared her throat.

Three headtorches shone into her eyes and dazzled her. Instinctively, Fen raised her hand to protect herself from the bright lights, but it was the sudden resounding silence that shocked her more.

What must have been only a couple of moments later, James greeted her with the not so friendly, 'Christ, Fen, we might have shot you, creeping up on us like that.'

'I can't see you, James, can you…' she waved her hand around until he and Clément had moved their headtorches. Hubert stubbornly refused to, but turned his face – and the beam of light – away from her and carried on chipping away at the mortar of what Fen could now see was a brick wall. 'What are you doing?' she asked.

'What does it look like?' James fiddled with his headtorch.

Clément took over, 'We are retrieving our treasure.'

'Treasure?' Fen had images in her mind all of a sudden of chests heaving with pirate gold, strings of pearls and precious gems.

'Our wine!' The booming voice of the older man carried far along the passageway, echoing as it went.

'How did you find us?' James asked, moving out of the way so that Clément could get back to work, helping Hubert chip away at the wall.

'I… well – I mean, I sort of followed Clément. You'd all left me in the kitchen.' Fen knew she sounded like the little girl who wasn't invited to play with the bigger kids. She reckoned she must look it, too, with her bare legs showing above her work boots and her long nightdress showing under her land girl jumper. Her eyes alighted on something familiar on the hard-earth floor of the tunnel. It was the ledger, the one she'd last seen in the kitchen dresser. 'So this is your hidden wine stash?'

Hubert finally lowered his headtorch and replied, 'Yes. When the Germans invaded, we knew we had to protect not only the wine from this domaine but Clément's and my personal collection too.' He paused, 'To think, after all of this subterfuge and believing we were safe, it could have still all been stolen by that bastard Spatz!'

'Why did you wait this long? The Germans have been gone from around here for almost a year?'

Hubert answered Fen's question, while Clément shook his head, 'Because Sophie kept telling us to hold on, hold on. Now, of course we know it's because she didn't want us to sell or drink or benefit at all from the wine we saved, she wanted it all for when she'd finished killing us off and could drink all the Romanee Conti herself, with the bloody Weinführer!'

There was a groan from Clément as he realised how close he, and probably Hubert, had been to losing their lives, and almost worse than that, their wine.

With the time for contemplation over, the four of them together formed a reasonably organised work party and chiselled and hammered the new wall down. The dust was indescribable, the mortar powder mixing with centuries-old cobwebs and becoming paste-like in the dankness of the cellar.

'No wonder you thought no one would come down here in the first place,' said Fen to Clément, who had paused to rest while the younger men carried on.

'You only found it by following me, eh?'

'Yes, and quite a surprise I got when I saw you seem to disappear behind a plum tree!'

'This church and the château have been like siblings these centuries past, it seemed only right that we should take our wine from our cellar and hide it here in the church's vault. Something for you to write about, eh?'

'I suppose I should come clean about that.' Fen dusted herself down a bit. 'I'm no journalist or travel writer, just a woman who wanted to know what had happened to her fiancé. I followed Arthur's clues here.'

'Well, you are welcome. Thank you for lending us him and I'm so sorry that we didn't look after him for you.'

Clément's kind words were almost too much for Fen to bear, but she did her utmost to keep her tears at bay, not least because her eyes were already smarting from the brick dust and ground-down mortar.

She nodded and thanked the old man, but then stiffened that upper lip and returned to the subject of the tunnel. 'Did you really build this tunnel from the château's gardens? All the way under the church?'

'No, no, no,' Clément shook his head. 'This tunnel is perhaps two hundred years old. It was very useful for the Comte de Morey when he needed to make a timely escape from Robespierre's men!' The old man smiled at the thought. 'Yes, it has been an old friend to us Bernards for many generations.'

'And the church doesn't mind? I mean, you having access to the vaults?'

'What is there but bones? And in any case, the tunnel has collapsed between here and our cellars, so we can't access this directly from the house. Hence the entrance by the trees.' He wiped the sweat from his brow and in so doing swept a streak of dirt across it; then, only half-seriously, he said, 'We pay our dues though by giving the church the best communion wine in the world!'

'Romanee Conti?' Fen was reminded of the parish church in Midhurst and Edith always refusing communion. *She'd have been up to the altar like a shot*, thought Fen, *if it had been fine Burgundy in the chalice*!

'Better than that,' Clément corrected her. 'Domaine Morey-Fontaine!'

'Hallo!' James called over, and beckoned Fen and Clément to join him. 'Here we are, we can get through. Coming?'

'Gosh, yes.'

'*Oui, allons-y!*'

Led by Hubert and then James, Fen and Clément climbed over the few feet of crumbling bricks and mortar left at the base of the opening. The small room, that once would have been part of the church's vault, was crammed full of bottles. They were stacked, head to tail, in cage-like shelving. Their glassy, concave ends stared at her like a thousand eyes, gleaming now in the darting lights of the head- and handheld torches. There were wooden cases stacked on the floor too and Fen brushed off some of the mortar dust on top of them.

'Lumme,' she exclaimed as she saw the name on the first wooden box – ROMANEE-CONTI and above it some other French words about the domaine and a line drawing of the vineyards with a low wall, dominated by a cross on a stake. There were other wines there too, the boxes showing the names of local villages and producers.

Clément was lovingly brushing the dust off the top of a stack of boxes, touching them as carefully as if they were newborns, while Hubert had already selected a bottle from the same case and was opening it with a corkscrew. Fen looked over and saw that the name burnt onto the wood was Domaine Morey-Fontaine – the Bernard family's own wine.

'A good vintage?' Fen asked.

'The best,' replied Clément, who felt it needed no more explanation.

To Clément, Hubert and James, the scene was not so astounding, for of course they had built the wall that had hidden the wine, but to Fen it was unlike anything she'd seen before. There was also something magical in this dark place, and Fen could see how the French regarded their wine as their treasure.

She watched as Clément and Hubert raised bottles from the shelves and looked admiringly at them, as artists would do at an exhibition – talking knowledgeably and with great respect about their comrades, while swigging from the bottle that Hubert had just opened.

'Ah, the Gevrey from '37! It was a blessed vintage.'

'An idiot's vintage. Do you remember you let Thierry have a go? Even he managed to make something divine.'

'Thierry had a great future.' His father blinked away a tear, mentioned something about dust and cobwebs and then changed the subject. 'But here is a '34 from Vosne-Romanee, now you are talking.'

'I'm relieved we saved these '28s and '29s, Clément. They will be worth ten times more now on the market, unless the Germans decide to give it all back to us.' Hubert gave a hollow laugh at his own joke.

'Ha, we should be so lucky. It will be gone by now, drunk by philistines who probably paired it with sauerkraut and weinerschnitzel!'

Fen listened as the two men talked of vintages and domaines. It wasn't that she wasn't interested in the fine wines, and had gratefully swigged from the proffered bottle too, but now the family had their 'treasure' back she felt like there was only one more loose end to tie up; solving the clues to find the relic and complete Arthur's mission.

She caught James's attention and showed him the letter Estelle had given her. She had folded it into three now, with only the middle section of the letter showing, not for privacy, but she suspected that if she read Arthur's final words at this moment she would utterly fall apart. There was no time for that now, and she knew, from witnessing bombing raids back in England, that once your adrenalin runs out – and there was buckets of it coursing through her body currently thanks to the rather dramatic capture of Sophie – that she would just want to sleep. *Perhaps*, her body was telling her, *that's no bad thing…*

She shook herself and looked up at James.

'I've stashed it, knocked about, in Greater Rutland.' James pondered the clue.

'I've been to Rutland, and whatever you can say about it, it doesn't look like this.' Fen couldn't help but shy away from a particularly large cobweb that was hanging from the ceiling, caked in dark, dirtied dust.

'So it's one of Arthur's clues…' James thought out loud.

'Yes. Right, let's think.'

They both stood there for a bit, shifting their weight from foot to foot.

'Ah,' Fen took the letter back from James and pointed to the words, careful not to damage her precious letter with her grubby finger. 'Knocked about. Could be an anagram, but the word *in* makes me think it's something hidden actually *in* the words.'

'Knocked about…'

'Ah, *about*, like turn about, or backwards… A ha!'

They both made the connection and saw the answer staring at them. With one look, they confirmed that they were on the same page, and with no further ado, James gestured out towards the opening in the broken wall. 'Ladies first…'

CHAPTER TWENTY-NINE

Although he'd given her a head start along the tunnel and up the steep staircase, James easily caught up with Fen and ran along at her side as she bounded up the broken stone steps of the terrace and along the wall of the château. There was no need for torches now as the moon had broken free from the clouds and was illuminating their path beautifully.

Fen slowed down by the time she got to the gate into the courtyard and finally stopped, resting her hands on her hips and panting slightly, as she stood looking up towards the central tower of the old building.

'See?' she asked James, waving her hand up towards the very top of the roof. 'TURRET.'

'Spelt out backwards inside the words *Greater Rutland*.' James wasn't panting as much as Fen was and allowed her to get her breath back before questioning her further. 'So? Now what?'

'Now we go and find that relic.'

'You think we might have seen it before, if it was just on the staircase?' James pointed out.

'I remember now,' Fen cut across him. 'The first day I arrived. I was standing here, in the courtyard and something glinted from the very top of one of those little turrets. It's not lying on the staircase, you loon, it's right up there.' She waved her hand, still holding the letter, right up at the topmost window.

Like two children at the start of a race, they barely waited for starter's orders before tearing across the grass, onto the stone pathway towards the inconspicuous wooden door at the bottom of the tower. James got there first, and heaved it open.

The clattering of their boots on the stone stairs filled the spiral staircase with noise, but neither of them cared or slowed until they had passed the normal landing that led to the ladies' and family bedrooms, then reached the topmost floor, where James and Hubert, and back then Arthur, had had rooms.

'So where are the turrets?' asked Fen, turning on her torch and running her hands around the solid stone walls. The steps stopped at this floor and the only door out of the circular room was the one that led to the attic bedrooms.

James answered her by tilting his head and looking up to the ceiling. It was flat and obviously false, as the tower from the outside had a decidedly pointed top. There was a trapdoor in the wooden struts above them and James reached up, fruitlessly, for the catch.

'Gah,' he shouted as, for the third or fourth try, he was unable to snag the small piece of leather that acted as a handle.

'Here, hold me up.'

Fen put her torch down and let James lift her up. One big heave and she caught the leather strap and gave it an almighty tug. A cloud of dust crowned them both and Fen coughed as she accidentally breathed it in.

'Blimey, how dusty is it up there?' Fen brushed the dirt from her shoulders.

'I don't think Arthur took the feather duster with him when he hid it,' James remarked.

Fen ignored his sarcasm and continued, 'Can you see anything?'

'No, you're going to have to go up. Ready?'

Fen was anything but, seeing that she was still in her nightdress, nevertheless when James knelt down, she knew she was expected to stand on his knee and prepare to be catapulted into the roof space. She gave a quick prayer of thanks for her sensible knickers and stepped up to the task. A few attempts later and she hoisted herself over the edge of the trapdoor and was able to sit, safely, with her legs dangling down, on the edge of the wooden floor.

'What can you see?' James passed her torch up to her as he stood on the floor below.

Hopefully more than you can… she thought as she tucked her nightie between her legs. Then she shouted down, 'What looks like another case of wine… Here, wait a moment.' She leant across and pulled the wooden case towards her. 'It's terribly light. No wine in here.' She manhandled the box onto her lap, held the torch in between her teeth and gently pulled off the top, which was easy enough as the nails that usually held the wooden lid down were barely hammered in at all.

She laid the lid down next to her and peered inside the box. It was full of sawdust and wood shavings, and sitting plum in the middle of the box was another envelope, addressed to her in Arthur's writing. She slipped it out and hid it up her sleeve, hoping the general darkness around her meant James hadn't seen; she wanted her last letter from Arthur to be private.

'Anything?' James voice echoed up to her.

'Yes.' Nestled in all the wood shavings and sawdust was a small tin, not much bigger than the sort of thing sardines came in. Fen passed it to James and peered down as he prised it open. Inside was a small, red velvet pouch.

James looked up at Fen, who shone her torch on the small cloth bag. He released the cord around the neck of the pouch and let whatever was in it drop into the palm of his hand. It was a small, desiccated piece of wood. Fen had half expected a choir of angels to sing, or at least Raphael and Gabriel themselves to make a cameo. But there was no heavenly fanfare, no clouds parting to unleash the hand of God, only a small piece of wood, now carefully being put back into its little velvet pouch.

'Well then,' James said, 'let's get you down from up there, shall we?'

'Yes, please.' Fen was shuffling her bottom across the floor towards James's outstretched arms when something caught her eye. 'Oh!' She stopped and stared across at the little turret window, one of four that was letting the moon's beams into the top of the tower. Dangling from a thread in front of the glass was a silver photo frame. It caught the moonlight as it twirled this way and that in the draughts from the windows and the open hatch.

Fen was mesmerised and watched it dance for a second, before pushing herself away from the trapdoor and scrambling over to it. It must have been what she'd glimpsed as she'd looked up towards the tower; the object that had been glinting in the sunshine. She recognised the photo frame then, and gasped. It was the one she had given Arthur the day he had left Midhurst, and the face illuminated by the moonlight coming through the window was her own.

EPILOGUE

Fen clasped the letter to her chest. She'd read it through dozens of times now and she feared that if she took it out of its envelope, unfolded and then folded it one more time, it would start to fall apart.

She placed it very carefully on her pillow as she continued packing her sturdy brown suitcase. Her stay had been a short one, though you could never argue that it had been uneventful. As she folded her jumpers and work overalls up, she ran over in her mind what had happened since they'd uncovered the murderer in their midst.

Sophie had been taken away to Beaune, where she would stand trial for murder. There had been a riot of sorts outside the gendarmerie in Morey-Fontaine before she was transferred, and Sophie had been hauled out in front of the baying crowd and, although not torn limb from limb, she had been branded with swastikas and had her head shaved – like the poor woman Fen had seen from the bus in Paris. A *tondue,* as they called them – a shaved one. Still, the shame would no doubt be short-lived as the gallows would see to that.

Clément was a man bereft. The war had taken two of his sons and his daughter-in-law had murdered the third. If there was any good to have come of the situation, it had been that the two sides of family, the Bernards and the Ponsardines, were now more fully reconciled and Hubert had moved into one of the smarter 'family' bedrooms in the château.

And, to Clément's credit, he still bounced young Benoit on his knee, his fondness for the little chap not lessened now he knew he wasn't a Bernard by blood. Perhaps his father would come back one day and claim him, but for now Fen felt sure that his grandfather and newly named Uncle 'Hubie' would do their very best for him, and Jean-Jacques of course.

Fen had wondered, as she emptied her clothes from the chest of drawers, whether Estelle would set her cap at Hubert, but for now she seemed to be up to her eyeballs just running the house, looking after the boys and cooking for the men. Fen had been tempted to stay and help her, but then she couldn't shake the memory of that woman's hands around her throat. Any warm feelings Fen might have had towards her had evaporated in that moment.

Plus, James had that look in his eye – restless, searching. Now Arthur had been revenged he'd been talking about moving on. His Baker Street HQ had wired him permission to take some leave and Fen felt inclined to join him. She closed the lid of her suitcase and snapped the catches shut. They would both need to be witnesses at the trial at Beaune, but after that, who knew? Paris perhaps, the City of Lights, a new start.

Fen sat down on the bed and winced as the springs did their best impression of caterwauling felines.

One more time, she told herself. With that, she carefully unfolded the letter and read Arthur's words again…

France, August 1944

My darling Fen,

Well, here it is, the little relic. A great deal in a small place – multum in parvo after all! I knew you'd find it – and only you. Get it back to Father Marchand and he'll restore it to the church. If you have no idea who I'm talking about, then give it to Clément Bernard – he's a good sort, as is Hubert his cousin, despite his boorish exterior and habit of drinking a bit too much of the communion wine.

In fact all of the Bernards are first-rate people, except… well, let us give her the benefit of the doubt, but if I'm betrayed by anyone around here, then my money's on Sophie. She's been sniffing round our plans and skipping off to see the Weinführer at every opportunity – if there's a sabotage we're planning, the Hun are one step ahead each time and I'm pretty sure her youngest son isn't a Bernard by blood, if you catch my drift. Still, enough gossip.

I know you might question why I'm risking my life for a piece of wood, but it's important to me that, on any level, the Nazis cannot win. It's not that I believe God can be harnessed by Hitler and Himmler, but they do, and I can't let them take one more precious religious artefact from a local church where it does nothing but good, to a place where it can do nothing but harm, even if that harm is just strengthening the pseudoscience of the Nazis.

And I respect these people. It's been day after day, hour after hour of skirmishes, gunfights and ambushes and, through all of that, the people of this small town have got on with their lives and shown strength that I admire more than anything. Fracan keeps baking, even though often enough his entire batch is 'requisitioned' by a passing German platoon; the children still play in the Place de L'Église while their mothers gossip in huddles by the church door; there's not much in the way of food, and the school has no heating through the winter, they can't even burn the textbooks to keep warm – the Nazis got there first. Men disappear in the night and single gunshots are often heard. We live on our nerves, but there is always a smile and a laugh, a cigarette to be shared and a story to be told. Life goes on.

I will try and send a letter to you at Mrs B's in case I don't make it home from here; I don't want you to be left wondering. I can't send you this letter – what I'm about to tell you now would be redacted to hell, but I want you to know what I'm doing out here. I'm part of what we call the Special Operations Executive. We're a roguish bunch of codebreakers and linguists, all handy with a pair of pliers and hopefully able to disrupt the occupation as much as possible.

I was so tempted to enlist you too, although I wanted to save you from all of this danger. I hope you have survived the war and are as beautiful and bonny as when I left you. I hope you've met James Lancaster now too – you know you met him that night at the Spread Eagle? If he's here and I'm not, I think you two should try and look after each other, if you can. Plus he's filthy rich.

I love you, I love you, I love you… forever yours,
Arthur

A LETTER FROM FLISS CHESTER

Dear reader,

I want to say a huge thank you for choosing to read *A Dangerous Goodbye*. I hope you loved dipping into Fen's world and helping her solve her first mystery as much as I loved writing it. Did you guess who it was from the clues?

If you want to keep up to date with all of my latest releases, please sign up at the following link. Your email address will never be shared and you can unsubscribe at any time.

www.bookouture.com/fliss-chester

I dedicated this book to my adventurous great-aunt, and although, as far as I know, she didn't solve any murders, she was a real character who worked around the world from the 1930s through to the 1980s! I like to think that a little bit of her has rubbed off on Fen and because of that her spirit will continue adventuring as long as I keep writing.

If you enjoyed *A Dangerous Goodbye*, and I really hope that you did, I'd be incredibly grateful if you could write a review and tell me what you think of my first Fen Churche mystery, plus you'll be helping new readers to discover one of my books for the first time.

I love hearing from my readers – you can get in touch on my Facebook page, through Twitter, Instagram or my website.

Thanks,
Fliss

FlissChester

FlissChester

socialwhirlgirl

www.flisschester.co.uk

ACKNOWLEDGEMENTS

Thank you to my husband, Rupert, not only for all the support you always give me as I write my books, but also for your wine expertise and rather worrying knowledge on how many ways you could kill someone in a winery. You also proposed to me all those years ago in the best possible way – with a personalised cryptic crossword! Thank you, my love.

Huge thanks to my stepsister Penny Lawson, who not only taught me how to do cryptic crosswords, but infected me with her love for them too. Our two heads together are always better than my one. For those of you without my stepsister on hand, do try the late Colin Dexter's *Cracking Cryptic Crosswords*, it's the best book for cryptic crossword beginners and will teach you the language needed to work them out.

Much of my historical wine research was found in *Wine & War* by Don and Petie Kladstrup. It's a genuinely fascinating book full of thrilling stories and anecdotes from France's great wine-producing families. *Les Parisiennes* by Anne Sebba is a wonderful biography of the women of Paris before, during and immediately after the Second World War. It's a treasure trove of research and information and a rich source of inspiration. By chance, I met Anne at a party at the London Library and was able to blurt out, 'Your book! It's on my desk!'… So thank you, Anne, for not only not looking at me too oddly that night, but for writing such an interesting piece of historical non-fiction.

Authors aren't the only ones who have a hand in creating the work you've just read, and it wouldn't be the book it is without the help of my agent, Emily Sweet, and my editor at Bookouture, Maisie Lawrence – your insights and advice are much appreciated and I hope you've enjoyed working on this novel as much as I did!

Lastly, my thanks to my family, my mum especially, who are incredibly supportive of my writing and don't glaze over too much as I talk about plots and murderous things. Mum – you've given me so much, but perhaps most poignantly and most recently a shoebox full of my great-aunt's pre-war love letters from her fiancé; so Great Aunty Glen and Great Uncle Mac, this book is for you.